DIRTY ANGELS

DIRTY ANGELS

ANDREW CLOVER

Hodder
Children's
Books

A division of Hachette Children's Books

First published in 2007 by Hodder Children's Books
a division of Hachette Children's Books

1

ISBN-13: 978 0 340 93097 7

Typeset in Bembo and Berling by Avon DataSet Ltd,
Bidford-on-Avon, Warwickshire

Printed in the UK by CPI Bookmarque, Croydon, CR0 4TD

The paper and board used in this paperback by Hodder Children's Books
are natural recyclable products made from wood grown in sustainable
forests. The manufacturing processes conform to the environmental
regulations of the country of origin.

Hodder Children's Books
a division of Hachette Children's Books
338 Euston Road, London NW1 3BH
An Hachette Livre UK Company

For Livy

Author's Note

This is Andrew Clover's first book, but he's written lots of films and cartoons, one of which was nominated for a BAFTA. He's also a stand-up comedian and an actor. He writes the Dad Rules column in the *Sunday Times*, and does the *Storyman* show on Radio 4. If you visit www.andrewclover.com you can hear his collaboration with David Walliams and Terry Gilliam and, Andrew's favourite, Fred Deakin from Lemon Jelly. Andrew lives in London with Liv, his mum, two dogs, and two very cheerful, noisy little girls. If you want to know more about him buy his second book, Dad Rules, which is published by Penguin in 2007. When not writing or doing stand-up comedy, Andrew is usually to be found walking round Hackney Marshes with his daughters.

1

I got problems . . .

I'm nearly fourteen, yeah, but I'm like four foot ten, and I sound like a girl. My best friend is Polly. She's four inches taller and she's got a deeper voice.

Everyone else in my school has got shady names like Kriss, Sal, or Eric. My name is Colin Hitchin. The guys call me Colin Bitchin. I got a big forehead and I'm well skinny and I got no shoulders. The girls call me Tadpole.

I don't like being boyed, but if I fight, I get so *mad* I start waving my arms and kicking, and then everyone goes 'He's tweeking! He's tweeking!' and then they call me 'Tweek the Freak'. Last time I fight, they don't shut up about it. Eric even makes up a *rap*. I'm trying to do my maths. He's sitting behind me whispering: 'Is he a tadpole?/or is he a bitch?/he's just a Tweek Boy/he won't never be rich./Bitchin fights like he drunk too much liquor/Bitchin fights like he was a window-licker.' It takes him all morning to make this up. When he's done it, Sal keep saying it over and over. I'm putting my fingers in my ears, and then Sal's going, 'He's put his fingers in his ears. He can't take it,' and I wanna say, 'It ain't that I can't take it, but I am *bored*. I'd like to cut out your tongue, and eat it, in pitta bread, with garlic sauce.'

But I know if I say that they're gonna rush me. So I don't say nothing.

All I want is to be normal, so no one's gonna start on me.

But whenever we do a test, I come top by miles, so then everyone says I'm a geek as well as a freak.

All I want is to be normal. I wanna walk up my street, past Yorkshire Grove, and I want the guys to invite me to play football. I wanna go past the girls chilling outside KFC on Albion Road and I want them to offer me a puff on their fag. I won't smoke. It stunts the growth and I don't need that. I just wanna be *asked*.

I just wanna be normal.

So how do you reckon I feel, when I find out I'm psychic?

2

I am.

First I just notice little stuff.

Like I get dreams where I talk to people who are dead.

Or sometimes I get feelings. Like ... It's Tuesday night. 7:30 pm. I'm coming home from karate. I'm about to walk down Defoe Road, and I get this *cold* feeling in my stomach, and so I go down Marston Road instead. Next night I'm walking down Defoe Road again. What do I see? A big yellow board up saying: *SERIOUS ASSAULT. Tuesday. 7:32 pm* ...

And sometimes I see ghosts, and sometimes I see stuff that's stranger than that.

You might think this is raw. Like I got Special Powers. I'm telling you, this *ain't good*.

It began three years ago. That's when it starts going pear-shaped with my dad ...

He's hiding away in the attic writing this book called

A History of British Crime (from the Romans to the Present).
He's up there, day in, day out, reading books and
newspapers about murderers and thieves and drug-
dealers. He don't talk. He don't wash. If you go up there,
you can't hardly move, 'cos he keeps ordering gadgets
from Japan on the Internet, so if you try to speak to him
you're gonna knock over a box, and he's gonna shout.
Mum and Dad are always arguing, and if I come into the
room, one of them always goes out, like it's all my fault.

Meanwhile I'm getting untold dreams at night.
Always the same dream . . .

*I'm walking up my street, and I got this feeling something
bad's happened to Dad. There's police outside my house, and
they won't let me in. Then Mum comes out and says: 'Colin,
let's go for a drive. There's something I want to talk about.'*

Night after night, I see the same thing. Does my
head. I can't work. I can't concentrate. I'm walking
around like I got a wet brain. This ain't like I got Special
Powers, it's like I got Special Needs.

So in the end I tell Mum about the dream and I tell
her she's gotta talk to Dad. But she don't speak to Dad.
She speaks to Dr Juvanji, and before I know it, he's
giving me drugs. So then, I'm still getting bad dreams at
night, and in the daytime it's like my head is filled with
porridge. I got big bags under my eyes. I look like an elf
on a methadone programme.

This goes on for three months.

Then one day I *am* walking home, and there's police outside, they won't let me up to our flat, and then my Mum comes out and says the exact words: 'Colin, let's go for a drive. There's something I want to talk about.'

She tells me Dad died, but she don't tell me *how* or *where*.

So it's after then that I set fire to the old gym. Dunno why. It makes me feel better for like two seconds, but then I go under. I don't cry. I never cry. But every night I'm dreaming about Dad. So when I wake up I feel empty, and I can't think about nothing 'cept how I wanna be eight again, and have him back. I tell all this to Mum and she says, 'I know, darling, I know.' But then she gets Juvanji to give me more drugs. Thanks, Mum. Why didn't you just believe me in the first place?

3

So now, three years on, I can feel it all happening again.

This is how it starts . . .

I'm having this dream where I'm in the park, and then someone arrives and tells me they're from heaven, and they got a message about my dad.

I wake up and I'm sweating and the sun is pouring in. It's that kind of hot weather where you can't sleep. Kind of weather where you feel you gotta be out all the time, or you're gonna miss it, but you don't know what you're trying not to miss so you just feel lost.

I get up and dress. I'm thinking about this mad dream, and I'm thinking I ain't telling *no one about this*.

But then I think . . . Maybe Polly. I could tell her. I'm thinking this weekend me and Poll could go down Hackney Marshes. We could pitch the tent next to the river where her mate has got a houseboat. Polly loves it there. We hide away in the long grass. She brings her guitar and makes up songs. I take my top off and practise my kicks. No one bothers us. It's perfect.

I eat breakfast with Mum. She's reading the paper. I'm reading my SAS Combat Manual. I don't say nothing 'cept to ask if we can get some Frosties, 'cos there ain't nothing to eat 'cept my Mum's lesbian muesli. She's in one of them moods where she's all silent and you gotta know *why* she's being silent or she's gonna get mad.

She puts down the paper, and says:

'Let's go to Malta this weekend.'

'Yeah . . . like we can afford that.'

'It's only nineteen pounds return,' she says. 'It looks nice.'

She turns round the paper. There's a picture of a man – lying with a gorgeous woman – in a boat – that's floating in shallow water – and you can see the shadow of the boat on the white sand at the bottom of the water. I'm thinking: I know if I was on that beach, there would be some waste man on a jetski. And there'd be English people stubbing out their fags in the sand. And even if I could be on that beach, alone, in that boat, I wouldn't have that woman with me. I'd have my mum. And I don't wanna hang out with Mum. I wanna hang out with Polly.

'I don't know, Mum,' I say. 'I just hate planes.'

'Don't be ridiculous,' she says. She's getting the

hump. That's the thing about my mum, you gotta agree with her right away or she takes it personally. 'Why don't you like flying?'

I'm thinking: Where do I start? I hate planes 'cos I hate sitting next to screaming babies and you ain't allowed to get away or gag them. I hate planes 'cos I hate all that *'put the mask over your face and breathe normally'* stuff. (How else am I supposed to breathe? Through my *ears?*) I hate planes 'cos when you look out the window, all you see is motorways and car parks and you feel like there ain't no land left.

I say: 'You know how much pollution planes make? A plane, flying to Miami, makes as much pollution as a car, driving for a whole year. So we ain't allowed to fly.'

'Everyone else does it, so why shouldn't we?'

I don't say nothing.

'Do you ever think what it's like for me?' she says. 'I need a break!'

Then she gets up, and goes into her bedroom, and bangs the door. I can hear her in there, crying, which ain't normal. Usually she just puts on the hairdryer.

I get my school stuff and my dad's SAS scarf and I shout, 'Bye, Mum', and I leave the flat. As soon as I shut the door, I feel tight inside, like I know something massive is gonna happen. I go down the two flights of stairs and I feel like I'm going to my death.

At the front door there's a big pile of pizza leaflets

and tickets for cab firms and also a magazine called *East – the FREE Magazine for the Hackney Community (sponsored by Keats Estate Agents)*. On the front, there's a picture of wallpaper and a dimmer switch. At the bottom, it says: *How to find that Dream Home*. I think there ain't no one who has dreams about dimmer switches. And if there is, they need punching.

I look through the whole pile of junk mail, 'cos there could, just could, be something good. I always look. That's why I'm always disappointed. Every day it's like I've looked in my Christmas stocking and found nothing but tangerines.

But today, at the bottom of the pile, there *is* something.

It's a postcard, addressed to me. On the front is a photo of a mountain and the word *Venezuela*. On the back, there's a drawing of a dog, and it's got wings. There's a speech bubble out the dog's mouth. He's saying: 'What's all this then? Woof!!'

That's heavy. There's only one person this card could be from ... My crazy Uncle Jimmy. My dad's big brother. Jimmy spends his life travelling round the world washing dishes in restaurants and getting into trouble. I used to send him these stories about Jack, the Brave Police Dog. Jack was everything I wanted to be when I was eight: he was a detective, he was a dog, he used to say, 'Ho hum, what's all this then, woof!'. Jimmy used to send me letters back about what he was up to.

And sometimes he visits. I love that, but Mum hates it. You never know how long Jimmy's gonna stay. And he stinks the whole house out with his manky clothes. And he's the kind of guy who says: 'Anything of mine, you share it.' The sort of people who say that, they ain't never got stuff you want.

4

I open the door.
It's *hot* out there.

There's someone sitting opposite my house. Some bag lady wearing a Chelsea strip. Her face is pink from the sun.

I check my watch. It's 8:35, which is late, and right away my stomach tightens up like a fist. If I'm late, then I gotta ride on the bus with everyone else. And when I arrive at school everyone's gonna be hanging about outside and they're gonna start on me. I walk up the street looking at the ground. I don't like to catch no one's eye. I pass two banana skins that've gone black and sweaty. I pass a smashed CD. I check what it is. Free thirty-day introduction to AOL.

Then I look up. A car goes by with its windows wide open. It's blaring out this track which goes:
'Everybody's doing it, so why can't I?
Everybody's doing it, so why can't I?'

Everyone is listening to this song right now. The singer is called Kimberley Galloway and she comes from down the road, so suddenly every muffin you meet is calling up newspapers to say, 'She was the first girl I ever kissed. I got pictures if you got cash.' Everyone's saying the song could go number one, simultaneously, in America and the UK, like that's supposed to show something. All it shows is that *all* the people can be *all* wrong *all* of the time. I ain't joking, the track is worse than 'Barbie Girl'. It's one of them tunes that tunnels in your brain like a worm so you can't forget it. You shouldn't call it a tune. You should call it a *brainworm*.

I know something bad's gonna happen, but I don't know what.

I pass a Bangladeshi bloke called Yussuf who lives further up Walford Road. He waves. I nod. No problem there. Yussuf's friendly. He's Sellotaping a sign to a lamppost which says: 'Find peace. Find Allah.' Yussuf is into Islam big time and he's got one of them funny hats and he's growing the big beard. He used to have his hair slicked back with gel, and he reeked of perfume, and he was well into girls. We used to play football together, and he'd tell me who he'd got off with the night before. But then one day he comes round and says he's converted to the Prophet and from now on I must call him Yussuf Mohammed Ali Khan. Before then I called him Lee.

Further up the street, I see Eric. He's white with a round head and shaved hair, and he always wears Arsenal tracksuits. He's messing with his bike, but he ain't really concentrating. He's looking at his phone, which is on the pavement, playing music. It's playing the same brainworm song.

Eric used to be my friend. I used to go round his house and we'd watch cartoons together. His mum let us eat fish fingers on the sofa and me and Eric would wet ourselves doing Scooby-Doo noises. Eric is great at taking the piss and doing impressions. I used to call him Scooby. Everyone else called him Gut Bucket. He used to be well fat and no one liked him. When we played football he was always in goal. He was rubbish as well. Sometimes his goal kicks didn't make it out the area. You know when a goalie has done a save, he always screams at his defenders? That's the only bit Eric could do. But he never minded if I practised my penalties on him. I liked him. But then he became a hardcore Arsenal fan. He started dressing in them blue Arsenal coats and talking about how 'we stuffed the Scum last night'. After that he started making other friends. He don't talk to me no more 'cept to rip the piss 'cos he's just dying to fight me. He loves fighting. If you ever hear someone shouting: 'Do you want some?' then soon after you'll see Eric pushing someone in the chest. He's also one of them people who can get you stuff. He gets cheap

DVDs and CDs from his uncle, and he's always selling them off round the school. He's basically a chief.

Eric looks up and sees me.

'All right, Bitchin',' he says.

'Ri,' I say. I'm keepin' it brief.

He holds up his phone.

'You seen these new phones?' he goes. 'They're giving them out free.'

'Yeah?'

'Well you get the first three months free. I can give you this one if you want. I got three more.'

'I don't want one.'

'Why not?'

How am I supposed to answer that?

'Cos I don't want a new phone, I already got one.

'Cos I hate new stuff, 'cos you gotta read the instruction books and I would rather stick pins in my eyes than read them things.

'Cos if I take something from Eric, I'm gonna have to speak to Eric.

'Why don't you want a new phone?' says Eric again.

' 'Cos after three months I'll have to pay, and I don't have no money.'

'Bitchin',' he says, 'you're gay.'

I'm trying to walk in a way that's not-at-all gay. I sort of drag my heels.

I turn into Stoke Newington High Street. There's no

sign of the bus, and there's about ten people at the bus stop – mainly guys from my school. Polly *ain't* there, but Sal and Kriss are. That ain't good.

I approach the bus stop carefully. I'm trying to see who might give me grief, but I'm doing it on the sly, 'cos I don't want *no one* to see me looking. Right away, I notice stuff that's strange. Nothing that's off-the-dial strange. But it starts to add up . . .

No one is talking, and everyone is acting like they're either (1) tired, or (2) stupid, or (3) they been getting drugs off Dr Juvanji. Plus, *everyone* is looking at their mobile phones. OK . . . normally a few people are on their phones – mainly girls, 'cos girls always need to be shouting away to show how popular they are.

Sal is right next to the kerb, staring at his phone, while eating a chocolate brownie. Sal is Turkish and he ain't no stranger to the inside of a kebab shop. In fact his family runs The Best Turkish Kebab Shop on Stoke Newington High Street. Sal is massive and hairy and he wears too much hair wax so you can see his scalp. He's only in our year 'cos he got held back for failing his exams. So he's already nearly sixteen, and he must be sixteen stone as well. Luckily he don't get into a lot of fights 'cos he's basically mellow. But when he does fight, he's lethal 'cos he knows how to use his weight. He sits on people. He's wearing a Galatasaray top which has got bright, shiny colours, so he looks like a hot air balloon.

I keep well away from him, and move round to the back of the group.

But that puts me near to Kriss, who's wearing a bright red Gap hat and a Chicago Bulls vest which shows off his muscles. Just like everyone else, Kriss is watching the video of the brainworm on his phone, but at the same time he's eating a doughnut. He only eats half of it, then he drops the rest on to his foot and without hardly looking he volleys it, left foot, down the pavement.

This is why I used to be friends with Kriss . . .

1) 'Cos he is unreal at football. One of his uncles was John Fashanu who played football for Nigeria. He's so good that I reckon he could play for England and I would love to go and watch him. I would tell everyone he was my friend.

2) I've known him since I was four and Mum made me go to St Matthias Church Sunday School 'cos she wanted me to go St Matthias School. We did a Nativity play. Kriss was the innkeeper and he got this purple robe off his cousin, and he acted like he was a pimp and all the rooms were full 'cos they were full of girls. He was hilarious. I was a sheep.

3) After Sunday School we used to chill out in Butterfield. I invented this army gang. He was captain and I was lieutenant. We used to wear these green baseball caps that his mum bought down in Dalston

Market. Whenever you did a game with Kriss, he always wanted to get the clothes right first.

This is why I ain't friends with Kriss now . . .

1) If you try and mess about with him he always says 'You gay? You chi-chi man?'

2) Kriss is probably the best-looking guy in my school, and he has a lot of power. If you fall out with Kriss, you're in deep trouble.

3) He's very good at fighting. He don't fight much though. Don't need to. He's only got to stare and people back off.

Kriss watches the end of the brainworm video and the music fades away. Then he turns and looks at me. Looks me right in the eye.

'Bitchin,' he says, 'what music you like?'

I hate being asked that question. It's like there's a right answer and you gotta know what it is. Normally I say I like whatever Kriss has said he likes, but I can't do that now. So I make something up.

'I like Sly Boy,' I say, 'also MP2, also the Kumquat Connection.'

Kriss keeps staring at me.

'I ain't heard of none of them,' he says. 'Do you like this girl?'

He clicks on his phone, and Kimberley Galloway appears. I really don't want to hear that song again. It's like eating more candyfloss when you've already puked.

'She's OK,' I say.

'She is buff,' says Kriss.

'She is *leng*,' says Sal. He's come over. He's like a wolf. He knows the leader is about to take down a deer and he's gonna get lunch.

'She is *leng food*,' says Kriss, still staring at me.

(*Leng food???* I ain't never heard that expression before. This happens all the time. It's like everyone's texting each other these new words and then all the suckers have to start using them straight away or they're gonna get done.)

'I'm gonna watch it again,' says Sal.

He presses a button on his phone, and the video starts playing on the screen. They all gather in to watch, so I gotta watch too. Kimberley is a blonde, white girl. OK, she is good-looking but she's a bit old. 25 at least. She's got a square jaw, and her eyes are a bit close together, and she's got a big bottom lip. She looks *greedy*. Looks like one of them girls that you see at airports, yelling at their boyfriends 'cos they want an upgrade. She's staring into the camera, and rapping, always with the same expression on her face. She looks fit, but stupid. Like a sexy cow. Her clothes and the background keep changing. One moment she's shopping. Then she's dancing with half-naked blokes. Then she's getting out of a helicopter. Something about this video, it makes me mad. I can't explain it.

The chorus goes:

'*I need it,*

I need it,

I seed it,

I need it,

Everybody's doing it, so why can't I?

Everybody's doing it, so why can't I?'

The song is so bad, it could be Christmas Number One. It's bad enough to get played in a fairground. But the other guys like it.

'She is potent,' Sal says. 'I would prep her, man.'

I'm thinking: Right, Sal ... Like she's gonna get prepped by a fat teenager who's still at school. But I don't say that, I just say: 'She's OK.'

'*OK!*' says Kriss, hitting me on the arm, and giving me a sly look. 'Bitchin – you chi-chi man?'

I don't say nothing to that. What I *wanna* say is ... yup, she's blonde, and she's good-looking, but I reckon she's a *witch*. Gotta be. I mean ... she's a singer, but she can't sing. And she's in movies, but she can't act. And she's got her own TV show, even though she ain't got nothing to say. How does that come about? 'Cos she's a *witch*.

The song finishes.

Right away, Sal presses the button, and it starts all over again.

'Man! Don't start it again!' I say. 'I can't take it

no more!'

Now they're all giving me a bad look. I don't like that look. It means that any second I'm gonna get battered like a piece of fish.

'What's your problem?' says Kriss.

'You taking the piss?' says Sal.

'No, I ain't. I ain't.'

They're still giving me a bad look. I gotta get away quick. But I gotta act like I ain't running away or they'll come for me later.

5

I act like I suddenly need to go to the newsagent's.

I nod hello to Hidir who's behind the counter. I get
myself a Twix, a Lilt and a copy of *Fight* magazine. As I'm
going out, I see some ginger in the security mirror. I
look up. Vernon Watkins is hanging out by the freezer
section. I get right away what he's doing. He's hiding in
the shop 'cos he don't wanna have to stand with
everyone by the bus stop. Same as me.

'All right, Vern,' I shout.

'Oh, hello, Colin!' he shouts.

So I go down and see him and he spreads his arms like
he's going to try and hug me. I back off. He's wearing a
tweed jacket and a shirt with a collar and some thick
glasses that I ain't never seen before. I can see why he's
hiding. If he turned up at the bus stop dressed like that,
they would set him on fire. He's dressed like a grandad.

He's also got this catalogue out on top of the fish
finger section.

'You know where to get cheap software?' he goes.

'No. What do you want?'

'*Chess Strategy for Masters*,' he says. 'You play against the computer, and then the computer tells you what moves you could've made. Then it tells you what different moves different Grand Masters have made in the same situation.' He looks me in the eye, dead serious. 'This could turn me into a Grand Master,' he says.

'OK,' I say, 'how much?'

'Two hundred and forty-nine quid.'

'That's cold.'

'Yip,' he says.

Suddenly I can't help myself: 'Verno, why the *hell* are you dressed like that?'

'I wanna look like Dave Brubeck.'

'What? Who is that?'

'He's a jazz musician from the 1950s. His music is amazing.'

'I'm sure, but them glasses make you look like a paedo.'

Vern ain't bothered by this. He must get so much stick he don't get hurt no more.

'I'll play you the record next time you come round,' he says.

I'm thinking, you're gonna be waiting a long time. Don't get me wrong. I like Vern, BUT . . .

1) His dad's a vicar. And he must be one of them

touchy-feely ones as well, 'cos Vern's always trying to hug people. When he does it to me, I back away like I'd back away from a Rottweiler.

2) He's got ginger hair and glasses. Looks like Harry Potter after a bad bleach job.

3) He's obsessed with chess. He's always getting chess books out the library. Don't get me wrong. I know people play chess. I also know people pick their noses and eat it. You can do it, just keep quiet about it.

4) He's got skid marks. Eric found 'em, and he passed 'em round the changing room.

5) He's dressed like Dave Brubeck, who musta looked like one of them old men you see staring through the fence at the girls playing netball.

6) Last time I went round his house, Eric saw me coming out, and he wrote *Bitchin and Vern are gay* on the bus stop timetable.

I turn. I see someone coming into the shop. It's Kriss and Sal. Right away I get the fear. I cannot get caught with Vern.

I walk straight past Kriss and Sal, who're getting scratch cards. They don't notice me. Result.

I come out. Still no sign of the bus. I got such a bad feeling I'm actually shaking.

So then I just stand on the pavement, taking deep breaths. I'm looking at my feet, thinking they look further away than they used to. Thinking, I hope no one's gonna notice me.

Then something weird happens.

I hear a voice. Sounds American. Sounds *shabby*. Sounds like Samuel L. Jackson from *Pulp Fiction*, and that guy's got the best voice there's ever been.

The voice goes:

'*Boy, you are a mess. You are all over the place like a mad woman's piss.*'

I look round. I'm looking at a pigeon which has got a stump for a leg. It's on the pavement pecking away at Kriss's doughnut. I don't see Samuel L. Jackson.

The pigeon stops pecking. It looks up.

Its eyes have gone grey-blue like there's a milky film over them. It looks at me.

It says: '*You need help, child. You need power. You better come and find the Master.*'

6

I'm thinking: Is this it? Have I actually lost it now? Do I need to see Juvanji so he can give me pills? Is everyone gonna rip the piss for the rest of my life? Should I just rush into the street and get squashed like a hedgehog?

But then I look up and I see someone crossing the street . . .

I'm saved. It's Polly.

Pollerina.

Polledora.

She's still on the other side of the street, but I can see it's Poll. For a start, she's got her guitar case on her back. That figures. Most Wednesday nights, Polly goes to Open Mic Night in the Lonsborough. Basically means she sings two songs to eight old men and a fruit machine. My job is to step in when the old men start grabbing.

I watch Polly crossing the street. She's got her own

shape. I ain't saying she's fat, but she's chunky. Strong. Her arms are as wide as my legs, mind you my legs are like sticks. She can waste me at arm wrestling. She's good-looking, though, and she's got her own style. The girls round here have got corn rows in their hair, and they wear track suits even though most of them don't walk further than the chip shop. Poll dresses like a crustie: DM boots, ripped jeans, long, dirty, dark brown hair which she's wearing loose. Today she's wearing a T-shirt which is tight round Polly's big breasts.

'Hi, Poll,' I say. And I give her a little kick on the arse.

'Hey, Gorgeous,' she says, and I smile. Not just 'cos she's called me Gorgeous, but also 'cos Polly's got a beautiful voice. Soft Ulster accent.

Now that Polly's here, straight away, the bus turns up, and the doors open right in front of us. Sal tries to push in.

'Sal,' says Polly, 'would you not push? That's bang out of order.'

She's always saying that, and no one messes with her when she's said it. We flash our passes at the driver, we go upstairs, and we go straight to our normal seat: on the right, at the front. She puts down her guitar. I sit next to her and I can feel my arm touching hers. I like that. Course, if I'd've known this is almost the last time I'm gonna sit next to Polly like this, I'd like it even more.

She looks at me. I look at her. She's got the thickest eyelashes I've ever seen.

'You OK?' she says.

'Yeah. Having these dreams that do my head.'

'Ah, you're so cute,' she says, and she grabs my head and puts it on her shoulder. This feels well gay, so I push her off. It feels like she's trying to be my mum, and I don't let my mum hug me so I ain't letting Polly do it neither.

'What's the matter with you?' she says.

'Well, I'm OK. But everyone else is being well strange.'

'How?'

'Well . . . everyone's got these weird new phones. And everyone kept talking to me, but no one was talking to anybody else.'

Right away Polly turns to the rest of the bus, and she gives a big smile. 'Good morning, everybody!' she says.

'Don't do that!'

'Why?'

'I don't wanna cause attention, or everyone's gonna start on me.'

'That's just what you think.'

Then she goes silent for a second. I know it won't last though. Polly's an iPod on random selection. What-ever she comes up with, it's always a surprise, and it's always good.

'I have this fantasy,' she begins. That gets my

attention. 'It's like a recurring fantasy. When I'm on a bus, I imagine that someone's gonna come, and they're going to shout "Everyone's gonna die, except you. You have ten seconds then you're going to be sent to a desert island *for ever*. You have ten seconds to find your companion! ten, nine, eight . . ." So then I have to choose who I'd take . . . Obviously, right now, I'd choose you.'

I'm glad she said that. But I can also feel myself blushing, and I'm hoping no one else can hear.

'Yeah,' I say, 'but . . . say I ain't here. Who?'

She looks round.

'Well, Kriss is the best looking.' I don't say nothing to this. 'But he's got issues. And Sal is strong, so he'd be good for cutting down trees. But maybe . . . I'd take *him*.'

She points out a skinny guy who's reading a novel. I ain't never seen him before. He looks about our age, but he definitely don't go to our school. Maybe he's going up to one of them Jewish ones that are north of Church Street. I don't want Polly taking him to a desert island.

'Who would you choose?' she says. 'Apart from me.'

I look at the bus.

'None of them. They can all die.'

'Colin,' she says. 'You're turning evil. Seriously. You are.'

She smiles when she says it. So I can't tell if she's

saying I'm evil-sexy, or evil-bad, and so I say nothing. And that's the end of my last normal conversation with Polly. After then everything is different.

I'm about to ask if she'll come camping this weekend, but Kriss comes over and sits on the seat behind us and he whispers something in her ear. I get out *Fight* magazine and pretend to read it, but I can't hear what he's saying. I'm looking at her left hand which has got a freckle on the knuckle that I ain't seen before.

And then the bus stops.

We're on Church Street next to the block of flats that are facing Clissold Park. This is the stop for our school.

We get up quick and get down to the door first. Everyone else follows behind us. So I'm still standing in the doorway when I see it . . .

A few metres away, there's flowers tied to the railing, from where a car killed a boy, a few weeks ago. Everyone can see that. They've been passing them for weeks. At first they'd go quiet when they went by, but no one knew the boy, so after a bit they ain't too bothered. So no one really notices the flowers which have gone all brown inside the plastic cover.

They also don't notice the ghost who's standing in front of the flowers.

He looks about seven. A little fat kid with a shaved head. He's crying.

Just seeing him, it makes me go cold inside. It's like

when you're out swimming in the sea, and suddenly the water goes freezing. Already I can smell him. People don't know that about ghosts: they stink. Have you ever taken the top off an empty pasta sauce jar, 'cos you're throwing the jar in the recycling? The ghost smells like that. He smells scared.

He's shaking his head and muttering.

'My dad's gonna kill me,' he says. 'Gonna kill me. And my mum, she told me to watch out. They're gonna batter me. So hard, they're gonna batter me.'

Vernon Watkins is at the front of the crowd walking to school. And he walks *right through* the ghost. That is wrong.

Meanwhile everyone else is stuck in the doorway behind me.

'Move it, Bitchin, you lemon,' says Sal.

'What's the matter?' says Polly.

'There's a ghost, right there,' I say.

And, just for a second, I see this look in Polly's eyes. It's like she's thinking: Oh God, here we go again. 'Oh dear,' she says. She's keeping her voice soft, the way you talk to an old person. 'What should we do for the ghost?'

'Shhhh, Polly,' I whisper. 'Everyone's gonna rip the piss.'

'If you don't want me to help, I'm going.'

'Polly, don't.'

'Why?'

'Cos I need you to stay with me or they'll start on me.

'Cos I wanna talk to you.

I say nothing.

'I have to drop my guitar in the music room,' she says. 'If I get there first I'll save you a place.'

And she goes.

I bend down and pretend to tie my laces, and I wait till everyone else has gone round the corner. Then I walk right up to the ghost. Now you wouldn't believe the smell.

'My dad's gonna beat me so bad,' he's saying.

'Listen,' I whisper to him, 'your dad ain't gonna beat you. And you don't have to keep standing here.'

'I gotta stay here!' he shouts.

'You've been dead for weeks. You should go.'

'I gotta stay here!' he shouts again.

Then I notice something strange. Right next to him, there's a machine. Looks like an air-conditioner fan. There's a little bottle next to it, that's filled with liquid. This machine is like the ghost: it ain't real. I try to hold the bottle. My hand goes right through it.

'Listen,' I say to him again, 'you gotta move away from here.'

He looks at me. For a moment it's like I'm his only hope. I start to walk. He moves one step.

'STAY RIGHT THERE!' I hear this loud voice. 'HOW DARE YOU MOVE FROM YOUR POSITION?'

I'm looking around. I can't hear who's talking.

On top of the block of flats there's something nuts. Looks like an old man, 'cept he's only three foot tall, and he's got something hanging off his back, looks like a cloak. Just seeing him up there scares me like you wouldn't believe. I actually feel a little jet come out in my pants. I think I'm gonna have a panic attack and I won't be able to breathe.

But then I see someone else watching me.

7

It's Vernon Watkins.

I'm thinking: Is this it? Is this the only guy I can be friends with now? Vernon Watkins, who is, *officially*, for the hundredth week running, Number One, in the Coca-Cola Sponsored, *Top of The Speng*, Charts?

'What's the matter?' he says.

I look at him. It's OK. It's Verno. He's the one person I can tell, 'cos I don't care what he thinks, and no one else is gonna talk to him.

'Verno,' I say, 'see them flowers? There's a ghost standing in front of them. Little boy.'

'Really?' he says. 'I thought it went cold when I went past.'

I'm so glad he believed me, I think I'm gonna cry. I don't cry. I never cry, but I get a pain in my throat like I swallowed a boiled sweet. Verno gives me a tissue which he keeps up his sleeve the way grannies do. And he puts his arm on my shoulder. That brings me to my senses. Anyone could come round the corner. I push away the tissue and shrug off the arm. I gotta get away from him.

'We're gonna be late,' I say. 'I'm gonna run.'

I jog towards school. Trouble is, Vern runs after me. So I ain't shaken him off by the time we reach the school gates, so I change tactics. I gotta walk. And hope no one's gonna see. But they have. There's a bottle bank next to the school gates. As I walk by through the gates, someone opens the lid and accidentally-on-purpose smashes a bottle near my feet. I look up, really really quick.

It's Trish Appleton.

She's the thickest girl in my class. At school Mr Barker once asked her for her date of birth.

'Twenty-eighth of October,' she says.

'What year?' says Barker.

'Every year,' says Trish.

If you look up 'chav' in the dictionary, they got a picture of her. She is famous in Stoke Newington, 'cos her mum had her when she was thirteen. She's got dyed blonde hair, loads of make-up, and she wears a tight white T-shirt which don't reach her hipsters, so her fat stomach is poking out the top of her jeans. I hate her. Not just 'cos Trish is a slosher, which she is. She'll get off with anyone. Long as they got a cousin with a car. We used to get on fine. When we were like three, or four, I used to see her in Hackney Downs park when I went there with Dad. She always had a runny nose. She always sat under the slide, and she put out all her dollies and pretended it was her home. If you came in, you had to pretend to be her husband. She used to call me Little Daddy. Now she calls me Tadpole. She's so two-faced she's got a mouth on the back of her head. When she's on her own, she's friendly. But if she's with anyone else, you're gonna get pied up. Trish Appleton has battered me more times than Kriss, Sal and Eric put together.

'Tadpole,' she says, 'are you getting jiggy with Verno?'

I pretend I ain't heard, I pretend I ain't seen the bottle. That ain't easy since there's a bit of glass on my shoe. I move off, checking my watch. Four minutes to nine. Vern is still following me.

But then I see Sharon Holdings. Bad bad bad. Luckily she's busy with a bloke from Year Ten. You can tell he fancies her, 'cos he's hitting her on the arm. Everyone fancies her. She's tall and blonde and looks like a model. I remember the first time she talked to me, she asked if she could borrow my pencil sharpener, and she was so good-looking I couldn't talk. She looks at me, dead quick, as I go by, but she don't notice I'm with Vern. So I'm OK till I reach the school building.

I'm OK.

But soon as I open the main door and see that long shiny corridor and I get that school smell of Pledge I feel like wetting myself again. I can't explain it. School scares me more than ghosts. I can feel there's something wrong but I don't know what it is.

When we reach Assembly, Polly sees me and Vern. She's got two seats next to her. I'm hoping she'll put her bag on one, so Verno will leave us alone. But she don't. She smiles at him.

'Do you want a seat, Vern?' she says.

He smiles and sits. I frown at her. Poll knows that sitting by Vern could get me in trouble. But that ain't why I'm annoyed. I'm annoyed 'cos I told her I saw a ghost and she didn't believe me. So we keep quiet till Assembly starts.

Mr Hearfield starts talking. He's our headmaster. He didn't use to be. He used to just be the Physics teacher, and he wore thick glasses, and brown shiny trousers, and he would say stuff like: 'If we apply three unit of pressure.' He wouldn't say 'three units', he would say 'three unit'. What a bandit. But then he started prepping Ms Harvey, who teaches Business Studies, and now he's headmaster and wears a suit. So he looks OK now, but he still ain't changed the way he talks. He can't pronounce his Rs, he makes them into Ws, so he pronounces it 'thwee unit of pressure'. Eric does a hilarious impression of him. Hearfield is going on about the old gym, and how some people've been seen going in, but it ain't safe 'cos it's filled with broken glass.

He says the school has 'devised a deal with a major supermarket retailer, who will be sponsoring a new hall filled with top-of-the-range gymnastic and sporting facilities for the whole school to enjoy . . .'

I ain't really listening. But then something happens which gets my attention.

Hearfield is going:

'Also, you may remember that, three weeks ago, all London pupils sat an IQ test. Well, I have exciting news. One of our community has scored the highest IQ in the entire Hackney and Stratford area . . .'

He pauses. Already I'm getting the fear. I know what's coming next. I hope I'm wrong.

I ain't.

He carries on: 'I want you to put your hands together for a vewy special boy – Colin Hitchin.'

The teachers all clap and smile at me. Polly nudges me and grins. Vernon Watkins whispers, 'Well done, Colin.' Most of the school clap as well, but, over the top of it, you can also hear Sal and Kriss and Trish going '*BITCHin!*' and '*Tweek the Freak!*' and '*Tadpole the tiny FREAK Boy*'. I'm holding my head in my hands and I'm sinking into my chair and I'm getting well hot. You know that feeling when you go into a hot shop in your winter clothes and you kind of prickle? That's what's happening now. Why did he have to say 'special'?

I can't take it no more.

I make out like I'm busting for a wazz, and I run out.

I go back into the main school corridor and I just stand there.

I gotta get it together.

I'm being like Karate Kid standing on his post. I'm taking deep breaths. In . . . Out . . . In . . . Out . . .

I'm staring down the corridor, looking at the locked door at the end of the school corridor. The one that leads to the old gym Hearfield was just talking about.

And then something happens . . .

Something comes out *through* the locked door.

It is a massive snake. Black with yellow colour.

It slivers slowly through the locked door.

Staring at me all the time.

Opens its massive mouth. Its tongue comes out. Reaching down the corridor towards me.

8

If I'da been thinking, I'd be going . . .

Is that real?

It can't be real.

Snakes ain't that big.

And they don't go through locked doors.

And they don't go to school.

And if they did, they wouldn't be allowed in the old gym 'cos no one's allowed.

But I *don't* think. I run straight into the toilets next to me. I stand at the sink, staring at the mirror, trying to be calm, saying it under my breath over and over: 'It ain't real it ain't real and I ain't gonna be scared.'

Then, I realize I've gone into the girls' toilets which, to tell you the truth, I've always wanted to see. They're the same size as ours, but they got pink tiles, and more cubicles, and also they got soap. I wash my hands with the soap. It smells like Raspberry Ripple, and I wash my face as well, 'cos I'm still trying to get my hands to stop shaking. And so basically I've stayed in there too long, and the worst thing has happened . . .

Sharon Holdings comes in. Bad.

And also Trish Appleton. Even worse.

'Ah . . . it's a vewy special boy,' says Sharon.

'Tadpole, what you doing in our toilets?' says Trish.

I don't say nothing.

Trish starts up: 'He thinks he's a girl, innit? 'Cos he sounds like one, innit?'

I don't say nothing.

Trish starts again: 'Wassa matter? You think you is so *special* you can come in here?'

I go: 'I had to come in here. There's a big snake down the other end of the corridor.'

'What?' says Trish.

'There's a big snake. Down by the old gym.'

Trish looks at me. 'Show me,' she says.

Trish and Sharon walk out. I follow. I peer round the corner.

It's still there. Its head must be nearly a metre across. It must be larger than any snake on earth.

But it ain't so big that Trish and Sharon can see it.

'You winding us up?' says Trish.

'No.'

' 'Cos I don't like people winding me up? I got enough stress, you know what I mean? You get what I'm saying?'

I never know if I'm supposed to answer when people say 'You get what I'm saying?'. They only say it when they've said something that's so easy to get you end up wondering if there's some hidden meaning, which ain't likely – this is Trish I'm dealing with. She's got less up top than the average guinea pig.

I say nothing.

Trish starts again:

'What were you doing in our toilets, Tadpole?'

'He was probably looking for somewhere to swim,' says Sharon.

Thanks, Shar.

'Is that what you were doing?' says Trish.

I don't know what to say. She's like a bomb. Any second she could go off.

'You not speaking to me, Bitchin?' says Trish.

'I wanted to wash my face.'

So then it kicks off. Trish goes: 'Right, well, we better wash your face. In the toilet.'

And they grab me and they drag me inside one of the cubicles. At first I like it 'cos Shar puts her arms round me to lift me up and that feels sweet. But then they push my head in the toilet, and they soak my dad's SAS combat scarf. So then I lose it, and I start wriggling and kicking and trying to push them off but then I *whack* my face on the toilet bowl. So then I go more mad still, and Sharon is holding me, and Trish is reaching for my pants, and I know what she's doing, she's trying to give me an Atomic Wedgie where they grab the back of your pants and try to stretch them over your head. Normally it don't work, but 'cos I'm so small they manage, and then they lift me up, and they hang me on the hook on the back of the toilet door. Then they laugh, and the door shuts, and they go. Leaving me on the back of the door. Hanging from my own pants. Which are stretched over my own head. I don't want no one to see this. This ain't good. I'm hanging there, I'm thinking: Is this it? Is this what I was scared of? Is this the worst it's gonna get? But then it gets worse.

9

I'm hanging there for ages. I can't lift myself off. And I can't get my pants to rip. Thing is: I don't want to make a noise, 'cos I don't want no one else to see me there. I hear lots of girls coming in, but luckily no one comes in my cubicle. And then it goes quiet 'cos everyone musta gone for the first lesson. So I just hang there.

But then I hear someone come in, and I can't tell you why, but I know it's Polly. That ain't ideal neither. I don't want Polly to see, but what am I to do? I speak: 'Poll?'

Polly pushes open the door and she looks up at me. She tries not to smile but her eyes sort of twinkle.

'Colin,' she says. 'What happened?'

'Nothing.'

'Here, stand on my shoulders.'

I stand on her shoulders, and I lift myself off the hook. Then I lean against the cubicle wall, and I get myself down. I don't look at her face, I'm rubbing my back and I'm avoiding her eyes.

She says: 'Do you want to talk to me, Colin?'

'No. Why?'

'No reason . . . You sure?'

'Poll . . . Can you keep a secret?'

'Come on.'

'Earlier I heard a voice in my head. And I saw a snake in the corridor.'

Polly looks in the corridor. Then she looks at me.

'Colin, maybe we should go to the doctor.'

'I don't need a doctor! You know I hate doctors!'

'Colin, they're not giving you brain surgery. They just give you a little medication to make you feel straight again.'

'I am straight again.'

'But you say you're seeing stuff!'

'I *am* seeing stuff! Why don't you believe me? I was standing in the corridor and . . .'

She puts her arm round me, and that bugs me.

'Calm down. I'm trying to help.'

'Don't treat me like I'm a child. I don't need help.'

'If you say so, Colin. You're the one who was hanging on the back of a toilet door like a wet towel.'

I need to get her hand off my shoulder. I take her hand, and I fling it off, and she hits her knuckles on the door frame.

'Don't get mad with me,' she says.

'I ain't mad with you. If I'm mad, it ain't always 'cos of you. What's your problem?'

'Colin, don't be an eejit.'

I just stare at her, and then I walk off.

We go to Biology with Mr Barker. I hear a few people whispering '*special boy*' and Eric uses a Biro to blow wet paper in my hair, but I pretend I ain't noticed and it's nothing I can't handle. First Barker shows us the locusts who've been shedding their skins. Then he's telling us about this fly that burrows its arse into the skin of cows, so the cow's got maggots growing inside its skin. Gross. He shows us pictures of the cows, and they've got big red boils.

Polly gives me a few looks, but I ignore her. Then at breaktime, I go and hide round the side of the old gym. That way I don't have to see nobody. Luckily Verno has leant me a book, *Lupacle At Large* by GP Taylor. The Lupacle is a guy who turns into a wolf when he gets mad and then he goes on the rampage. This calms me down a bit.

10

Soon as school finishes, I leg it away. Normally I go and see Polly after school and we sit about eating cereal and reading, but I ain't doing that now. I'm avoiding Polly. I know she's gonna tell me I was out of order for shouting at her when she helped me down from the Atomic Wedgie. She'll wanna make me say sorry, and I don't *never* say sorry. Forget it. I've reached Chick Pizz on Albion Road, when I get a text. I know who it's going to be, before I even look.

It says: **Meet in Clissold nxt to weeping willow? P x.**
I text back: **B there in 10.**

The weeping willow is over the far side of Clissold near the ponds. Me and Poll like it 'cos it's like a tent and there's loads of shade when it's sunny. As I walk I see this little gardening hut. The door is usually locked but now it's hanging open so I look inside. I just see forks, and slug pellets, and bags of fertilizer. Also I get this shed smell that I ain't smelled since my grandad was alive. So then I walk across the park, and I see Polly leaning against the tree. I can see she's still got on her DM boots and her black jeans even though it's so hot. Polly thinks she's got fat legs, so she don't show them off. She's got bare stuff with her. Polly always brings stuff.

Also she's got someone in front of her. I can't work out who she's talking to. Then I recognize the bright red Gap hat. Kriss. He's leaning on his bike and moving like he's telling her something important. Just then Polly smiles. Kriss chucks his bike down, and he puts his arm round her neck like he's pretending to strangle her but you can tell he's just hoping for a feel. She laughs and hits him back. I don't believe it. I see what's happening. She fancies Kriss. When did Polly get so horny all of a sudden?

But then Polly musta said something 'cos now both of them turn and look at me. Kriss gives me a long look. It's like he's planning something. Then he picks up his bike and he cycles off. Polly looks back at her book.

When I get close she looks up and says, 'Hey, Col,' with a smile.

'Hi, Poll,' I go. I wanna act friendly to show I ain't pissed off with her, but I ain't saying sorry.

I sit down next to her.

'You can lean on this,' she says, and passes me a

rolled-up coat. Then she gets out two drinks. 'Do you want apple or mango?'

I say apple 'cos I know she likes mango. I like it about girls that they've always got their own favourite drink. With my mum it's banana soya milk. She always smiles when I get her that. I do it when I need cash.

'What were you talking to Kriss about?'

'It's a secret.'

'Fair enough. But you can tell me.'

'I definitely can't tell you.'

We don't say nothing after that. But then this squirrel appears nearby. It's checking to see if we're gonna lob it food.

'Did you see that story in the *Hackney Gazette*?' I go.

'About how crack dealers are hiding their stash and squirrels are digging it up?'

'Yeah.'

Polly knows the exact article I'm thinking about, even without me saying.

'That was hilarious,' she says. 'Reckon your mum wrote it?'

'She don't really write. Just edits.'

'Mind you,' says Polly, 'if I was a crack addict, I'd be smoking the crack. I wouldn't be leaving it out for the squirrels like some kind of twisted Cinderella.'

I laugh. Then I'm thinking: Is this it? Are we friends again? Do I still need to say sorry?

I don't need to think much longer, 'cos Kriss and Sal cycle over. Kriss has got a mountain bike, and he's doing a long wheelie. Doing a Zorro, we call it, 'cos it looks like you're on a horse and you're making it rear up 'cos you're riding into town to beat the crap out of everyone. Sal's on one of them tiny stunt bikes. Most people ride them in Hackney. If you're nang, you got a small bike. 'Cept Sal's so big he looks like an elephant on a skateboard.

They both stop in front of us. Sal takes out a can of Coke and swigs it.

'Wassup, Bitchin,' says Kriss.

'Wassup, Kriss,' I say. I'm thinking: What does he want?

'We gotta hand in Maths coursework on Monday,' he says. 'You done yours?'

'Yip.'

'Will you go home and get it, so I can copy it out?'

'I dunno, Kriss.'

'You're good at Maths, you know what I'm saying? You been turning up regular . . . If you like, I can come round your house later.'

'I dunno.'

'You two coming to Sharon's on Sunday?'

'What is it?'

'Birthday, innit? Meeting at Nag's Head Islington six o'clock, then going back to hers.'

'OK. Did she tell you to tell us?'

'D'int she tell you herself?'

'No.'

'Well, come, bruv. Bring the Maths then.'

'OK.'

'You can come as well, Poll.'

Kriss is like that. Even though it ain't his party, he's still inviting people. Sal's already finished his Coke. He burps and chucks it over our heads.

'Don't do that,' says Polly.

'What?'

'Chuck stuff in the park.'

'Everyone else does so why can't I?'

'But there's six billion people in the world. Imagine if they all chucked a can of Coke in the park.'

'But they don't, so it don't matter, innit?'

'Yeah but you do matter,' says Polly. 'Imagine that, whatever you do, six billion people are doing the same thing.'

'What you talking about?'

'It means, Sal,' I say, 'if you picked up one can of Coke, then you'd be tidying the world.'

'What?' he goes, and he looks at me.

Why did I do that? I've broken the basic rule: don't stick your neck out.

'I ain't gonna tidy the world like I'm some waste gash,' says Sal.

He's looking at me like I'm a baby with two heads. Suddenly I don't wanna chat about anything. I want to give him a Bucking Bronco kick to the head. But then I think three words: Tweek the Freak.

'What is Eric doing?' says Kriss suddenly.

I look round. Eric goes by on one of them bikes that don't have a crossbar. He's got this new fog horn on his handebars. It lets out a long Tarzan sound. He's charging towards the edge of the pond, where a couple of swans are eating bread. When he gets to the fence, he jumps off.

'Check this out,' says Eric. 'This is the biggest seagull I've ever seen! I'm gonna chuck a stick at its head.'

He makes to pick up a stone.

'Don't you dare!' says Polly. Right away, she gets up. She's sprinting over. Polly ain't no athlete. She's jiggling away. Kriss and Sal grab their bikes and go over. I walk over as well. No one hates swans more than me, but that don't mean I want Eric to chuck a stone at one.

Eric sees Poll coming, and he grins. He ain't got a brick. He just picks up a stick. Polly runs at him, and she tries to grab it straight off him.

'Give it to me!' shouts Polly.

'I was joking!'

'No you weren't! That is so out of order,' says Poll and she pushes him in the chest.

'What you doing, you pikey bitch?' says Eric.

'I'm not a pikey bitch,' says Poll.

'You are,' says Eric. 'You and your mum buy clothes from catalogues.'

'We buy clothes from Oxfam,' says Poll.

'You're admitting it?'

'I'm admitting nothing,' says Poll, 'I'm boasting.'

Polly don't let it drop. She tries to grab the stick off Eric. 'Cept now he definitely ain't gonna let her get it. She's almost fighting with him. I don't know what to do. This is Polly. She's my best friend. But surely she can see Eric is thick, but he ain't that thick. It *was* just a joke. And I can't see why Polly is trying to grab the stick off him. And she looks like a lemon. She does, I swear, and I don't know why Polly has to act like she can tell everyone what to do.

'Just leave it, Poll,' I say. 'He was joking.'

'So you're taking his side?' says Poll, turning on me. Polly is so Irish sometimes. She's always gotta be fighting someone.

At that point Eric chucks the stick away. He don't chuck it at the swan. But he chucks it in that direction, just to show he ain't gonna be told what to do by nobody. Now no one knows what to do. We're all tense. It's like we're gonna have a fight about anything. Then Kriss turns to me:

'Bitchin, don't mess me about. Go and get the Maths.'

'I don't wanna.'

'I'll lend you my bike.'

'I don't wanna.'

'Why?'

'I just . . . don't wanna walk across the park right now.'

'*Why?*'

'I . . . just got a bad feeling about it.'

'Why?'

' 'Cos . . . I ain't going over there . . . It ain't safe. Any second now, a bomb is gonna go off.'

'What the hell are you talking about?'

I don't know why I said that. The words just came into my head.

'What you chatting about?' says Kriss.

'Nothing. Don't matter.'

'You're a freak,' says Sal.

11

Me and Poll go back to the tree. She gets her book out and starts reading again. You can tell she's vexed with me 'cos I didn't take her side. She knows I was embarrassed about her. Polly Knows Everything. And I'm riled 'cos she won't tell me what Kriss was saying. I get the magazine out, but I can't relax. It ain't just 'cos we nearly got in a fight. It's worse than that. I feel so tense inside. My stomach is clenching.

Something is definitely about to happen.

Something big.

I don't think I'm gonna get hurt, but somebody definitely is.

I hope it's nobody I like.

Something's gonna happen.

Any second now it's gonna happen.

What's it gonna be?

Am I making it happen 'cos I'm expecting it?

What's it gonna be?

I'm panicking.

I'm staring at the big house, where they got the café.

Then it happens . . .

Suddenly the house is surrounded by a massive orange flash.

Bits of brick and window are blown thirty metres in the air.

Then there's a huge ball of smoke.

Then the noise hits us.

BOOMMMM!

'Jesus H Christ, and Mary Mother of God!' says Polly. 'Do you think it was a firework?'

'Sounded like a *bomb*,' I say.

We watch. No one's moving. Then someone's shouting. Then people are running. Then Kriss, Sal and Eric are riding over, screaming:

'BITCHIN! BITCHIN!'

They come right over and skid their bikes in front of us.

'Bitchin!' says Kriss. 'How the hell did you know that was gonna happen?'

'What *has* happened?' I go.

'Did you have something to do with it?'

'What do you mean?'

' 'Cos if you did you are gonna get smacked up so bad!'

'What? What has happened? Was it a firework?'

55

'That was a *bomb*. I think someone's hurt. And you knew it was gonna happen.'

'What do you mean?'

'Do you know who put it there?'

'No!'

'Then how the hell did you know about it?'

Kriss is all sweaty and his eyes are wild. He is definitely gonna tosh me up. Any second now. I gotta tread careful. We gotta drop the subject quick.

Then Polly chucks me right into it. 'You did say "maybe a bomb will go off". Why did you do that?'

Silence. Now everyone's looking at me. I gotta say something. I think up several excuses in my head, but none of them work.

'I don't know,' I say. 'It's . . . Something's happening to me, yeah. It's like I keep seeing stuff that ain't there, and I hear stuff, and it's like I know things that are gonna happen, even before they do . . .'

Silence.

Eric is grinning a bit. Why is he grinning?

'What you saying, Bitchin?' he says. 'You think you're *special*?'

He thinks 'special' is the funniest word in the world.

'Eric, you're a comedian,' I say. 'I'm serious. You could write for Graham Norton.'

Eric looks confused.

'You saying he's gay?' says Kriss.

'No . . . I ain't. I'm just saying I think *I'm* psychic.'

Now Sal and Eric are grinning. You can tell Sal don't know what psychic means.

'What? You is psycho?' says Sal.

'You is sicko?' says Eric.

'No it's just . . . I know stuff. And I'm having these weird dreams, where I meet people from heaven, and they give me messages about my dad.'

Sal goes: 'Is your dad *dead*, Bitchin?'

'Yes, Sal,' I say, 'my dad is dead.'

Sal says: 'How did he die?'

'I *don't know*!'

'Did he top himself?' says Sal.

Thanks, Sal. You are as subtle as a boner in a sauna.

'Have you seen *his* ghost?' says Kriss. He's taking this more serious than the others.

'No.'

'Maybe he's too small,' says Eric, 'or maybe he's *special* as well.'

'Leave it,' I shout. 'You would never say that, if my dad was alive!'

Sal goes: '*Why?*'

'My dad was in the SAS.'

'What's that?' Sal goes.

And of course I fall right into it.

I say: 'SAS. That's the Special Air Services.'

Right away, they're all laughing.

'Special Air Services!' says Eric. 'Is that where they get a load of mongers, and they chuck them out planes?'

I'm such a fool. I know I should back out, but they're talking about my dad. I go: 'No! *He was in the SAS!* They flew into Kuwait and they engaged with Iraqi forces!'

'They got engaged with Iraqis?' says Eric. 'Then did they marry them?'

Right. They are boying my dad. They're asking for this. I'm going to *rush* them. I know the way this is gonna work. I'm gonna jump kick Sal, and I'm gonna follow it up with a straight right to Eric's head, and then I'm gonna kick Kriss in the balls. I know how this is gonna work. I seen Jackie Chan do this in *The Tuxedo*, and I practised it in my bedroom.

I get merked.

In no time my knees are bleeding, my hands are bleeding and I'm lying on the floor and Eric's got me in a headlock and he's gobbed in my mouth.

Polly grabs his hair.

'Jaysus Christ!' she's shouting. 'Leave him alone.'

She pulls him off, and he gets up.

Eric is saying, 'My God, he tweeked. He totally freaked!'

And they all walk off saying 'Spazzamatazz!' and '*Freak* boy!'.

Polly puts an arm round me.

'You OK, Colin?'

'Will you stop asking if I'm OK? Course I'm not OK.'

'I'm trying to help, for Christ's sake.'

'Well don't. I don't want no more of your help. Sticking your fat face in everything. For God's sake, I don't wanna see you no more. Leave me alone.'

And I get up and go.

As I walk by the café, people are rushing around looking pale.

And a police car is turning into the park, and coming this way.

And then this Asian woman is being carried from round the back of the café on a stretcher. She's bleeding from her head and she ain't moving.

Suddenly this shape comes out of her body.

I get what it is. It's her ghost. She's floating near all the people who are just gawping. She's waving her arms and shouting:

'How can they do that? How can anyone do that? My children! My children! What are my children going to do! Oh, please, God, please, God, look after my children!'

Already there's a smell coming off her. It's a smell of anger. I'm getting it myself. I'm thinking of Eric's face leaning over me and gobbing in my mouth. I'm thinking I want to hurt him bad.

I gotta get away quick.

12

It takes me ages to walk home. I'm getting that thing that happens after a fight: I'm shaking bad and my hands are bleeding and my knees are getting stiff from where I got thrown to the ground. I stop off on Albion Road and I buy some stuff, like a magazine and chewing gum, but it don't calm me at all. And then I stop on Allen Road to puke. And then I see Kriss and Sal at the other end of the street so I go into Butterfield and I sit under the trees. Then I do go home and I try to read my book but I can't concentrate 'cos my head is rammed. Then suddenly I think my mum's gonna come home, and I don't wanna tell her I got banged up and if she sees me she'll know. Then I think maybe I could go round to Vern's 'cos he's great at cleaning cuts and putting on plasters and stuff. But then I realize there's only one person I want to see, and that's Poll. I know I told her I don't wanna see her again, but she'll understand. I just been pied up by Eric, I wasn't thinking straight. She'll know that. Won't she? I go straight round to Polly's house. I even try to run. But my legs are getting well stiff so I can't.

She lives at the other end of my street on a big estate which is five storeys high and all round a big yard which has got a couple of swings, four big trees, and a car park that's always filled with broken glass. I go up the stairs which always smell of piss and then up to Polly's on the fourth floor. I knock on her door, but no one comes to answer it. I knock again. Nothing. I'm about to knock again, but then I start thinking . . . Maybe they ain't heard me. Maybe they *have* heard me and they don't wanna see me. Maybe if I knock again, then it'll look like I'm a stalker. Maybe I should go.

I knock again. Polly's mum arrives. Sharleen. She always looks rough, but now she looks like a tray of cat litter. Blue towelling dressing gown. Fag ash down the front.

Straight off, she says: 'What's the matter with her, Colin?'

'Dunno. What's happened?'

'She came home an hour ago. She didn't say hello. Didn't have her tea. Nothing. Went straight to her room. I went down there, she was writing something. Here,' she gives me an envelope, 'it's for you. Next thing I know she's fallen asleep. At five-thirty on a bright summer afternoon! I say, "Madam, are you not going to

61

have some tea?" and she's come on all peculiar. I can't get her out of bed. It's like she can't move. You come and talk to her. I'm not bein' funny, I don't know what to do with her.'

That's good. I like it when adults want me to help them. Also I like it that we're going to Polly's room. Normally me and Poll have to sit in her living-room which stinks of fags. We walk down the hallway. Sharleen knocks on the door, and she puts on this bright voice:

'Hello, Polly? Colin's come round.'

Sharleen pushes open the door.

Right away you can feel something's happened to Polly. She ain't asleep. She's sitting up in her bed, cross-legged, not moving. She looks all saggy, with her shoulders all slumped. She don't turn round as I come in. I walk into the room, and sit on the bed. Polly don't even look up. She's staring at a magazine in front of her. She ain't reading it, it's like she's pretending.

'All right, Poll,' I say. I feel a bit of a tool with her mum standing there. She pipes up pretty quick anyway:

'Polly? Polly? Aren't you going to say hello to Colin?'

'Polly,' I go, 'I need to talk to you.'

Sharleen suddenly loses her temper.

'I've had enough of this. I'm going to go down to run my bath, and if you're not up by the time I get back there's going to be trouble.'

I wait for Sharleen to go down the passage, then I start.

'Poll, it wasn't a firework you know. It was definitely a bomb. I think someone got killed. I saw their ghost.'

But Poll don't look up from her magazine. This bugs me.

'Poll,' I go, 'why did you ask me how I knew about the bomb? You really dumped me in it, gal. You could tell they were gonna get me.'

She still don't look at me. Keeps staring at her mag.

'Come on, Poll . . . Ain't you gonna say you're sorry?'

Still nothing. This ain't working. So suddenly I'm saying stuff I don't mean to say:

'Look, I know I shouted at school, yeah . . . And I know I was harsh and I ain't saying sorry. OK . . . no . . . sorry. Truly. But . . . I don't know what's happening to me and . . . Listen, I really need to talk to you . . .'

The last bit comes out funny. It's like I could cry any second, so I shut up, and just look at her. Then I realize I'm looking at Poll's breasts, and that makes me feel weird so I stop. Suddenly I want to tell her all about my mum, and my dreams, then I think I've told her so many things, and if she ain't gonna be my friend no more, she'll still know all these secrets. Suddenly I lose it.

'POLLLLLLLLLLLL! Listen to me, you cow!'

Even that don't seem to bother her, which is lucky.

I'm glad I shouted though. She comes to life, and she turns over the page of the magazine.

'I want that,' she says, pointing at this handbag, 'and I want that, and I want that . . .' At first, she is really pointing at things – not just the handbag, but also some shoes, and then some hair stuff – but after a bit, she ain't even pointing, she's just waving her finger around in the air. I watch her doing this for a while, and then I sniff, and I get a good whiff of the rank smell in the room. Suddenly I think I hate Polly and I hate my mum and I hate everything and there ain't nothing to be done about it. I can't even be bothered to get out of that stinking room, I might as well just stay in there and die.

Sharleen appears, still wearing the dressing gown. She's heard me shouting.

'Colin? Colin? What's the matter?'

She can't work out if she's annoyed with me, or with Poll. She reaches forward and she grabs Poll, and she pulls her to her feet, hugging her, the way they do on *The Bill* when they've taken a body from a river. Polly don't stand up. Her mum shakes her a bit. This wakes her up, and she talks again.

'I need that, I need that, I need that,' she says. And then she flops down again.

'Colin?' she goes again. 'I can't bear it. What is the matter with her?'

I don't know and I'm scared.

13

On the way home, there's helicopters going over making nuff noise. I hate them things. I go in Hidir's shop. Spend all the money in my pocket on a Ribena and *Martial Arts* magazine. Head home. I'm turning the corner to Walford Road, and I see Yussuf. He's right opposite the Jewish synagogue, where everyone dumps their rubbish. He's sticking another of his notices on a lamppost with Sellotape. It says: 'Join the one true faith. Turn yourself to Islam.'

'Good evening, Colin,' says Yussuf. 'I hope you are well.'

He pronounces it 'vell'. He sounds like Abu from the *Simpsons*.

'Yussuf,' I go, 'you taking the piss?'

'What do you mean?'

'Yussuf, you're putting up your sign right outside the synagogue. You seen them Hassidics? They won't fight you. They'll just ram you with their Volvos.'

Yussuf looks at me calmly.

'Then I will be dying for my faith,' he says, 'and when I enter the Kingdom of God, there will be seventy-two virgins waiting for me.'

'Yeah, but they'll all look like your mum.'

He lets that go. He's the calmest man in Hackney.

'By the way, Colin,' says Yussuf, 'there's a man waiting outside your house. Been there for the last hour.'

I look up the street. I can see someone sitting on the front wall.

It's Uncle Jimmy.

'Omygod,' I say, 'it's my Uncle Jimmy.'

'Oh . . . I thought he might be a little deranged.'

'He's definitely deranged. He's out to lunch, but he's on the case. Laters, Yussuf.'

I walk off.

'Jimmy!' I shout.

Jimmy turns, and sees me. He stands in the street, and waves his arms in the air.

'Colin Hitchin, as I live and breathe! You brave beauty! Come and give me a hug!'

I don't exactly run 'cos my legs are hurting. But I speed over, and he comes skipping towards me and he picks me up like I'm a little kid. Then he hugs me. I get the smell of Old Holborn and sweat and shirts worn for the third day running. It feels good. Then he holds my face in his hands and he looks at me. I look at him. His grey hair is hanging down to his shoulders and he's also got a thick droopy moustache. That's grey as well. His face is grey and very skinny. But his eyes are good. Full of life.

'How're you doing, boy?' he says.

'Not great.'

'You look shite. What's going on, pal?'

'Nothing. I just ain't happy.'

'That's OK. People are only happy in adverts.'

'Yeah, but, Jimmy . . . Bad stuff is going down, and I think I'm going mad.'

He smiles. 'Good. Sounds like we'll get on well.'

We go up to the flat.

It takes Jimmy five minutes before he's messed the place up. He's taken his boots off, he's rolled himself a fag, he's taken off his big stinky overcoat so you can see his T-shirt underneath. It says Bob the Builder. Thank God Mum ain't around to see this. She'd be spraying air freshener for an hour.

'Where've you come from, Jimmy?' I ask.

'Venezuela. I'm a bar manager in a little place on the coast. Well . . . I was.'

'What happened?'

'Usual story. You know . . . I told the owner he wasn't paying the kitchen staff enough. I got into a fight over a woman. Someone wanted to kill me. I ran off. So anyway . . . three days ago, I'm staying in this cheap hostel somewhere in the mountains. Lying in a hammock actually, but feeling like any second I could die. And it hits me: I need to see my family, before anything happens. And the only family I've got left is my brother's widow, your luscious mommy, and her crazy, beautiful son. You. Actually I . . . had a feeling you might need my help.'

'Why might you die, Jimmy?'

'Dunno . . . Well I just . . . I have a feeling I might have cancer.'

'You got a feeling?'

'Aye.'

'Why don't you go and see a doctor?'

'That would definitely be the sensible thing to do.'

'Do it. Ain't no point hiding.'

'Listen, pal, I hate advice. Specially when it's right. The way I see it: life is a game, and we're all playing. But I've fallen so far behind. I'm ready to start again. Now, do you have a light?'

I look in a drawer and I find this brass lighter of Dad's. Jimmy lights his rollie.

'Nice lighter,' he says. 'Could come in useful.' He winks and passes it back. 'Where's your mum?'

'Work.'

'She coming back?'

'This evening.'

'How is she?'

'Stressed. Always on about broken showers and stuff.'

'Is the shower broken?'

'Yeah.'

'I'll take a look.'

He goes into the bathroom and starts fiddling. Jimmy's like that. You'd think he wouldn't know how to run a bath, but he loves anything mechanical. While he's fiddling with the tap, he says casually: 'She seeing anyone?'

'She's got two boyfriends. One called Malcolm, who publishes magazines. And another called OB. He wants to be a famous TV presenter and he thinks Mum can help.'

'Only the inadequate become famous. Only the greedy become rich. The greedy *and* inadequate become President of the United States.'

I smile at that.

'So,' says Jimmy, 'tell me how you're going mad.'

'I know stuff.'

'Like what?'

'Like, I said "there might be a bomb" and there *was* this bomb . . . Do you think that . . . 'cos I said "there might be a bomb" . . . I *made* there be a bomb?'

'Excellent question. I think if enough people say there'll be a bomb, there'll be a bomb.'

'Plus I keep seeing weird stuff, like ghosts, and snakes.'

'OK. Good,' says Jimmy. Nothing throws him.

'And this morning I saw a pigeon that was talking like Samuel L. Jackson.'

'There are four explanations there. One: The pigeon was Samuel L. Jackson in disguise. He's a great actor. It could be done. Two: The pigeon was doing an imitation of Samuel L. Jackson. Three: You were hearing a voices in your head, and if you are, I'm proud of you. Or Four: Someone was projecting their voice through that pigeon. That's called psychic interference. That seems most likely. If it happens again, you tell me straight away.'

'And now my best friend is lying on the bed like she's lost her mind.'

'Who's that? Polly?'

'Yes.'

'Oh good. I'm glad she's still your best friend. I liked her. Irish, isn't she?'

'Yip.'

'There you go. A Celt like me and yourself.'

'So what's going on?'

'Everything you describe, Colin, sounds like a psychic phenomenon. You have to understand, that this world is just a copy. Around us is another world that's more real. A shadow world. The land of ghosts and angels. The land of the lamia.'

'Lamia? What is that?'

'The lamia is your imagination, but it's more real

than that . . . Say you've lost your hat. You're thinking: Did I leave it under my bed? Did I leave it at school? Suddenly, in your mind, you see it, fallen down the back of the sofa. Part of you is actually looking behind the sofa: your lamia. The lamia is a mental projection of you. It's the part of you that lives for ever.'

'Like my soul?'

'It's like the soul. It's like the angel inside. 'Cept that sounds too religious, too nice. Lamias are very social. They care about each other, so from that point of view they're good. But the lamia is naughty. Shady. Unhinged. Your lamia does everything you *want* to do.'

'OK,' I go, 'if I got an angel inside, how come I can't feel it?'

'Most people can't. But it's there all right. A copy of you. Dressed like you. Holding copies of the same things you're holding in your pocket.'

'Jimmy, this don't make sense.'

'Of course it doesnae make sense. Sense is merely for fools and accountants. You've got to go beyond sense, Colin. Go beyond reality. Go beyond time. Time is merely a filing system, created by fools, to stop the morons from panicking. I'm very proud of you, Colin. You're making excellent progress.'

'You don't understand. People at school already think I'm a freak. And if I tell Mum about this, they're gonna give me drugs.'

'Don't hide from your talents, Colin. You've got a most special gift.'

'Don't start that, Jimmy. I'm just normal.'

'When the phone rings, do you know who it's going to be?'

'Well . . . that's different.'

'Why?'

'Well . . . 'cos if the phone goes at six-thirty p.m., it's probably Polly. 'Cos she's had her tea, and she don't understand her homework. If it's one a.m., it's you – in a bar somewhere, all loved up on rum and Coke.'

'That's great. You actually see me drinking rum and Coke?'

'It's what you drink, innit?'

'How do you know?'

'I just notice stuff.'

'That's all it is: noticing stuff. Everywhere the world is full of magic, but most peoples' eyes are covered in a veil of fear and lies.'

'Jimmy,' I say, 'I can't be talking right now. I need to find what's happening to Polly.'

'That's exactly what I'm trying to help you with, Colin. Because it sounds like something's happened to Polly's lamia.'

'So what we gonna do?'

'We're going to go round there and find out.'

'I just did that, and it messed me up.'

'That's 'cos you walked there. I want us to go round with our lamias.'

'How we do that?'

'That isnae easy. It could also be very dangerous.'

14

'I ain't gotta choice, Jimmy,' I say, 'I gotta find out what's happened.'

'OK,' says Jimmy. 'Have you ever heard of astral projection?'

'No.'

'Sometimes called "remote viewing". It's about entering the world of the lamia. Do you want to try that?'

'How do we start?'

'Think about when you're falling asleep. Before you drift off, you just feel light. That's where I need you to be. Between sleeping and waking. The in-between world. Then you leave your body, and move your mind, entirely, *into* the shade. Into the lamia. And then you concentrate. You believe utterly what's happening.'

'Is this safe?'

'It may not be safe to leave your body for too long. But we'll be fine, unless someone messes with our bodies while we're trying to work. That's very bad.

But no one can reach us here. Your mum's out for a while. Right?'

'She ain't normally back till eight.'

'So let the adventure begin.'

'You sure you know how to do this?'

'I'm a world master at this.'

I'm about to refuse, but then I look at Jimmy. It's hard to believe anyone's a world master at anything, when they're wearing a Bob the Builder T-shirt. He ain't dangerous. I got nothing to lose.

'Come on then, Jimmy. Let's give it a try.'

'Good lad. The first thing is you got to really relax. Let's go back next door. You may want to lie on the floor, with your head on a cushion. I'll do the same.'

We both lie on the floor in the living-room facing up towards the dusty lampshade. He looks at me.

'Do you trust me?'

I look at his eyes. They're red. 'I trust you,' I say.

'Good. Close your eyes and relax.'

I do.

'See your breath, filling your body, making you relaxed. Imagine the air pouring in through the top of your head is platinum gold. Breathe out, and imagine the air coming out has come through the bottom of your feet, and it is cold and full of minerals, like air from a cave. See that. Gold air coming down, cave air coming up. You are empty. Just a receptacle for breath. Breathe. Relax. And in your mind say the magic word "hazoom". *Hazoom.*'

I'm doing it. I'm saying hazoom. And it works. I'm so tired anyway I'm feeling well weak. My mind is getting light like I've been swigging cough medicine. He keeps telling me 'to step away from the body, step into the lamia'. I ain't really listening. I'm just feeling more and more calm.

After a while, I get this feeling that I'm light, like I'm on a lilo floating in the sea. I hear a voice:

'Colin? Colin? Can you hear me?'

It's Uncle Jimmy's voice, but here is the weird part: I'm not listening to his real voice. **I'm listening to his voice, in my head***.*

'If you can hear me, reply to me, in your head.'

I think: 'How'm I supposed to do that?'

Right away I get a reply: 'Good! That's it. Now listen . . . This is not Uncle Jimmy talking to you. It is Uncle Jimmy's lamia. And you're hearing with your lamia. You are your lamia, and you've left your body behind. I want you to float up. Up. Up. Remember the lampshade. Keep going till you can feel it just brushing against you. Can you feel that?'

'Yes.'

'Good. Right. Turn over in the air, so the lampshade is brushing against your back, and face down at your body.'

I do it. Least, I think I do it.

'Good. Now, in a moment, you are going to open your eyes in your mind, in your lamia, and you're going to look down at your body. Keep calm, and now look . . .'

I open my eyes, and I see something incredible . . .

I am hovering two and a half metres in the air.

Just hanging there like I'm held up by invisible wires. Looking down at my body. I can see a bruise starting under my left eye from where I got the bogwash. I can't believe it.

I look round the room.

Suddenly I see a creature watching me through the opened window.

Looks like a massive bird, three foot tall.

'Cept it's got the head of an old man.

It's holding its wings open like a crow that's too hot.

I scream.

And then my stomach drops away.

I think I'm gonna throw up.

I open my eyes.

I'm back in my body, lying on the floor.

I turn to Jimmy. He's lying beside me, watching.

'You OK?'

'I saw this . . . thing watching us from the window.'

'That happens all the time. Must be waiting for you to sleep.'

He turns to the window.

'Be off with you,' he shouts, 'there's nothing for you here.'

He's shouting at the open window, but I can't see nothing in it no more, so Jimmy just looks like a nutter. Looks like a tramp in the park.

'Right,' he says, 'shall we try again?'

'I don't wanna see that again.'

'You can't avoid them. They're everywhere, all the time.'

'What are they?'

'That was a shakfiend. They prey on your fear. They want to drain you of life. Don't give them that pleasure.'

'I can't do this. I can't be seeing something that wants to drain me.'

'The world is full of things that wannae drain you. Mosquitoes. Viruses. Maths teachers. Shakfiends are always there. The only difference is you're letting yourself see them. Don't worry. We're gonna keep away from those bastards.'

'You sure about that?'

'You can't get anywhere if you're scared, 'cos you tense up. Let's calm down. Let's start again. Say hazoom.'

I'm still scared of the shakfiend. But also I wanna

know what's gonna happen. So I say it again. Hazoom hazoom hazoom.

Soon the tingly feeling comes back, and I feel myself lift up again. Again, I open my eyes. I'm looking down from the corner of the room like a CCTV camera. I look at Uncle Jimmy's body lying there, and he looks sweet, the way people do when they're asleep. Then I hear the voice again, from behind.

'Well done, Colin. I said you were talented. It took me a year's practice before I could do that.'

I turn around, and I get a shock. Another Jimmy is standing in the corridor, leaning against the wall, smiling. His lamia. Looks like a ghost. He ain't black and white, like a ghost you see in a film. He's got colour. But he don't look solid. He also looks a lot more fit and handsome than Jimmy himself.

I smile.

'You look good,' I say.

'Oh, thanks. It's how I truly am.'

He turns and I see something surprising. He's got wings stuck on his back. Like big swan wings. 'Cept the feathers are black.

'Why have you got wings, Jimmy?'

'Because I'm a lamia. I'm an angel.'

'You can't be an angel.'

'Why?'

'You got egg in your moustache and you smell of fags.'

'Fine. I'm a dirty angel. Why don't you come down off the ceiling and look at yourself?'

I look down.

'How do I get down from here?'

'Just spread your wings and think where you want to go. Everything starts in the brain. You'll get the hang of it.'

I float down and I go straight to the mirror in the hall – the one Mum looks at, just before she leaves the house. I look wicked. I'm wearing the same clothes as before. But I look better. Taller. Good. And I've got wings on my back as well. I turn sideways and look at them. They're white and blue. They look good. I'm rolling my shoulders, trying to move my wings. Suddenly I find the muscle. My wings open wide.

I look at myself, and I smile. That makes me lift up again. Jimmy glides into the living-room, over our bodies, and he goes to the open window.

'Shall we go out?' he says.

'I dunno. I don't want to see no more of them creatures.'

'Wait,' he says. In the window, Mum's got two basil plants growing. He rips them both up and he gives me one. 'Stuff that in the button hole of your shirt,' he says. 'It'll dissuade them a little.'

I do, and he does the same. But then I notice that the basil plants we took – they're still there.

'How come the plants are still there?'

'Like I say, the real world is just a copy. We've taken the lamia of the basil plant, but their bodies are still there.'

'Don't things die, if they lose their lamia?'

'Not right away. It's like laptops. They can carry on, for a while, without getting plugged in.'

'What about people? Do they keep on living, if their lamias get hurt?'

'They don't die right away. But the people will be like vegetables.'

'Can they live? Can they work?'

'Only in television. We must get to Polly before that happens to her.'

We both lean out the window and look around. No sign of the shakfiend. It is weird out there. 'Cos everyone in the street – they all got lamias too. The people are walking down the street. Sometimes you can see their lamias flitting in and out of their bodies. Sometimes they come right out and they fly round in the air. An old West Indian bloke is walking along holding an umbrella. His lamia is all raggedy. He comes out of his body and screams: 'Why don't you listen to me? How dare you ignore me?' But his body is walking on, all quiet.

Something's happening to me. I'm trying to stand in the living-room looking out, but it's like I'm being sucked out the window. I hold the frame to stop it.

'Hang on a second, Jimmy,' I say. 'I don't want Polly to see us if we go round. Don't want her to think we're spying.'

'She won't see us. Her lamia might see us, and then that'll feel like she's just thought of us.'

'How do we get there?'

'Fly.'

'How?'

'As easy as thinking. Just spread your wings, know where you want to go, and let yourself float out the window.'

Jimmy lets go of the frame, and I watch him float up and out of the window and right over the middle of the street. I can't believe it. It looks like he's just lying in the air, three storeys up.

'Come on, Colin. Know you can do this.'

And I let go of the window. My feet leave the floor. My head goes out into the fresh air. I open my wings. I rise up. I rise up. I don't look down. I keep staring into Jimmy's eyes. But I know I'm out of the window, and hanging above the street.

'Good boy, good boy, good boy.'

He turns till he's standing upright in the air, and holds out his hands. I come towards him. It's like when I learned to swim, and I'd make for my dad and hang on. I hold his hands and keep staring into his eyes 'cos I don't dare look down.

'Good boy. Now remember. We have left our bodies behind. We can go wherever we like. All you have to do is to believe it.'

'All right, boss.'

'Good. So now you can look down.'

I take my eyes from Jimmy's and I look down.

I'm ten metres above the street. Jesus. A Telewest van is driving underneath.

'It's all right,' says Jimmy, 'you're not gonnae fall down. You can hold my hand if you like. Till you get the hang of it. Which way is Polly's?'

I point over the top of our house.

Jimmy smiles at me.

'Lead the way,' he says.

And he flaps his big wings, and I flap mine. We float up past our house. Soon we're higher than the gutter. I look down and see a plant growing out of it. Then we cross over the roof of the house opposite. And then we're flying over the back gardens. I check the sky for shakfiends. There ain't none, but the sun is coming out and shining through clouds. I look down and I see Yussuf, who's doing his salutations in the garden. His lamia is right beside him. Doing it too.

15

So we're drifting down Walford Road, but flying over the back gardens, which ain't places you normally see.

In one there's bushes and all the grass has been trampled down by a big Rottweiler that's panting away in the corner. I hate Rottweilers.

In the next there's a pond and there's loads of gnomes.

In the next there's paving, and a naked woman is lying on her back facing up. She musta rubbed herself with suncream 'cos her chest is shiny. I can't see her lamia. She must be asleep.

We keep going. At one point a wood pigeon is flying along underneath us, going at the same speed. Then it turns up, and it looks like it's surprised to see us, and it dives. Long as we don't pass any swans in the air. They give me the fear even more than Rottweilers.

Then we're coming up to the High Street and

you can see the cars and buses rumbling along underneath and it don't feel safe to be hanging in the air above all that. Now we rise up and go over the five storeys and now we're floating into the middle of Polly's estate.

Some kids are playing on the swings. Doing the Chopper: that thing where you lean over the swing then you twist the seat round and round and then it spins. Their lamias are inside the kids' bodies but you can sometimes see them. Also there's a supermarket lorry parked in the middle of the car park.

And on the top of the block of flats, there's a shakfiend. That scares me again. But it ain't doing much. Just sitting there like a big ugly pigeon.

Soon as it sees us, it jumps off, and flaps towards us.

'Jimmy!' I shout.

He turns. He sees it.

'Stay cool, laddie,' he says, 'stay calm. They don't like the trees,' and he flies to the big oak tree outside Polly's house. He lands on one of the wide upper branches. I land next to him. You can feel the tree moving in the breeze so I hold on to a small branch as well.

The shakfiend flies back the way it came, and it settles down where it was before.

'Which one is Polly's flat?' asks Jimmy.

I point to a flat nearby. I can see Polly's bedroom from here. She's got her blind down. I can also see the frosted glass of Polly's bathroom window which is slightly open. And I can see the kitchen window with a blind that's half down but I can still see the taps and the sponges.

Suddenly I gasp.

There's a ghost staring out of the window of the flat that's right next to us. She's got a tea towel on her head and a mean expression on her face.

She's looking out and talking:

'I don't see why she should have all the fun,' she says. 'Just 'cos she's taken what's mine. Don't see why.'

I can smell her as well. It gives a bad taste in my mouth like when you drink orange juice just after you brushed your teeth. It makes me feel like I used to when I got jealous of Vern 'cos he got chosen for the Annual Cub Convention in the Lake District when it shoulda been me.

The ghost woman takes a swig from a bottle, then she jumps out the window. She falls down to the tarmac and lands smack on her head.

But then right away she's back where she started. Still staring. Still mumbling: 'Don't see why she should have all the fun . . .'

'Stop looking at her,' says Jimmy, 'she's sucking you in. It's not healthy.'

I turn. 'Can you see her as well?'

'Course. We're lamias, we see all ghosts. And I tell ya, there's a lot to see round here. Far more than I'd expect.'

'What happens, Jimmy?' I ask. 'When you die, do you just stay here?'

'No no no. When you die, you . . . travel off. That's what should happen anyway. Ghosts are lamias who've got stuck. They're imprisoned by their dank self-obsession.'

'Maybe someone's keeping them?'

'They do it to themselves. Ghosts are dwelling on what's happened. Trying to make you dwell on it as well. That's why you shouldnae stare. They've got very bad energy. Ghosts are always from people who've been killed, or from people who killed themselves.'

I'm about to ask him more, when something happens.

16

*P*olly's blind opens. You can see Sharleen inside. She goes out of the room. Now you can see Polly through the window, lying on her bed, watching the telly, magazine on her lap. It looks like she's looking at us, 'cos she's got the telly on her chest of drawers, right next to the window. Her lamia is sitting next to her, doing much the same.

It's weird. The lamia looks the same as her, but a bit older. She looks curvy. Womanly. Also exhausted. Her wings are pink and brown.

'That's her,' I say.

'Oh dear.'

'What?'

'Watch.'

Polly's lamia gets off the bed, and leaps against the telly, clonks her head against the glass. Then she goes back, and sits next to Polly. After a few seconds, she does it again. She looks like one of them flies who tries to get out of the window but smacks into it head first.

Jimmy nods.

'Television,' he says. 'Lamias hate it more than anything.'

'Why?'

'Stifles them. Normally your lamia acts out anything that's in your imagination, but television acts it all out for you, so the lamia just crashes into the glass. That's why when you watch telly, you get tired.'

Jimmy floats over to the windowsill, and then he shouts through the glass:

'TURN THE TELLY OFF. YOU'RE NOT ENJOYING IT.'

But Polly does nothing. Jimmy comes back.

'She's not responding. We need to get in.'

'Shall we try the bathroom window?'

'Good lad.'

We float over to it. It's only open a few centimetres.

'Right,' says Jimmy, floating towards it.

'Jimmy, we'll never fit.'

He grins at me. 'We're lamias now. We can travel through anything. That's a perk of the job.'

He winks at me and then pushes his head right through the glass and disappears inside. I follow. The glass is all cold. But soon I'm in and I'm looking down at Polly's ugly blue bathroom sink, which has got toothpaste splattered all over. The bathroom smells of toilet cleaner and mouthwash.

Jimmy drifts out into the corridor. I follow him. He's at the door to Polly's room, leaning on the door frame. I stand next to him.

And there's Polly and her lamia, both looking sad. Her lamia seems to see us. But then she gets up, headbutts the screen, and sits down again.

'Don't look at the telly,' says Jimmy, 'or you'll start doing the same. Stay back in the corridor. In fact, wait here.'

Jimmy goes down to the living-room, where we can see Sharleen through the open door. She's smoking and doing the crossword. I hear him shout: 'GO AND TURN POLLY'S TELLY OFF. THE NOISE OF IT IS ANNOYING YOU.' Jimmy comes back, followed by Sharleen. She goes straight over to the telly, and turns it off. Then she opens the window. Then she looks at Polly.

'Are you going to tell me what the matter is?' she says.

Polly says nothing.

Sharleen sighs. You can tell she ain't really thinking about Polly though. Her lamia has stayed in the living-room. Sharleen goes back. Now the telly's off Polly seems to get some strength.

But something happens.

There's a flapping of batty wings, then the shakfiend appears at the window.

Polly's lamia don't stand for this. She charges right at the window, waving her arms and screaming. 'Bog off,' she's shouting. 'Go! I don't want to see you again!'

The shakfiend scarpers.

Poll's lamia goes back and lies beside Polly, who looks well tired. Polly and Sharleen can't have heard the lamia shouting 'cos neither of them react. Polly's body picks up her magazine, and pulls it on to her lap. She reads and her lamia reads too, although she also keeps checking the window. Suddenly Jimmy reaches out and grabs me back, so now we're in the corridor, peering round the door.

'Stand back. This could be very dangerous.'

'What?'

'I've seen this before. It's that magazine.'

'What about it?'

'Didn't you see who was on the cover?'

'No.'

I look over. The magazine front cover says in big letters: EVERYBODY'S DOING IT SO WHY CAN'T I? There's a picture of Kimberley Galloway. The Brainworm Queen.

Polly opens the magazine, and it's got that new magazine smell – all fake and plastic, but nice as well.

A bit like glue. Poll flicks to the Kimberley story. The caption says: 'Go Solo. It's the only way.' A picture shows her on a beach in the Caribbean, leaning against a chopper wearing a black bikini. I can do this thing where I just look at a page and I've read the whole thing. In five seconds, I've read the whole page, which says Kimberley's left the band of scrubbers she used to be with, and that she's making a load of money, and how she's got a new album called 'I Gotta Fly Away 'Cos this Place is Swag', and it's talking about her new single and saying that it's gonna go straight to number one. At the bottom of the page, the caption says: 'Overleaf, Kimberley models her new swimwear range.'

Polly turns over the page, and I see a double-page spread . . .

Kimberley's kneeling on the sand. I don't like to say it, but she's looking tight. She's on a beach, wearing nothing but a black bikini. She's got her hands behind her head, bunching up her blonde hair. And she's kneeling up like the photographer is standing over her, and she's staring into the lens. So if you're looking at the picture, it looks like she's kneeling in front of you, and she's staring into your eyes, staring at you like she knows what you want and she wants it too. I know that look. Me and Eric once stayed up late watching a documentary about strippers on Channel Five. Most of it was boring. You had to wait for ages while the strippers said they were businesswomen and they weren't being exploited, but when they finally shut up and got their kit off, they all did that look that Kimberley's doing in the picture.

Then something weird happens . . .

There's this little sachet of perfume glued to the page. It's called Desire. Polly opens it up and squirts it on her wrist. This grimy smell comes out. Smells like dirty pants and crumpled sheets. The smell of Mum and Dad's bed when you climb in on a Saturday morning. Something about it trips me . . .

I feel the way I did when I got a crush on Sharon Holdings, and I used to sit behind her at school, and I'd just look at her ponytail going down her back, and her shoulders. And I'd want to touch her, and I'd know that I was bad, and that even looking was making me worse. And Sharon Holdings knows this, 'cos one day she turns to me, and she goes: 'Colin, you perv. If you wanna look at me any more, you better buy me a present.'

Polly keeps staring at the picture.

Like she's hooked.

And there's something about that smell, I can't explain it . . . It makes me start to hear the song. Like the picture is singing the song. Or maybe I've just heard the song so much I know it by heart. I'm

hearing the drum beat in my head that starts it off.
I'm hearing the lush violins and the flutes. And then
I'm hearing the words . . .

> *'I'm an individual.*
> *I'm an individual*
> *I got individual needs . . .*
> *My street gets me down.*
> *There's fear all around.*
> *So I'm gonna fly me away.*
> *I'm getting buff*
> *Gonna get myself some stuff*
> *And I'm gonna fly me away.*
> *I ain't gonna come a cropper,*
> *Gonna buy a dirty chopper*
> *And I'm gonna fly me away.*
>
> *I hate em 'cos they started it*
> *Gonna get myself a private jet*
> *I need it,*
> *I need it,*
> *I seed it,*
> *I need it.*
> *Everybody's doing it, so why can't I?*
> *Everybody's doing it, so why can't I?'*

I don't know why, but this time the song don't sound

too bad. Then something wrong happens.

It's like the picture's come alive.

Kimberley is rising out of the page. *Slow at first, but then getting quicker. It's like she's got a long snake body, covered in soft yellow-gold scales. It rises up, and Kimberley is swaying around in front of Polly and her lamia. She's moving her hands through her hair. She's waving them slowly by her side. Sometimes her snake tongue comes out and flicks out, but even that looks good.*

I'm seeing two things at once.

I'm seeing Polly, who's just looking at the magazine, like she's gone to sleep.

And I'm seeing her lamia looking at the Kimberley snake, who's writhing about. It's opening its mouth and flicking its tongue through its yellow teeth.

I'm hearing the chorus again: 'Everybody's doing it so why can't I?'

Suddenly, the snake lunges forward.

It opens its mouth, and it bites the eyeball of Polly's lamia.

Then I'm hearing the chorus again: 'Everybody's doing it so why can't I?'

Then it bites the other eyeball.

Polly's lamia falls down like it's dead.

After that the snake fades back into the picture. And the song fades in my head.

No one moves.

I just watch from the doorway.

The shakfiend flaps back into the window. He stands there a moment, licking its tongue over its flakey old-man lips. Then he jumps across the floor.

He picks up Polly's lamia in its mouth like a dog picking up a dead cat.

And then he turns for the window.

Right away, I jump in. The shakfiend jumps straight on to the window ledge.

I dive over, and I grab him by the wing. It's all slimy and disgusting and the shakfiend is trying to shake me off. So I keep hold of the wing. But he swipes its yellow teeth at me and I let go.

'Jimmy,' I shout, but he don't come.

The shakfiend tumbles through the window. I lean out and see he has fallen to the ground. He's running up the pavement on his little legs, flapping his wings, looking like a swan trying to take off from the water.

I turn. Jimmy is cowering at the back of the bedroom.

'Come on,' I say. 'Quick.'

'It would not be wise to follow,' says Jimmy.

'We ain't gotta choice. That's Polly. That's Polly, for God's sake! Come on.'

I look out the window.

But now I can see no sign of the shakfiend. Nor of

Polly's lamia. I can just see the supermarket lorry and the broken glass in the car park.

I look round. Now Polly's lost her lamia, she's collapsed like an inflatable doll with no air.

And it's at that moment, I black out.

I can't see nothing.

I feel sick.

I can't breathe.

17

And suddenly I'm back in my living-room. My mum is kneeling over me, shaking me. She's lifting up my head. I'm puking all over her lap. My head is beating – bang bang bang – and my mum is shouting: 'Colin! Colin!'

I look at her. Mum hugs me tight and starts to cry.

Then she grabs Jimmy.

'Jimmy! What the hell have you done to Colin?'

And now Jimmy comes to as well.

He looks like a wreck. He immediately starts to puke too. But he holds it together. Springs up to the kitchen sink and does it there. Then he cleans it out.

My mum is angry. She's white hot.

'You shouldna done that,' says Jimmy. 'That was very very dangerous. Oh God. That hurt.'

Mum is staring at him.

'Have you been drinking? Have you? Or have you been giving him drugs?'

'No, it was just . . . Just a little . . . guided meditation . . .'

My mum turns her attention to my puke. Most of it is caught on her coat. She carefully takes it off, and stuffs the coat into the washing machine. Then she takes off her skirt. She's wearing blue knickers. Jimmy can't believe his luck. He's getting a right eyeful. Then she disappears to the bathroom.

I go over to Jimmy by the sink and wash my face.

'Thought you said she wasnae coming home!'

'I didn't think she was.'

'It's lucky we weren't too far away. Our lamias must've just about made it in time. You can die doing that.'

'You said it was safe!'

'Well it is safe, basically.'

'What is safe?'

My mum has come back into the room. She's holding a new dress. She's staring at Jimmy like she hates him.

'What is safe, Jimmy?'

'It was just . . . meditation. That's all. Alison,' he says, 'it's good to see you. Been a long time. You're looking beautiful, as ever.'

Mum walks over to Jimmy, and she slaps him hard round the face.

'If I hear you've been anywhere near my son again, I'm calling the police. Get out.'

Jimmy stares at her a long time. But when he talks, it's quiet.

'OK. I'm sorry. Colin. See you around. Remember . . . Never succumb to the temptation of being scared. You're bigger than that. I love you both. Bye.'

He's about to go. But then he says:

'Here, Colin, give us a hug.'

And I step forward and hug him. He turns and whispers:

'Hazoom before you sleep, and you'll lucid dream.' Then he says something else, but I don't catch it. I think it's 'Speak to the Muslim', which makes no sense.

Then he goes.

Mum turns to me.

'Right. You. Sit down. We need to talk.'

No, please don't make me talk to you. Can't you just punish me?

I follow her into the living-room.

'Sit down,' she says.

The sofa is piled up with her books about interior design. I put them on the floor and I sit down.

'Listen to me, Colin. I don't want you doing anything like that again.'

'Why?'

Mum sits at the table, and faces me. But first she brushes her hair with her hand. That's Mum. She's got something important to say, so she wants to look good before she says it. She talks:

'I came home one day and found Jimmy and your father lying on the floor, just like that. Shortly after that Dad started to go over the edge.'

'I thought Dad was sent over the edge from fighting for the SAS in Kuwait.'

'Colin,' she says, 'your father wasn't in the SAS.'

'Yes he was!'

'He was in the SAS Territorial regiment. That was a part-time thing, and he stopped doing it when you were five. It was Jimmy that ruined him.'

'When was this, Mum, that Jimmy came?'

'When you were about eight.'

'So maybe Dad was going wrong before then. Maybe Jimmy was just trying to help him.'

Mum looks at me very seriously:

'Jimmy's a gifted hypnotist, but he's unbalanced. He makes you see things that aren't there.'

'What if they *are* there, Mum? We went round to Polly's and we saw her getting attacked and then it was like she collapsed.'

'Polly's mum called me not long ago. Polly was fine then. Just a bit depressed. Sharleen thought perhaps you'd upset her.'

'Oh.'

'Jimmy has spent time in a mental hospital, did you know that?'

'No.'

'For all I know, Jimmy was giving you drugs. You're having enough trouble at school already. If you have another of your episodes, we've got to go straight off to Dr Juvanji again.'

'Mum, don't do that.'

'Prove to me you don't need it.'

'I know what's real and what's not. I'm not a fool.'

'Well, good.'

I go quiet after that.

'Mum,' I say, 'I know you blame me for it.'

'What?'

'Dad.'

'Don't be silly!'

Mum gets up. She starts packing her stuff.

'I've got to go,' she says.

'Where?'

'*Afternoon With Margie* . . . oh heck.'

'What?'

'The tube's down.'

'Why?'

'More bombs have gone off. I'd better drive.'

'Mum, if bombs've gone off, it'll be gridlocked out there. Take the bus.'

'*I don't feel safe on the bus!*'

Mum looks totally stressed.

'Colin?' she goes on. 'Can you call Sharon Holdings

and get a number for her dad? I want to see what kind of deal he can offer me for a trade-in.'

'What's the matter with our old car?'

'It's finished.'

'Why?'

'Tyres keep going down . . . When you need to clean the windscreen, no water comes out.'

'So? Change the tyres, and fill it with water.'

'*I don't feel safe in that car!*'

She's really on edge.

'I want something bigger. Something safer.'

'Mum, go on the bus.'

'*I need to keep away from other people!*'

'Mum, you're getting well vexed. You better calm down, or you're gonna end up in a mental hospital yourself.'

She goes off like Hiroshima:

'That does it. You're grounded. You're not leaving the house.'

She goes to the door, and slams it. Bang. It's quite an exit. She messes it up though. Ten seconds later, she knocks on the door again. I open.

'I forgot my keys,' she says. 'Can you pass them?'

I get the keys and lob them to her. Then I watch her going down the stairs. She looks pathetic.

I go back in the house. Now what am I gonna do?

I turn on the telly.

It's the news: 'Another bomb has gone off outside Regent's Park tube station, bringing London Underground to a halt. It's also been confirmed that the blast in Clissold Park last night has taken the life of the cleaner of the Clissold Park café, Miyassah Abdullah Sayid. And a further huge explosion has gone off in ancient woodland close to Stansted Airport. The Government has urged people to keep away from all parks and woodland areas. Meanwhile Friends of the Earth have made a statement saying the Stansted blast clears the way for the construction of the new runway to the airport. A spokesman for the Government says that they "vehemently refute these opportunistic claims", and have launched a "full and immediate inquiry" into the tragedies.'

I can't watch the news. It always depresses me. I start flicking through all the cable channels.

Who Wants To Be a Millionaire? Stupid people trying to get rich. Then . . .

The Weakest Link. Stupid people getting insulted. Then . . .

A Place In The Countryside. Stupid people moving house. I reckon I'll watch this for a moment. Someone's got to. I watch a family of rich spengs who want somewhere nice and quiet with a big garden. Then they find one. Then they say it's too far from the shops.

I turn the telly off. Every time I turn it on, it makes

me think that bombing people is the right idea.
Sometimes I hate the world so much I don't know what
to do.

18

L ater. I'm lying in bed thinking. I look at the clock
beside my bed. It's got green digital numbers. Says:
11:01 p.m. I'm fed up of thinking about Polly and
lamias and the way my Mum hugged me when I came
back from the projection. I just wanna get calm. I just
want to go to sleep. So I'm taking deep breaths.

Do you ever notice what happens when you go
to sleep?

You're lying there. You're hearing cars go by in the
street. You're hearing drunk people come back from the
pub. But then slowly you don't hear nothing. It's like
your head is a room, and someone has shut the
windows, and put blankets round the door. Your head is
quiet, and it's time to start showing films on the wall of
your mind. It's time to *dream*.

That's what happens.

I feel myself get lighter and lighter, and then I feel my
mind is drifting out of my body and I'm lifting up across

the room. Now I don't know if I'm dreaming it, but it's like I'm *seeing* it . . .

I drift up to the window, which is open 'cos it's hot.

And then I drift out like I'm a piece of dust. As I go out the window, I feel something brush against the window frame, and I see I got my wings. I open them wide, and then I drift away from the house, and then I turn slowly back and I go over the roof of our flat. Then I go across the road, and I can see Eric's dad driving up in his car, then I go across the other side of the street, and then over more roads, and it's like I know where I'm going:

Clissold Park.

I need to get there.

Soon I'm flying up Albion Road, where there's a bus stopped at the bus stop. And then I'm coming over the church and the trees and into Clissold Park. I go over the tennis courts and the café and the swampy river that's filled with supermarket trolleys and terrapins that try to bite the feet off ducks. Then I go into the main park where there's normally nothing but grass and big oak trees.

It's like there's a fair going. There's bare people, and all of them look blissed. They got a big bonfire going, and everyone is running about and hugging and talking.

I land next to a shed. It's the one I passed earlier that was filled with gardeners' stuff.

Now the door is open, and you can see stairs going up up up and light is coming down and beautiful music. It don't make sense.

Someone comes out. It's Dawnelle.

Now that ain't right.

Dawnelle is ten and she's from Montserrat. She was my neighbour and I used to go round there all the time 'cos they were always having parties which always had big aunties giving out stuff called goatwater which made the grown-ups well drunk. Us kids wanted to try it too, but they wouldn't let us. I like Dawnelle. She is mellow. She used to be, anyway.

She died three years ago.

Car accident. Went out with her gran and grandad and they smacked into a lorry on the M25.

'Hello, Colin,' says Dawnelle in her laid-back Montserrat voice.

'Hello . . . is that Dawnelle?' I say.

'Well I think I used to be,' she says, smiling.

'But are you still Dawnelle?'

She smiles. 'Mmmm . . . what was she like?'

'You had pictures of Freddie Ljungberg on the wall. And you were mad about Lee Ryan.'

'There ain't much of that Dawnelle left now.'

'What've you got instead?'

'Less Dawnelle, and more of everything else.'

'What happens through that door?'

'That's heaven,' she says. Like it was nothing.

'Heaven? So the people up there ... are they all dead?'

'We don't call it dead. We call it liberated. It's nice. We can come and go as we please.'

'Can I come in?'

'When it's your time, I'll be waiting for you.'

'Is my dad up there?'

'I ain't seen him. But I'll look out for him for you, and I'll tell you how he's doing.'

'Thanks, Dawnelle.'

And then Dawnelle walks up to me, and she hugs me. It's nice. I can smell coconut oil in her hair.

'Listen,' she says, looking at me in the eye, 'I got a message for you. Take this,' she says, and she gives me something. It's my dad's brass lighter. 'And when the time comes for you to fight, you fight hard. Then afterwards, jump into the eye.'

'What? Jump into the eye? What does that mean?'

'I don't know. See you!'

Then she turns and goes back up the stairs.

I watch her go.

Then I turn round and I look at the crowd of people

*on the grass. Now I see something I didn't see before:
nearly all of them are kids. Some of them are babies.
Some of them look the same age as me: thirteen.
Everyone's having a heavy time.*

There's a boy in front of me – looks about six.

'What's going on?' I say.

'I don't know,' he says, 'I'm just a fireman!'

'Where's your hose?' I say.

*'A robber took it,' he says. Then he laughs,
and runs off.*

*I'm watching, and I see that there's also a
few grown-ups around. They're larging it as well.
I see a tiny old woman – about my size – she
looks Filipino.*

'What's going on?' I say.

*'We're just gathering,' she says, smiling. Then she
holds my hand in both of hers and says: 'Your mother
is very worried about her flat. Don't worry. It will sort
itself out soon.'*

She squeezes my hand and disappears.

*Then I hear a loud voice with a Glasgow accent.
Sounds a bit like Billy Connoly. Sounds even more
like my dad.*

'Colin!' it says.

I turn.

*It's Uncle Jimmy's lamia. He's pushing his way
through the crowd. He's wearing a long red robe, and*

a bowler hat. He comes and hugs me as well.

'Colin,' he says, 'have you found out anything more about Polly?'

'No,' I say.

'Oh well. Let's ask around. But let's both have a bit of fun as well. Bit of a dance and a sing. When in Rome . . . get sunglasses and a moped, and ride around like a fool.'

'What you talking about, Jimmy?'

'A stitch in time . . . makes a hole in the time-space continuum.'

'What do you mean, Jimmy?'

'I'm a poet, Colin. Nothing I say makes any sense at all. That's why I'm always right. What's all this then, woof!'

He gives a manic laugh, then he waves his arms, and dances off into the crowd.

I don't care. I know there's someone else I need to see, and I'm walking round trying to find her. I'm at the edge of the park, near the railings, when someone touches me on my shoulder. I turn.

It's Polly. 'Cept it ain't Polly, it's her lamia with the pink and brown wings. She's wearing a black dress with a strap round her neck. She's got black eyeliner round her eyes, and her hair is long and it falls down on her naked shoulders.

'Colin,' she says, 'I'm so glad I've found you.'

'What happened?'

'The shakfiends have been trying to take me away all day and I've been fighting them. Then they took me off to this warehouse, but I escaped.'

'How did you get away?'

'They don't like the trees. If you stay in the trees they keep away. I was so scared, Col. I thought if they took me away I would never see you again.'

I smile. 'Here I am,' I say.

'Here you are,' she says.

She puts her hands on my cheeks, and she kisses me on the lips.

Then she stops and just looks at me.

Then she holds my T-shirt in her hands, and she leans back against the railings, and she pulls me to her, and she kisses me again. I can feel her breasts against my chest.

Her eyebrows look very bushy from this close and her cheeks smell of lemon. I'm thinking . . . What is she doing? Is she just being nice? Just kissing me like a big sister? But then she turns her head sideways, and she kisses me again, 'cept this time she opens her mouth, and I can feel the inside of her lips which are wet and soft. And I close my eyes, and it hits me . . .

She really is kissing me. Kissing me 'cos she wants to. Kissing me 'cos she **wants** me. And then her tongue comes out, and it just licks gently against *mine. And our tongues touch. And I stick my tongue out more, and I'm touching her lips, and the tips of her teeth. And then she sticks her tongue right out, right into my mouth. It's amazing. I feel all orange inside. It's like when you eat a doughnut and you get this warm feeling, 'cept the feeling ain't just inside, it's everywhere.*

Then something happens.

Suddenly there's three shakfiends on the other side of the fence. One of them holds on to Polly's legs through the fence. The others climb on the fence and they're trying to lift her up and over.

I grab hold of the wing of the one that's lifting her and try and pull him down. He swipes his yellow teeth at me and I lose the grip.

Then I hear a noise like metal jangling.

It's like my feet have been grabbed from under me. They're grabbed backwards.

Next thing I know, I'm flying out of the park, feet first.

I'm flying into the air, and away from Clissold, fast as a speeding motorbike.

No. This ain't right. I gotta get back. I gotta get back. I gotta save Polly. I gotta kiss her again.

But in seconds I'm flying back across Albion Road. I'm shooting over my house.

Then I'm whipped back in through the window.

Bang. I'm dumped back on my bed, and I'm hearing the jangling again.

I open my eyes.

I look at the clock beside my bed.

It says 11:02 pm.

I hear the noise again, and I know what it is.

It's my mum's keys in the door.

She's coming home.

And she's woken me up. Thanks, Mum. You got it right again. The job of the mum is to screw things up, just when they're getting good.

19

My mum's got someone with her. I can hear her saying: 'Shh, I don't want to wake the Angry Goblin.' Thanks, Mum. Bit late to be worrying about waking me. And if you call me the Angry Goblin to my face I'm gonna call you the Vain Bitch.

I hear them go down the corridor, and into the living-room. Then I hear the pop of a cork. Then the cluck cluck cluck sound of wine poured in a glass. Then music.

I am mad at my mum for waking me.

I get up and I do twenty press-ups, then ten more on my knees.

And that's when I see something on the floor . . .

My dad's brass lighter.

The very same one Dawnelle gave me in the dream. The one I gave to Jimmy earlier. That is weird. I pick it up and put it on the table next to my glass of water.

Then I look at myself in the mirror. I'm looking

good. I look like Johnny Depp, but with long hair and a massive forehead and much smaller obviously. Like Johnny Depp's freaky baby brother. His goblin brother. Then I do a few kicks and blocks. I go through the basic red-belt kata.

Then back into bed.

I wanna sleep.

I can't sleep.

I feel sticky and hot.

I get out of bed again. I realize I'm still wearing the pants I had on all day, and I wet myself a bit when I saw the ghost near school. So I pull my pants off. Then I notice I got some hairs growing down there. Six of them, about a centimetre long. I'm thinking: Is this it? Am I now a man? Is this what I've been waiting for so long? 'Cos I been starting to think there might be something wrong with me. Most guys in my school – they got hair two years ago, which has been well embarrassing 'cos I've been completely bald. Plus I'm way smaller. My blade looks like a slug that's been covered in salt. For two years it's been a nightmare when I have to shower after PE. Usually I keep my towel wrapped round till the last minute. Kriss's always known something was up, though, 'cos if I'm standing waiting for the shower, he always comes and flicks me with a wet towel, and then if I try to fight him off then my towel falls to the floor and everyone laughs.

I look at myself for a bit, and I feel good.

Now I'm thinking I might have lush dreams. I might kiss Polly again.

I get into bed. I close my eyes and I wait to sleep.

Nothing happens though. It's like there's a switch inside me, and it can only be clicked once a night.

But after a long long time, it happens.

I'm light.

I lift up from my body. I float above it.

I turn and see my body. I see the black eye I've got coming from where Trish Appleton gave me the bog wash.

Then I turn for the window.

That's when I get the first massive shock.

A shakfiend is standing on the windowsill, staring at me.

His face looks ancient. Ninety years old at least. He's got a big beaky nose and big ears and that gross skin that old men have. It's got little tufts of white hair and you can look through it, and you can see the purple veins underneath. He's doing that thing that really old people do where they let their mouths open so you can see their purple tongues.

He's about three foot tall, and he's got bent hairy legs like a monkey.

And he's got enormous wings like a bat, 'cept they

ain't black, they're made up of the same white and purple old-man skin with the little tufts of hair. Even though his face looks old, his body looks well strong. He's got muscles like rope. 'Cept there's something well wrong with his breathing. He's wheezing away like his lungs are about to collapse.

I don't know what I'm supposed to do with him, but I can't pay him much attention. I need to be with Polly so she can lips me. So I just wriggle through the window and get ready to fly back to the park.

But he reaches up his wing, and he grabs me with this little batty claw.

I go: 'What the hell are you?'

He says: 'I'm a shakfiend, young man. One of the Master's host.'

He sounds like this ancient bloke who lived in the flat downstairs. He was always saying stuff like: 'You better watch your lip, young man.' He was always polishing his car and he would confiscate the ball if you kicked it against his wheels.

'You gotta leave me,' I say. 'I need to get back to the park. Dawnelle's got a message about my dad.'

'The Master has cancelled all visits to the park. The trees are not healthy,' he says. 'You're coming with me.'

And he jumps up and he grabs me round the neck

with his hairy monkey legs. Then he flaps his big purple wings in the air.

And he takes off.

He drops away from the flat, and just when it looks like we're gonna smack into a fence he flap flap flaps his scrotty wings and we lift.

He lifts more, then circles round, and flies fast over our house.

We come over the rooftops, and are heading straight into Yorkshire Grove, which is this tiny community garden opposite our house. It's just a five-a-side football pitch surrounded by trees. There's something about the garden: the shakfiend don't like it. When he's going over the tree he starts wheezing something terrible, like he's gonna have an asthma attack. So he changes directions till he's flying over the street.

I can't see too good 'cos he's crushing my face with his legs. I try to get away, but I can't do it. He just clamps his legs tighter.

But I can see where we're going.

He avoids Butterfield Park, and he's going towards my school.

At the end of our school astro-turf pitch there's a big old disused warehouse. He's heading there. He flaps down over the car park. Over a wall that's covered with rusty barbed wire. And in through a big broken window. He drops me on the floor with a smack. Then he lands on top of me.

I'm lying on my face with my chin on the dirty concrete, but I can turn and see a little. We're in a huge room with broken windows on either side. It smells damp and there's dead pigeons on the floor.

Also there's about a hundred kids in there. They're all quiet and freaked 'cos each one is marked by a shakfiend. My one grabs me by the back of the neck and he's pushing me down a corridor with loads of little rooms off it. He chucks me into one, and he slams the door.

I'm looking round.

It looks like an old prison.

There's a tiny window with rusted bars.

There's a dead mouse in the corner. You can see its little white teeth.

A few mozzies are flying round in the air.

There's nothing else in the cell.

I sit.

I rub my neck. That shakfiend hurt me bad.

I sit some more.

Then something happens.

The door opens.

The shakfiend reaches his wing inside the door. He's holding something in his little clawed hand: a plastic bottle. Like a Lucozade bottle filled with see-

through liquid. *He's shaking it out and all the liquid's going over the floor. It looks like water, but it smells rank. It smells a bit like that scared ghost-boy next to Clissold Park. Something about that smell, it makes you want to lie on the floor and wait to die.*

*I don't know **how** it happens, but suddenly . . .*

A film starts playing on the wall. It's like my own personal cinema. A good quality one at that. The sound is quality. Picture is quality. It's like watching an IMAX. It all feels so real, it's like I'm inside the film, or the film is coming from the inside of my head, just like the voice of Samuel L. Jackson did. Which ain't too hard. 'Cos it's a film that I've carried round in my head for a while.

It's the film about the time I got news about Dad.

20

It's two and a half years ago. I'm walking home through Butterfield Park, coming from Polly's house. I'm wearing some trainers I chucked out ages ago. Polly's walking beside me, but we ain't talking.

Butterfield ain't a big park like Clissold. It's one of them little ones, with a big grass area, about fifteen trees, and a couple of middle-aged ladies watching their dogs curl out turds on the flowers. I like it. Me and Verno have got a den in the corner. We know all the best trees to climb. This is Our Place.

It's March. The trees are covered in little buds. The skies are grey. It's too cold for people to be out, so there's just a couple of tramps sitting on the benches, talking into their cans. Not many plastic bags in the bushes.

It's March 14.

I know how old I am. I'm eleven years eight months three days.

I'm right back inside the film now. I'm thinking what I was thinking on that day.

I'm scared that Mum's gonna be mad at me, 'cos I stayed at Poll's and I didn't ask Mum's permission. I'm wondering why Mum didn't call to find out where I was. And most of all I'm bricking it thinking that Dad's gonna murder me for what I done. And I'm guilty as hell about it too. Polly knows something's up, but she knows what I'm like, she knows I don't wanna talk, and so she's asked nothing.

'I'll walk you home,' she goes, 'then later we'll go skating at Lea Valley Ice.'

'OK,' I say. Nothing else. It's a Saturday, so we can do what we like.

We're walking up my street, and we see policemen waiting outside my house.

'That's my home,' I say to one of them. 'I need to go in.'

'You can't go in,' says the policeman. 'Please wait outside.'

He goes in. I don't try and follow. It's like I already know what's happened. It's funny how you know. Polly does as well. 'Cos right away she takes my hand and she squeezes it hard and she don't stop.

I sit on a step a few doors away. Polly sits down with me. Now she's got my hand in her coat pocket, and she's still squeezing it like she's scared to let go.

Then Yussuf comes over and he puts his hand on my shoulder and then he sits with me as well.

Eventually Mum comes out. Her eyes are red, but when she sees me, she smiles like an air hostess. That ain't good. If you ever see your mum smiling, then you know something lethal has gone on. All mums are liars. Whatever they're feeling, they're gonna do the opposite. My heart is beating hard and my hands are shaking. I know something's up.

'Colin,' says Mum, 'let's go for a drive. There's something I want to talk about.'

I don't say goodbye to Polly and Yussuf. I just get in the car. And Mum takes me all the way to Epping Forest. In the car, she talks about little stuff . . . Where've I been? What did me and Polly have for dinner? That's mums for you. They're keeping things so firmly under control they can talk about dinner, when they should be telling you what's going on.

Finally we park in Epping Forest, right next to the pond.

And finally Mum talks to me. She don't give me details. She says stuff like: 'As you know, your father has been ill for a while. Well, now he's gone . . .'

Mum don't say how Dad's been ill.

She don't say where he's gone.

*She **does** say: 'I'm never going to love anyone else again.'*

'We were gonna go camping again,' I say, 'this summer. We were going to stay on Ben Nevis, and we were gonna do survivalist training. Just like Dad learned in the SAS.'

'I know,' she says.

Then I say: 'I just wanna see him one more time.'

'I know,' she says.

Then we just sit there in silence watching a swan beating the hell out of a couple of ducks.

Mum don't say nothing about what I done neither, and I definitely don't bring that up. It don't matter. Mum don't want to **say** the truth. She don't want me to **know** the truth. The worst thing is . . . It don't work. 'Cos she's trying to stop me thinking about it, but I can't stop thoughts getting in my head, 'cos my head ain't watertight. Right away I'm starting to guess what's gone on. I'm starting to invent. I'm starting to see it all in my mind and some of the stuff I see is probably ten times worse than what actually went on. I think that's when I first started to really hate my mum. 'Cos she didn't tell me.

21

I watch the whole film through: from me and Polly walking through Butterfield, right through to when me and Mum are sitting in Epping Forest watching the swan attacking the ducks. Suddenly the film stops.

It goes black.

I look around, and it's like I've been drugged, and the effects have just worn off. I'm back to normal. Well . . . I'm back in the warehouse where the shakfiend took me. I'm sitting on the floor of the cell, and my legs are really hurting and I've got pins and needles something chronic. It don't make sense. A moment ago, I was eleven, and I was in Butterfield. Now I'm thirteen again, and I'm in the warehouse, 'cept I don't even know I'm in the warehouse 'cos I don't know if this is a dream or if it's really happening.

I look round. Where the plastic bottle got poured out on the floor, that's dried up. It don't even look wet no more.

The door opens again, and the shakfiend is there.

'Why did you make me see all that?' I say. 'And what am I doing here? Am I even here?'

He don't bother to answer the questions. Just waits for me to stop talking. Then he starts:

'The Master is extremely interested in you. You got his attention with burning the gym. Now he is in a position to offer representation to one of you young people.' The shakfiend's sounding like Hearfield. 'This is a very significant opportunity. He has a highly exclusive client list, which includes the President of the United States, Mr Murray, billionaire owner of Flyanair, and a noted singer-songwriter who is currently about to go number one in the charts on this and the other side of the pond. If he grants his help, you go very very far indeed.'

'I just wanna go home.'

He takes me out the door.

22

I walk slowly into the warehouse, and there's other kids coming out with their shakfiends. They all look the same as me – like someone's sucked out their brains with a straw. I turn, and I get a quick look at the long corridor behind me. There's more kids coming out, and all of them are quiet.

'Cept for one.

He's screaming at his shakfiend: 'How dare you? How dare you? Leave me alone. Leave me alone!'

The shakfiend is shouting back at him.

'You better watch yourself, young lad. If you cause any trouble, I shall have no resource but to take you off to see the Master.'

'How dare you?' the guy shouts again.

And suddenly the shakfiend jumps on him. There's a mess of scratching, biting, punching. You can't really tell what's going on. It's like when pigeons fight in the trees. You just hear the wings flapping. In a few seconds, the guy is bleeding, and weak like he's been knocked out.

Now the shakfiend jumps on his head, and holds him round the neck with his legs.

'Out the way,' he shouts. And all the shakfiends push us back against the wall.

Now the fighting shakfiend starts flapping his wings, and running down the corridor, dragging the boy with him along the floor. Eventually they take off, and the shakfiend swoops past me like a huge white bat. As they go by, I recognize the boy. He's the one from the bus. The one Polly fancied. The shakfiend flies to the window. He stops there a moment, and then he takes off into the night, dragging the boy with him.

I definitely don't make no trouble after that.

I let the shakfiend take me home. As he flies across Stoke Newington, I'm trying not to think about what I've seen. I'm just staring at the full moon.

23

Next thing I know, I ain't staring at the full moon, I'm staring at the light bulb on my ceiling.

I'm back in my bedroom, and it's morning. The clock says 7:21 a.m. It's like more drugs just wore off, and I'm back to another reality. Is this real? What is real? This definitely feels real. It smells real. I can smell trainers under my bed. I'm looking at the clock next to my pillow. I reach out, and I touch it. What's happening to me?

I lie in my bed putting it all together. I see I been dreaming, and I see that the second the dream finished, I woke up. Smack. It's like the dream was a wave and it's dumped me on the beach. Smack. Like it's telling me: 'Right – that's finished . . . Now you lie there and think about what's happened.'

I'm hearing a banging sound. I know what it is . . . It's my mum's bed, next door, hitting the wall. That is gross. I jump straight out of bed, and I do press-ups. I only do fifteen this time, 'cos I'm feeling weak, and then five more on my knees and then I just stay on my hands and knees, panting. I realize I can still hear Mum, which feels wrong. So I get dressed quick, and I put Dad's old lighter in my pocket, and I get out. I'm wondering who Mum's got in there – OB or Malcolm?

I go through to the kitchen and start checking clues right away . . .

1) Mum's already been up. I see a toothbrush on the kitchen table.

2) I see the coat over the back of a chair: her denim jacket. She musta worn that last night.

3) She's got the radio playing XFM. The music sounds like a Japanese thrash band.

That settles it. It's OB. If it was Malcolm, she'd have her leather coat and Classic FM, Music for Old People. Malcolm is rich and old. Mum sees him 'cos she thinks he'll find her a job: get her editing *Marie-Claire*, instead of the *Hackney Gazette*. OB's young and Australian. Mum hangs with him 'cos she wants to pretend she's young. It's true, I swear. Mum's nearly forty but she spends *loads* on anti-wrinkle cream and blonde hair dye, and she *loves* having OB 'cos he's twenty-eight and very good-looking although he's so thick he's more like a pet than a boyfriend. He says stuff like 'How's it hangin, Big Guy?' and he wants to be a TV presenter. He hangs with Mum 'cos she's got this really tragic thing that she does every Wednesday, when she goes on a show on Living TV called *Afternoon With Margie* and she does this two-minute spot called Teen Fashion. Not that my mum knows about teen fashion. She's the one who tried to stop me going to Polly's party in my karate outfit.

I need to sort out my head. I go through to the kitchen to make breakfast. There's still no Frosties, just the muesli, 'cos she still ain't gone shopping. I eat some of that and I read one of Mum's books, *Detox Your Life* (all about how, if you want a better life, you should eat broccoli). I chuck that on the chair and then I look at my mum's other books, but they're all about houses. My mum is mad about design. She's always coming home with new paints. She paints one stripe on the wall, then she leaves it. If I ask her if she's gonna paint the rest of the wall, she always says, 'I'm still weighing it up.'

I put all her books on the floor, then I spread my karate books on the table, and I work out some new moves. I'm trying not to think about what's happened: about going round to Polly's flat, about the dream of kissing her, and the dream about the shakfiend, which sure as hell didn't feel like a dream at the time.

Then Mum comes in wearing this red silk gown she ain't worn in five years. She's humming. She musta had a good night. She comes over and kisses me on the top of my head. Right away, that winds me up. Then she smiles.

'Good morning, Colin.'

'Hi, Mum.'

'Did you sleep all right?'

'Mmm . . . not really.'

'Oh dear.'

'I woke up when you came back. And then I had some chronic dreams. Have you ever had a dream which feels so real you don't think it was a dream?'

'Darling, have you got enough to eat?' she says. She ain't listening to me. She's looking in the mirror. My mum is so vain. She thinks she looks like Meg Ryan, but she looks more like Leslie Ash, the one from the Homebase ads with lips like slugs. She's sticking out her top lip like she always does when she sees a mirror. I'm getting angry. If she don't listen to me again, I'm gonna blank her.

Just then she notices the black eye I got from the bog wash.

'Did you hurt your eye?'

'Mmmmm . . . *Might*'ve got hit playing football.'

I only say '*might*'ve got hit'. 'Cos I want her to say: 'Colin, are you quite sure no one's bullying you?', and then I can tell her the whole story. I ain't trying to hide what happened, but I ain't boasting about it neither. I can't say to Mum: 'Actually I got rushed by two girls and they held me upside down in a toilet please please will you do something about it?' I got pride.

She don't pick up on it.

'I'll do toast and egg in a moment,' she says.

'Don't worry,' I say, kinda under my breath, 'I'm sure you got other stuff to do.'

'What's the matter?'

'I know you've got OB in there waiting to *snat* you.'

'Don't use filthy language!'

'What did I say?'

'You said . . . *snat*.'

'Wass dat mean? It don't mean nuffin', Mum. I juss made it up. You maybe think it's disgusting 'cos you is thinking dirty thoughts. *Probably* 'cos you got OB in there, waiting to ride you. Ride you like you is a Postman Pat car in the corner of Woolworths.'

I'm getting cold. I know I am. But she's winding me up. I can't help it.

'Don't . . . Just . . . Shh. Keep your voice . . . Yes. Actually OB *did* stop by last night at the studios. We travelled home together.'

'Course he came to the studios. He's using you 'cos he wants to go on TV too.'

'So what?' she says, all casual. You can tell I'm getting to her though. Rubbing sand in her eyeballs.

'Mum,' I go. 'Only losers go on TV. 'Cos they feel they got something to prove.'

She don't know what to say to this. She can't deal with the way I've come at her this morning. I've come at her with cruise missiles. Destroyed her parliament.

Pchooooo. Destroyed her TV station. *Pchoooo*.

She tries a new direction.

'Colin, why don't we go out and see a film tonight? Just you and me.'

She's offering the white flag.

'Mum,' I go, 'do you think dreams can be real?'

She don't pay no attention to this. See, this is what gets me . . . She says she wants to talk with me, but the second I ain't insulting her, she ain't listening. She's getting out sugar to put in the tea.

'Can you clear up your books?' says Mum. 'I'm fed up of all this mess.'

That's no big deal. Every mum hates mess, 'cos all mums need to stay in control. They're dictators. Lying dictators. I clear up one book. But I kind of slam it down, like to say: I'm doing this, but I ain't happy about it.

'God, I need a holiday,' says Mum. 'I need space. I feel stuck in here.'

'OK then,' I say, and right away I go to the cupboard, and I get out the long stick for opening the hatch to the attic. I poke it at the little hole, and start trying to open it. She goes off like a firework.

'What the hell are you doing?'

'If you think we need space I'm gonna go start using Dad's attic. I'll move my stuff up there.'

'Don't be ridiculous.'

'Dad ain't using it, is he?'

'I'm not having you going up there.'

'You can't stop me.'

'No, Colin. *No!*'

She runs at me. She grabs the stick off me and puts it back in the cupboard. Her hands are shaking.

'Mum,' I say, 'don't you think you're losing it a bit?'

'Look, I'm not surprised you're getting bullied at school if you behave like this. *Why* are you always attacking me? What is the matter with you?'

After that she takes the two cups of tea and she leaves the kitchen, and slams the door. Result. If she loses her temper, she's always the one who apologizes after. I know I was out of order, but when she's got OB round, then I can get away with it.

I go to my room and dress. As I unlock the front door, OB himself appears. Mum must of sent him out for a man-to-man chat. He's just wearing a pair of beach shorts, that's he's holding on to with one hand, like they don't do up properly. He's got one of them stripes of hair on his belly. Looks like a caterpillar is trying to crawl into his shorts.

'Hey, Big Fella,' he says, 'how's it hanging?'

'In your pants, probably.'

'What?'

'Forget it.'

'No, what did you say?'

'Look, it was just a joke, OB. I could explain it to you, but you're probably too thick to get it.'

'Now come on, Cozzer . . .'

'Don't call me Cozzer, you jockey!'

I don't say nothing more. I grab my dad's SAS combat scarf. Put it on. I pick up my rucksack. I hurry down the stairs. I gotta get out of here.

24

First thing I do when I shut the front door: call Polly. No reply. I call Polly's home.

Her mum answers. 'Hello?'

'Mrs McBrien, it's me, Colin.'

'She's no better.'

'Right. OK.'

'You can come round after school.'

'OK.'

'Take care, Colin.'

'You too, Mrs McBrien.'

So then I spend the morning noticing Polly ain't there. She ain't there at the bus stop. She ain't there on the bus, and I sit upstairs on my own. She ain't there in Assembly. She ain't there in class. So when I ain't heard something right in French dictation, there's no one to copy off. And when I'm bored, there's no one to write me notes like *Doing a gig tonite, will U come?* or *It's hot, let's go to the Marsh.* When Barker gives out the text books, I take hers for her. And when it's breaktime, I go round the corner and hide.

After lunch we've got Hearfield for Double Physics. He's usually late 'cos he's off doing headmaster stuff. Verno sits beside me, which I ain't that happy about but he is incredible at Physics and it's my worst subject so I reckon I can copy off him. As we're waiting for Hearfield, Vern's writing in the back of a book.

Everyone else is talking about the bombs, and what they're gonna do.

'I ain't walking in the park no more,' says Eric.

'I don't do walking,' says Trish. She wouldn't go in the park anyway. 'Cept maybe to lips someone in the bushes. 'But I don't care. I'm going to Miami at half-term. We might stay there for ever.'

'I ain't gonna walk nowhere soon,' says Sharon Holdings. 'My dad's gonna get me a jeep, soon as I'm sixteen.'

This don't surprise me. Sharon Holdings gets everything she wants. And her dad runs Holdings Motors on Stoke Newington High Street.

'I can already drive,' says Sal. 'I take my uncle's truck.'

'Are you still gonna go to the park, Colin?' says Kriss, bringing me into it.

I turn. He's looking at me, real serious. Everyone stares at me. You can tell they wanna ask me about the bomb and how I knew. I look at Vern, who's keeping out of the whole conversation. He's no fool. I notice he's got these big zits in his ears. One of them has gone white and green at the end so it looks mouldy. Trouble is: Eric's now looking at Vern as well.

He says: 'Vern, you know you got mouldy ears?'

Everyone laughs and Trish comes over to look.

'That's it!' says Trish. 'We're gonna call you Mouldy Ears.'

'Mouldy Ears is in the house,' says Eric, and everyone laughs more.

So I can see the heat is off me for the moment. Verno's gone red like he's trying not to cry. But he carries on writing in his book. He's trying to make out he ain't heard nothing, that way he don't lose face 'cos he ain't reacted to everyone boying him.

Hearfield comes in.

Vern keeps on writing. I dig him in the ribs and I whisper, 'What you doing?', and he goes redder still. So I grab the book off him and look at it. It's called *Classic Opening Gambits from the Chess Masters*. I look at the back cover, and I check right away what he's up to. He's making a list of the fittest girls in the school. He's got Sharon Holdings at number one. Fair enough. She looks like Scarlett Johansson. In third position, Vernon has written *Polly McBrien (when she smiles she gets dimples). Plus, got the nicest lips*. Soon as I see that, I can't explain it, but I don't want to embarrass Vern no more, so I just give the book back. Then I write on his jotter:

Can I come round yours after school?

He writes back: *Be my guest.*

Then Hearfield starts talking all about energy and physics and equations, and I can't stick it. I drift away. I'm thinking of my dreams.

After ages and ages, the bell goes. Everyone starts packing up and talking. But Hearfield says: 'The bell is for my benefit, not yours . . . Right, you may now vacate the premises.' So then everyone legs it out. But I take my time 'cos I don't wanna see no one as I leave. I'm avoiding Sharon Holdings and Trish Appleton since the wedgie. I'm avoiding Kriss, Sal and Eric 'cos they could ask me about the bomb or just rush me. I'm avoiding Vern for now, 'cos if we're seen together then it makes more trouble.

When I get downstairs, there's some parents, with a baby in a buggy. It's a fat little thing, with massive cheeks, and jam stuck to its face. As I come slowly down the corridor, it's staring at me. I stare back.

Then suddenly its eyes change so they look grey-blue.

And the baby speaks. But it don't sound like a baby. Sounds like Samuel L. Jackson. It says:

'*I'm telling you, child, you got outstanding potential. Outstanding potential. But you need to get yourself some friends. You need to get yourself some power. That's the way of the world: the power of the many, into the hands of the few. Be one of the few. I'm waiting for you. Find me.'*

Then the baby's eyes go back to normal, but I'm still freaked.

I gotta get out of here.

I walk over to Polly's. At first I've got a tight feeling about it, but then I get more hope. I reckon she'll be lying on her back reading a Thomas Hardy book. I'll come in and she'll say: 'This Jude the Obscure's a miserable bastard!' Then she'll chuck the book clean out the window and we'll go to her kitchen and we'll eat beans and I'll tell her Vern's got her at number three and she'll say: 'That's funny, 'cos I've got him at number one.' Then we'll take the piss out of Vern for a bit. Polly likes Vern, but she's always killing herself about his weird clothes. Her favourite joke is to go out the door, and then she'll say: 'Who am I?' Then she'll come walking in wearing something stupid she's found from the back of a cupboard, like a cravat, or a big scarf. Last time she did it, she wore a normal jacket, but she wore it inside out and back to front, so the zip was at the back. And a bike helmet on her head. She stood outside the door saying, 'Who am I?', and then when she came in, she was laughing so much she started to cry.

I get to Polly's block of flats, and I go straight in. I've got a key. I got one to feed Polly's cat when they went to France, and I never gave it back. As I get to the top of the third flight of stairs, I *know* everything's gonna be OK. I'm holding a little carton of mango drink. I've got a grin on my face ready to tell her about Vern.

But then I meet a stretcher coming down the stairs.

It's Polly.

It's like I'm winded. I just stand against the wall and let them come past.

I see Polly's face and it looks green. I remember what Jimmy said: You can carry on without your lamia for a bit, but not for ever.

Sharleen's coming down the stairs behind the stretcher. Her eyes are red.

'What's happening?' I say.

She puts on a normal voice like everything's fine.

'She's in a coma,' she says. 'They're taking her in for tests.'

'OK,' I say. I'm doing it too. Pretending I ain't worried.

25

When I get out of Polly's block, the ambulance has already gone. So I go into Hidir's and I get myself a sandwich and crisps and I get another mango carton for myself even though I don't like it much. I eat the crisps and stuff the packet in the pocket of my combat trousers. Then I don't know what to do, so I go round to Vern's, which is just next to St Matthias church.

As I come trudging up Princess May Road I can see the church in front. It's got a tall steeple made out of bricks that've gone black. I ain't been to the church for ages. I went there when I was four. Mum wanted me to get into St Matthias School so she started to act like she was dead religious. She kept saying 'We've got to catch the eye of the vicar' and she used to sit at the front and sing loud. When they prayed she'd kneel and hold her head in her hands like she was crying. Kriss would be sitting behind, flicking my ear. We didn't know Verno then. He used to give out the squash at Sunday School.

The funny thing was, after we'd been going to St Matthias for a year there was a stabbing at the school and after that no one wanted to go there no more and it shut. Me and Mum went to the church one more time, and it was really sad. Just a few old ladies holding hymn sheets. Like bingo, but you don't win nothing. Kriss still went, 'cos his mum went, and she's the only person he's scared of. She's religious as hell. Everyone is scared of Kriss's mum. She's called Glendora and she drives a 73 bus. No one messes with her. If a suicide bomber got on the Number 73, Glendora would smack his butt and send him home.

I know I said I'd visit Vern, but suddenly I don't want to. Only just then an ancient people carrier drives up. It's Vernon's mum. Sue Watkins. Mrs Mouldy Ears. She's got one of them Baby On Board signs at the back. Like if she didn't have the sign, everyone would ram her.

She gets out.

There's two types of white ladies in Stoke Newington: the ones what wear tight tops and go to the pub with their kids and sit there smoking – chav mums, Trish Appleton's mum. And there's the posh ones that have got kids called Molly and you see them in the health shop looking worried – stressed mums, like my mum. Mrs Mouldy is definitely the second kind, too. She's got five kids and Vernon's the oldest. They're all getting out of the car as well. Two ugly sisters, and then an ugly boy, Mrs Mouldy is holding a baby, and she's also pregnant. Why are the Mouldies so keen on keeping their genes going? You just know the next baby's gonna be ugly as well.

Mrs Mouldy sees me and comes towards me, smiling.

'Hello, Colin, why don't you come in? I know Vernon can't wait to see you.'

'OK.'

She puts the baby down by my feet.

'Would you hold Daniel's hand? I need to get out the shopping.'

So I hold the hand of the youngest Mouldy. He's like a monkey that's been peeled. He's got food stuck to his face so it looks like he's got a rash. But Mrs Mouldy is looking at him like he's beautiful.

'It's amazing,' she says, 'he can walk!'

I'm thinking: Wanna impress me, tell me he can fly. Tell me he got out of his high chair and spent the day soaring a hundred metres above Hackney. But I don't. I just go in, holding Daniel's hand.

Vern sees me coming down the path and he steps forward and hugs me. 'Cos I'm holding the kid's hand, I can't back off.

'Welcome, Colin,' he says.

'Ri, Vern,' I say.

'Come in.'

Mrs Mouldy takes the rest of her minging kids to the living-room, so me and Vernon've got the kitchen to ourselves. There's little signs up everywhere saying stuff like *God Is Watching*. I'm thinking if God is watching Mr and Mrs Mouldy making all them ginger babies, he must be feeling well sick.

Vernon is so pleased to have a guest, he rushes round making Marmite toast and Nesquick.

I get down to business.

'Vern, listen. Poll's gone weird. She's in a coma. Before that she was just sitting there, not doing nothing, just acting like a monger.'

'My dad says that there's loads of kids doing that round this parish,' he says, looking concerned. 'They just stay in their beds, and no one can get them out. Apparently doctors come, and they can't find anything wrong, and they can't do anything.'

'What do you think we should do?'

'I know exactly what we're going to do,' he says. 'We're going to get my dad's church on the case. We'll get St Mary's church on to it. We'll involve everyone in the whole diocese and we'll have a joint prayer.'

I'm thinking we don't need prayers. We need lamias with knives who can storm the shakfiend place and get everyone back. But I don't know where the shakfiend place is, or where they are, or what they're doing.

'Do you think that'll do it?' I say.

'I think it's the only thing that will do it. The most important thing is love.'

'Vern, don't give me that. The most important thing is truth. Finding the bad guys and beating the crap out of them.'

Vern is looking at me seriously.

'I know you're very worried about her,' he says, putting a hand on my shoulder, 'but there's nothing you can do now. Come on. Come upstairs and I'll play you some music.'

It's weird. When Vern is at school, he scuttles round like a mouse. But at his home, he takes control. He takes me up to his room and he turns on a side light.

'Take a seat,' he says, so I sit on a beanbag.

In the corner he's got one of them ancient record players.

'This is Johnny Hodges,' he says, '*I Got It Bad, and That Ain't Good.*' Vern puts on this weird accent, like he's black and he's from New Orleans. I feel embarrassed for him, like I did the time he accidentally called Hearfield 'Mum'.

So I just sit there on the floor, and I listen to the music.

It's good. It's incredible. But it don't help. 'Cos now I can't stop myself thinking about Polly. I lie there, and I think of all the reasons I like her . . .

1) 'Cos I can be myself with Poll. When I talk to Kriss,

I feel I gotta talk like Kriss. With Poll, I can use the words I wanna use and I can tell her the worst stuff. I even told her I burned the old gym and I never told that to no one else. She told me I shouldn't have done it. But she never told on me.

2) 'Cos she's an only child, like me. Her dad disappeared when she was four. He got a job on an oil rig and he never came back. So Poll knows the score. I don't ask about her dad. She don't ask about mine. That's why we're friends.

3) 'Cos I like it when I go round her house and she sings just for me. Sometimes when she sings the same songs to the old guys in the Lonsborough I think, you guys can't hear that, it's *my* song.

I'm thinking all this and then I realize I might cry. I don't cry. I never cry. But I get the lump in my throat, and I start sniffing a lot. At one point I see Vern looking at me, but just quick, on the sly. Then he turns off the light, and he lies down on the bed and stares at the ceiling. Now no one can see me, and I do it. I cry. Then I think of more reasons I like Poll . . .

4) 'Cos most girls stay in groups and they whisper. Polly don't do that. If Polly got something to say, she says it. She ain't afraid of no one. One time Eric called her a slag, so she put him in a headlock, and she ran him against a wall. Eric was so surprised he didn't do nothing. No one messes with Poll.

5) 'Cos she don't laugh unless she finds something hilarious. Unlike most girls who always want to be screeching with laughter all the time, like they reckon if they stop laughing, everyone will see what losers they are. Poll is funny though. When we were in Year Two, Polly only wanted to hang with the boys. And so Trish Appleton said, 'Why do you hang with the boys? Girls are more mature than boys.' Polly said: 'But girls play hopscotch and skipping games and that stupid thing where you wrap string round your fingers. Does that show you're mature, or that you're wrong in the head?'

6) 'Cos she's so proud of her clothes, even though they're cheap. She goes down to Camden Market, and she'll buy some weird coat that belonged to a Russian soldier. It'll still smell of soldier, but Poll don't care. She'll cover it with her own smell, which is some lemon thing from the Body Shop. Sometimes I smell that smell on someone else, and I wanna tell them they ain't got the right. That's Polly's smell.

7) 'Cos she's getting nice breasts. She's cool with them though. She don't show them off like Trish Appleton, but she don't walk round with her arms folded neither.

8) 'Cos she gets dimples when she smiles. I like that. And I like Polly. I don't *love* her, don't get me wrong. But she is nice. She is fresh. She is salad. She's my best

friend. She's got nice hair and nice lips and I would like to kiss them. Maybe I will. But maybe she's vexed at me 'cos I shouted to her to leave me alone. I didn't mean that. I gotta straighten that out. She'll understand, won't she?

Suddenly the music's finished, and I can tell Vern's about to get up and turn on the lights, so I wipe my eyes quick on my sleeve.

'Did you like that?' he says.

'Yeah, Vern, it was real.'

'Do you want me to make you more toast?'

'No. I gotta go. Thanks, yeah?'

'That's OK. Come back tomorrow, I'll play you more.'

'Yeah, wicked, Vern,' I say.

He looks at me. For a second, I think he's gonna give me a hug. I leg it quick.

26

But when I get home, I don't know what to do. I'm tired but I don't dare go to sleep. So then I just sit for about three hours. Too tired to move. I'm holding Polly's exercise book I got back from Barker. She's written her name on the front – Polly F. McBrien – in loopy handwriting, with a circle instead of the dot on the 'i'. I write it underneath the same way. Then I do a whole column of them down the page. Then I do more columns of them till the front cover is filled with identical signatures. It looks good. Then I do the back page and the inside cover. Then the buzzer rings. Probably Mum. Even if she's got her key, sometimes she can't be bothered to look through her bag. I press the button. Then open the door. Then sit down again.

Kriss comes in. He stands in the living-room and looks at me. This time he's wearing a yellow velour tracksuit and he's got a bandana round his head.

'You got your Maths, Bitchin?'

Kriss don't never say hello. Probably reckons it's gay.

'All right, Kriss,' I say. 'You aint been here in a long time.'

'Innit. What you doing?'

'Nothing.'

'Safe . . . You got your Maths, Bitchin?'

I haven't figured out if I'm gonna let him have my Maths yet. I don't wanna hand it over like I'm his bitch. I want him to do something for me, but I don't know what.

'Ain't you playing football today, Kriss?'

'Game's off. Bombs, innit?'

'You're unreal at football. You could play for England.'

'My uncle played for England.'

'I thought he played for Nigeria?'

'That was John Fashanu. Justin Fashanu played for England. Got two caps.'

'Why you never told me about him?'

'Chi chi man, innit?'

'Oh . . . so?'

'You get me?'

'No.'

'You can't have a footballer who's gay. How are the rest of the team supposed to take a bath with him after the match?'

'Maybe he wasn't interested in them.'

'Forget him, bruv. I ain't talking about him.'

'What happened to him?'

'Hanged himself.'

'Oh no . . . Poor guy.'

'Them guys should be put down like babies with webbed feet. You get me? You get me?'

Kriss is getting well intense. Staring at me. Like I gotta give the right reply or I'm gonna get pied up. Suddenly he goes . . .

'You OK, Bitchin?'

'Yip.'

'I didn't touch you, bruv. In the park. So don't get mad with me about it. It was Sal and Eric, innit?'

'Yeah. But you coulda stopped them.'

'Yeah.'

'Next time you gotta stop them.'

'OK.'

'I'll find my Maths,' I say.

We go into the bedroom. There ain't much room in there, so he sits on the bed. I look through my bag and find the right book. I hand it over. Then I sit next to him.

'You gotta make some mistakes, otherwise they'll know.'

'OK.'

He starts copying it out. I'm checking that he's changing a few things. Kriss ain't a fast writer. He uses capital letters whenever there's words. Takes him quite a long time. After a bit, I just lie back on my pillow and dream.

Finally he chucks my book on the floor, and he folds his book up and stuffs it in his pocket. He turns to me. Since Kriss never smiles, it's impossible to tell what he's thinking.

'You OK?' he says again.

'Yeah. I'm just a bit worried about Polly.'

'Why?'

'They took her to hospital. She's in a coma.'

'Why?'

'Dunno. No one knows. That's the trouble.'

'That's cold.'

'Yeah.'

'Do you like her?'

'Yeah.'

'But have you prepped her?'

'No.'

'Why don't you prep her?'

'I dunno.'

'Do you lips her?'

'No.'

'You tried to lips her?'

'No.'

'Why?'

'I dunno. 'Cos I don't know that she likes me. And if I did try to lips her, maybe I wouldn't do it right. Or maybe someone would see and they'd rip the piss. Or maybe it'd ruin what we've got.'

'Maybe. But I think she does like you though. I seen . . . sometimes she tries to hug you, or touch you, and you push her away.'

'Yeah.'

'Why you do that?'

'Dunno.'

'Bitchin, you ain't gay?'

Kriss is back to his favourite question.

'I don't think she likes me like that, Kriss. I think she likes you.'

'Reckon?' he says. And he smiles. I wouldn't have cared if he ain't smiled, but now I'm bleeding inside.

'Do you like her?' I say.

'She's OK.'

'Yeah.'

He smiles again.

'She's got wicked jugs,' he says suddenly.

'She has,' I say. Maybe it's OK to talk about Polly to Kriss. I don't mind talking about her. It just gives me the fear when I think he might do something. Kriss is very good-looking.

'Do you want to lips her?' he says.

'Maybe.'

'Do you want to prep her?'

'Dunno.'

'But don't you want to get out her wicked jugs and see them and like go blurblurblur between them?'

'I guess.'

'You getting the horn, Bitchin?'

'No!'

'You are!'

'I ain't!'

Suddenly he puts his hand on me, and squeezes.

'You are though. I can tell!'

Oh my God, suddenly I see it.

'Kriss,' I say quietly, 'you can tell me the truth 'cos I swear I don't care either way. Are you gay?'

Oh my God, I shouldn't have said that.

He lifts me up by my shirt. He holds me in front of him. I think he's gonna spit on me. Then he chucks me back. Slams me into the pillow and I whack my head on the wall.

I shut my eyes. But when I open them, he's gone.

So after that I sit some more. I watch the room get dark. I'm tired, but there's no way I'm going to sleep. No way.

At midnight, Mum comes in. She's got someone with her. Sounds like Malcolm. They go off to the bedroom, but there ain't no noise. Must be Malcolm.

I sit some more. No way I'm gonna sleep.

I keep thinking over and over about what's happened. At first I'm so mad at Kriss. If he's gay, then he's the biggest hypocrite I ever met. Then I think, if he's gay, I feel sorry for him. That's a big secret.

And then I think about what Kriss said ... Sometimes Poll tries to hug me and I always push her off. Why do I do that? Then I think about what Mum said about Dad: *'I'm never going to love anyone else again.'* I don't never want that to happen to me. Maybe if you love someone, they die. Maybe if you kiss them, you kill them. I know that sounds mad. But Polly is important. I can't take the risk. After a bit, I'm getting it mixed up in my head. I gotta avoid Polly. I gotta stay awake, 'cos of Polly. If I fall asleep, I'm gonna kill Polly.

Then I fall asleep.

27

I'*m drifting out of my body.*
  I turn.
  A shakfiend is standing in the corner of my bedroom,
wheezing away like a perv. Waiting for me. The second
I see him I know I shoudn't've slept.
  I turn and run for the door.
  He takes one jump and he lands on my back. I
smack my head against the side of the bed.
  He drags me out the window. Once again.
  I'm pulled out into the night air.
  He flies me through Stoke Newington.
  He takes me back to the prison cell.
  Slams the door.
  He returns a couple of minutes later. Chucks a
plastic bottle on the floor.
  I'm ready for it this time. I know I can't fight it. I
sit with my back against the wall. And I wait to see
what's gonna happen. I know that stuff on the floor is

159

gonna drug me. I know my mind's gonna flip, and I'm gonna see mad stuff about my dad.

And that's what happens.

But it ain't the same film as yesterday. This ain't the day I heard my dad had died. This is the day before. The last time I talked with him.

Right away I'm there . . .

I'm eleven again. I'm standing outside our home on the pavement. I'm feeling tired 'cos I ain't been sleeping 'cos of the bad dreams. It's Friday. I've just come home to get my football boots, but Hearfield, who's our coach, has called me up to say I ain't playing. I'm pissed. I'm pissed with Hearfield. I'm pissed with Kriss, who's our captain, 'cos he's got all his friends playing with him. He's got Eric in goal, 'cos Eric's got a whole load of Arsenal away strips and that's what we wear. And now he's got Sal in central midfield, which is my position. Kriss just likes having Sal around, 'cos he's so big it makes Kriss feel like he's got security. OK, I'm smaller, but I'm way better at football than Sal. I'm quick. And I'm several metres faster up top. I'm like a mouse. No one can stop me. I just dodge past their legs. I should be in the team. So I need Dad to call up Hearfield and tell him to give me another chance.

I'm on the pavement and I see Yussuf coming up the street. 'Cept he ain't Yussuf. He's still Lee. He don't have his Muslim beard. Don't have his funny hat. He's dressed in an Arsenal tracksuit, and he's got his hair all slicked back and he reeks of perfume. He waves at me, but I say nothing. Lee taught me all the football tricks I know. He says I'm like Joe Cole: I'm small, but I got a low centre of gravity. So I know he'll ask me about the match and I don't want to tell him why I ain't playing. So I go into the house before he can come over.

I need Dad to call up Hearfield to sort it out. I go up the three flights of stairs to our flat, and go in. The flat don't look like it does now. On the side there's a picture of my mum and dad kissing on top of a hill. The living-room is covered with Dad's papers. And my mum's holiday brochures. And Dad's whisky bottle.

There's a waft of Old Holborn smoke coming down the stairs.

I climb up the ladder . . .

At the far end of the room, sitting at his desk with his back to me, is my dad. Black T-shirt. Hunched shoulders. Clumps of hair on the back of his neck 'cos he ain't shaved it.

I step over piles of papers and I stand at Dad's side watching him. His eyes are flicking quickly from word to word as he reads a paper. I've thought about my dad so much in the last few years, but now I see I've forgotten about the little tuft of grey hair in front of his ears, and how one eyebrow goes higher than the other.

'Colin,' he says, 'can you bring me fresh coffee? I've got to get this done.'

He passes me this crusty mug which has got grey coffee dribbled down the side.

'Dad,' I go, 'I need to talk to you.'

'I'm researching something,' he says. 'Do you know what the biggest industries in the world are? Number one: arms. Number two: drugs. That's what we're up against.'

He trails off and he writes in the margins of one of his coffee-stained books.

'Dad?' I go. 'They kicked me out of the football team, Dad. We're playing a match today against a school in Newington Green.'

Dad looks at me a second.

'Right,' he says, but you can tell he ain't gonna do nothing. He just wants me to go.

'Dad, can you call up Hearfield? It ain't fair.'

'He sounds like an arse, son.'

'Yeah . . . so do something about it.'

'Life's tough, son. Get used to it.'

'I ain't getting used to this. If I ain't back in that team, I'm gonna fight Kriss.'

'It doesnae pay to stand up for yourself.'

I forgot this . . . All dads do is give advice. I

don't need advice. I need him to kick the crap out of Hearfield.

'Dad,' I go, 'I told Polly to come and watch the game. But now I ain't even playing.'

'Call her up.'

'I can't call her up. I feel like a fool. It ain't fair, Dad.'

This does it. Saying that gives me a lump in my throat, and I think I'm gonna cry. Dad looks at me.

'Look, I'm too busy for this. Did you know, in the eighteenth century, if you got hanged it might take you five days to die? So the families of the criminals, they'd hang on to their legs to try and help them die quickly. Know that?'

Thanks, Dad, that's really cheered me up. Sorted me right out.

And he starts to talk. On and on and on and on. I've forgotten how bad dads are. You tell them you is vexed about football. They give a four-hour talk about the eighteenth century.

I can't take it. I butt right in:

'Dad, why don't you ever shut up? I need to play in that game!'

And he turns on me.

'It's bad enough with you waking up every other night and then fighting at school! How the hell am I supposed to work with you disturbing me all* *the time? And your mummy is badgering me to take her on holiday. Tell her from me we don't have the money. So both of you can just leave me alone!'*

I don't say one more word. I go to my bedroom, and I call up Hearfield on my mobie. He says I can do the oranges at half-time and maybe come on as substitute. Result. So as soon as he says that, I get my stuff, and I leg it to the game.

Polly's waiting on the touchline, and loads of dads, but not mine – he never comes. Eric's dad is there and he keeps shouting 'Close the angles!' whatever that means. Sal's playing in my position, but he don't run, he just stands round shouting 'Push up!' and 'Man on!' He's winding me up so much, I tell Polly we should move.

Near the pitch there's an empty kids' park with a few swings and a slide. So I give Polly my stopwatch, and then we play a game where I have to do obstacle courses, and she has to time me. I make up a course: run up the slide. Ten push-ups by the swings . . . run round to the sandpit . . . ten sits-ups. Polly says, 'You have to do everything in two minutes, or your family die.'

I kill my family several times, and that feels evil, but in a good way.

Suddenly we see it's half-time and the game has stopped and everyone is watching me and laughing. Eric starts shouting: 'Bitchin, you chief, all you gotta do is bring on the oranges, and you aint done that.'

So me and Poll stop mucking about and we go back to the game.

Right after half-time, Kriss scores a goal, so now we're drawing one all. Ten minutes to go, Hearfield takes Sal off and tells me to go on. And suddenly I'm scared. All their kids are massive, they ain't never the same age as us. They're freaking me out. Plus, they all smell like the changing-rooms in their school, which stink of bleach. And the guy I'm supposed to mark is the biggest of the lot. He gets the ball, and he's running through on the goal. And Kriss is screaming at me: 'Bitchin, tackle him, Bitchin!' Suddenly I'm so tired, I can't move. But the guy is running at me. And now everyone is shouting. I know I'm gonna screw up. And I can't help it, I just wet myself. I can feel it running down my leg into my socks. And the guy goes by, and he scores. And then Kriss comes up to me, and he's shouting at me. Then someone sees I've got wet shorts, and they all laugh at me. And then I really lose it, and I rush them and try to fight them all. The other team are killing themselves, 'cos I'm the smallest kid by a mile and I'm trying to beat up my own team.

Soon as I get home, I go up to Dad's attic. But Dad

ain't there. Just all the pages from his book and his brass lighter and his tobacco. I pick up the brass lighter. I don't think about it. I set his work on fire and then I chuck it in the bin. I watch it burn for about ten seconds, and then I realize what I'm doing and I chuck cold coffee over it, and put it out with the rug. And then I'm cacking myself even more to think what Dad's gonna do. So I rush out.

I go and hang out outside Polly's house. It's like I wanna see her but I don't even wanna knock at her door. So I'm just standing on the grass near her flat. And there's all these glass bottles lying around. And I'm just chucking them at the pigeons, smashing them. And Polly comes out, and she watches me chucking the bottles, and she goes: 'You're never gonna hit the pigeons like that, you should get your dad's gun,' and I go 'Well I might' and then she goes, 'But let's do it after. If we go in now, we can watch You've Been Framed.'

Polly knows I love You've Been Framed. We both do. I like the ones where cats try and catch torch beams on the wall. She likes the ones about babies that fall asleep with their faces in the yoghurt. So we go in and watch TV. And I stay at Polly's for ages, 'cos I'm scared of going back and seeing my dad. And the weird thing is, Mum never calls. And Polly's mum don't come home. I think she's out drinking. So in the end Polly just says, 'Why don't you sleep here?' She gives me a tracksuit to wear as pyjamas and I lie down on her floor.

As soon as I lie down on the floor, the film ends.

28

The drugs wear off. I'm back to the present. I'm back in the prison cell. This film makes me feel even worse than yesterday's. This is stuff I ain't wanted to think about for a while. 'Cos it makes it clear: it's my fault. All my fault.

After a few minutes, the door opens again. The shakfiend smiles: 'Have you thought about the Master's offer, because—'

'Stop,' I go, 'stop right there. What the hell is going on?'

'The Master is going to offer his help to one individual with outstanding talent—'

'Who is the Master? What does he want from us?'

'He wants to offer representation to one talented individual.'

'So you keep saying. Why did you make me see that stuff about my dad?'

'We don't stipulate what you see. Now if you wish

to take advantage of the Master's offer, then all you have to do is find him. He can make you rich. He can make you powerful. Find him.'

'Who is he?'

'He's a very powerful being. And he can give you the future you wish for.'

I see I ain't getting through to him. I'm pressing the button, but there ain't no battery in the remote. I get a different idea.

I go quiet and let him take me out of the cell.

This time I see someone else kicking off.

It's Polly.

She's shouting:

'It's bang out of order! How dare you do that to me? How dare you?'

Her shakfiend is threatening her. 'I need a bit more control, a bit more discipline from you, young lady, or I'll take you to the Master!'

'Shut up! Shut up! Get your paws off me! You're bang out of order.'

I start screaming: 'Polly! Polly! Get away from him! I'm gonna help! I'm gonna help!'

But suddenly my shakfiend jumps on my back and I'm flattened to the floor with my face pressed against the concrete. I'm looking round and trying to see. Polly is taken out of the window by her shakfiend and I can't tell where they've gone.

I lie on the floor a long time. It's good. It gives me time to think it all through. To make my plan. I don't know it's gonna work, but I gotta take the risk. Eventually the shakfiend says:

'Are you calm, young man?'

And I'm ready. 'Yes, I'm calm. I apologize for the disturbance. It won't happen again.'

The shakfiend looks me in the eye like he wants to know if I'm taking the piss.

'Good,' he says.

So I behave as quiet as I can. Do everything he asks me to do. I act totally calm as the shakfiend lifts me up and jumps out the window. And I don't give him no trouble as we fly off, heading back home.

He's just going round the corner of Butterfield Park when I make my move.

I twist fast, and I push against his legs.

It works. I get away.

I fall down into Butterfield Park.

Bang. I land on the mud, and I scramble away under a bush. And you know what?

I was right. The shakfiend don't like the park.

I'm huddling under the bush. He's on the path outside the park, looking at me through the metal railings. He was wheezing before, but now he's sounding dread.

'Come out!' he's going.

I've got him.

'Why can't you come in the park?' I say.

He ignores this.

'You can't stay in there for ever, young man,' he says, 'and when you come out, you'll wish you weren't born.'

'I'll come out. But you gotta do something first.'

He's going purple in the face.

'I can't . . . I can't breathe.'

'OK, I'll come closer, but I'm staying in the park. And when I'm satisfied, I'll come out.'

'What do you want?'

'I want you to tell me what's going on.'

'It hurts!'

'Good. So be quick. Number one: who's the Master?'

'He's our leader.'

'Is he like you?'

'No. He's far bigger than us. And more intelligent. We're not even the same species. We are to him as dogs are to you. We help him. He breeds us.'

'Where's he come from?'

'He's . . . he's from another civilization. From another planet.'

'I don't believe in extraterrestrials. That stuff is for geeks.'

'Why shouldn't you believe in extraterrestrials?

They're around you all the time. What do you think mosquitoes are?'

'Mozzies?'

'Yes. They're related to us.'

'Never mind that. How long has the Master been here?'

'Long time. Three or four thousand years.'

'So why does no one know about him?'

'Most people can't see us. They're unaware of us. And he's been hiding. He's been gathering his power.'

'He's getting stronger?'

'All the time. And he's working on something to increase his power.'

'What?'

'I don't know. He could be making a bomb. I don't know.'

'How many of you are there?'

'A few hundred thousand.'

'And how many like him?'

'About a hundred. They're spread all round the world. There's only one in London. But soon he's hatching!'

'*Hatching?*'

'Yes. He's waited thousands of years, and now he's almost ready.'

'And then there'll be more of you?'

'More of **him**.'

'So what does he want?'

'We are not privy to his ultimate goal.'

'And why are you taking us to the cells?'

'We have to keep you separate. Humans are communal creatures, social. You want to mix. You want to know what each other is doing. You want to help each other. We can't let you do that. We have to keep you apart.'

'That's cold.'

'We're making you think for yourselves. That's helping you.'

'Why have you only got teenagers?'

'It's most effective that way. We catch the teenagers, and stop them massing in the park. After a period, most of them lose the instinct to gather.'

'But why are you making me see all that stuff? All the visions?'

'We just present you with the liquid. You're not even supposed to know it's happening.'

'So what's the point of it?'

'We merely have our instructions. As soon as you fall asleep—'

'Wait. Stop. How do you know we're falling asleep?'

'We can hear it. You emit electricity when you fall asleep. That's why when people fall asleep, their bodies twitch. *So we circle round, waiting to hear that, then we take you to the cell, you have the liquid, you have your visions.'*

'But why? What are you doing to us?'

'The Master is looking for someone special, someone he can help. He's especially interested in you. He's said your talents are vast. You could be one of the most significant people on the planet. You should take up his offer. Find him.'

'I don't wanna find him. If he's anything to do with you guys, he must be evil.'

'Please. I need to get you home now . . .' He stops. He's really having trouble breathing. *'I need to get away from the plants.'*

'Why?'

'Too much oxygen. It scalds our lungs. The Master as well. That's one reason he hides away.'

I don't know what else to ask. Suddenly I'm feeling so tired. I want to get back to my body. I want to get back to my bed. I need to rest. I move towards the railings. On the other side, the shakfiend is looking like his lungs are about to burst from his throat.

'Come on then,' I say, 'take me home.'

I go over to the fence and I slip through the bars. Then I let him take me home, and I get back into bed.

29

Soon as I get back into bed, the same thing happens. Smack. I'm awake. Lying in bed, running it through in my head. Now it all fits together: lamias . . . the voice . . . Polly. And it all comes to the same thing. I gotta find Jimmy again, 'cos I need his help. Then I gotta find the Master, 'cos he's got Polly's lamia. And if Polly don't get that back, she's gonna stay in a coma for ever. But right away I'm getting the fear about going to see the Master. I reckon if I find him, then I'm either gonna end up dead, or totally different. But I don't care. I'm scared, but at least I know what I've gotta do. I once seen Kriss taking a penalty at football, and that's the way I feel now. I'm an Ice Man. I know what I'm doing. I'm calm. I can see how the world's got messed up, and I'm on a mission to sort it out.

I go down the corridor. Luckily Mum's got Frosties at last, and I eat three bowls. I need sugar. I need energy. On the table there's more of Mum's design books, and also a copy of her new *Hackney Gazette*. On the front there's a picture of Butterfield Park, with a caption saying 'Council Approves Butterfield Redevelopment'. There's an artist's impression of what's planned. It's basically a supermarket, with a few flats over the top. At one end there's a gym, one of them little ones with running machines lined up next to a TV screen. There's a picture of a skinny lady on the running machine. She's grinning. She looks just like Mum.

Mum comes in. Same red dressing gown as yesterday.

'Morning, Colin.'

'Hi, Mum . . .' I say, in my new Ice Man voice.

'You OK?'

'Yip. Still getting the dreams. But I feel that—'

'Oh dear,' she says, cutting me off.

'Mum,' I go, 'why are they knocking down Butterfield Park?'

'Well . . . the site would raise four million, which can then be spent on climbing frames, schools, improving the parks.'

'If you want to improve parks, why build a supermarket on one? Ain't gonna help.'

'Of course it's going to help—'

'What, like, in the supermarket, there's gonna be slides and swings? Maybe a special section for squirrels?'

'Colin . . . Don't try to be clever, OK?'

'I don't need to *try*. I am clever.'

'Do you realize there are disabled people who can't get to Stamford Hill for the shops?'

'Soon there'll be more. 'Cos if there's no parks, everyone'll get *so fat*, they won't move . . . London will be filled with gut-wobbling kids who'll have to get lifted out of the house on cranes.'

'Come on. Butterfield's squalid. There's nothing but drug addicts there.'

'Why are you so keen? Do you get money from it?'

That stops her in her tracks.

'What a strange thing for you to ask . . . Why would I get money?'

'You edit the *Hackney Gazette*. You're a councillor.'

Mum goes quiet. Then she says it:

'I shouldn't really tell you this, so you must keep it quiet . . . Actually, a major supermarket are sponsoring a refurbishment of the *Gazette*. And they also want to set up pan-community sporting events, so they need a local figure to organize it . . .'

'How much?'

'They'd give a consultancy fee of twenty-thousand pounds.'

'Don't take their money.'

'Come on. Everybody else does, so why can't I?'

'Bu—'

'Have you thought what we could do with twenty thousand? Look at this flat! Do you think I like washing my hair in a bath with a broken shower? Do you? I want to redo this place, but I can't. And how am I supposed to get a better job when I haven't bought any new clothes in two years?'

'Have you actually called up Malcolm and asked for a job?'

'Shh. Don't talk about Malcolm.'

' 'Cos you got OB in there?'

'I might.'

'I don't care who you got in there. I'm just glad I don't have to see them. But call Malcolm and ask for a job. Better way of getting one than just riding him.'

'Shut up,' she says suddenly, 'shut up! God, I want to get away from here. And clear up your mess!'

I stand up.

'Mum,' I say, 'I will.'

And I leave home. And I go to school.

30

As I walk to school I call Mrs McBrien but there's been no change. So Polly ain't at the bus stop, and nor is anyone else I know. I pull out my book and right away I get into it. But then I notice there's someone lingering nearby. I look up, fast as I can. It's Sal. He's hanging around like a wasp who can smell jam.

'What you reading?' he goes.

I hate that. Whenever you get a book out, some spid comes over and says: 'What you reading?' It's like you're putting up a big neon sign saying:

COME AND TALK TO ME

(This applies to any moron out there.

My head is like a skip. Come and dump

your rubbish inside.)

'What's the book about?' says Sal.

'Lupacle,' I say. I know he don't know what that is, but I ain't explaining. I'm thinking: Get out of my face, or I'm gonna have to read my sentence again. And I

179

don't wanna be reading nothing again. I don't wanna be looking up till I've reached the end.

'Oh,' he says, and he goes into the shop.

When the bus comes I decide I ain't going upstairs to sit where I sit with Polly, 'cos everything's different now. I don't have Polly now, and I'm the Ice Man. So I sit downstairs next to the old ladies with their shopping. As the bus is about to pull out, someone comes running. It's Vern. He is wearing a trilby hat, which he's holding to stop it blowing off. He comes in panting, and sits right next to me. I don't know if the Ice Man would sit next to King Spod in a hat, but I guess I'll let it go.

Vern says: 'Look. I stayed up late doing these.'

He reaches into his bag, and he pulls out some paper. It looks like parchment, and it's covered with weird writing done in italics.

'What is it?'

'Prayers for Polly,' he says.

'Why is it in weird writing?'

'I used a calligraphy pen. You don't need to, but I thought it showed more intention.'

'Right.'

'I'm going to go round the churches after school, and I'm going to distribute them. By tonight one heck of a lot of people will be praying for Polly's soul. Beseeching the Lamb of God to come down.'

I nearly laugh at that. I have never, in my whole life, heard an expression more gay than the Lamb of God. 'Thanks, Vern,' I say.

'Here,' he says, 'I did one for you.'

And he passes one of them over to me, like he's passing over a page from the original Old Testament. I don't know how I'm supposed to take it, so I fold it up carefully, and I put it in the pocket of my trousers.

At breaktime, I'm about to do my normal trick: go and hide round the side of the gym, but then I think: no, I won't. So I sit on the steps of the school, and I read my book. I get right into it, and in a few minutes I've read right to the end, but I wanna read more, so I even read the back cover, and the acknowledgements, and the 'If you liked this, you might like to try . . .' section.

Then I put the book in my pocket.

I look up, and I'm watching everyone. Sharon Holdings is sitting on the bank of grass at the edge of the playground, and there's people gathered round her. Including Trish Appleton. I ain't even talked to her since the bog wash. I think it through . . . I can't run away from them for ever. If I rush them, then they're gonna fight back. And there's no way I can slag them off 'cos Sharon Holdings is much too popular. And Trish Appleton ain't popular exactly, but she's Sharon's mate. The way I see it, I only got one choice: I need to stand next to them, and make out it was no big deal. Take the stress out of the situation. I go over. But I go over slow. I don't want too much attention. When I come, Trish smirks a bit, but she don't say nothing.

Trish says: 'But what you wanna *do* for your birthday?'

Sharon says: 'I think I might get off with someone.'

Suddenly you could hear a pin drop. Sharon ain't like Trish. No one's ever seen her get off with anyone. That's OK by me. She is so good-looking I feel a bit faint just looking at her. If I start thinking of her snogging people I'm gonna be falling over. No one has talked since Sharon has said this.

Then Eric looks Sharon in the eye, and he says: 'Sharon, are your legs tired?'

'No, Eric, why?'

' 'Cos they're running through my mind all the time,' says Eric.

I don't know where he got this line. Probably *Home and Away*.

Sal says: 'Eric, man, that was cheesy.'

'Shut up,' says Eric.

'No, man,' says Sal, 'you is smelling of cheese, bruv.'

'Least I ain't smelling of garlic sauce,' says Eric.

'Shut up,' says Sal.

'Make me,' says Eric, and he's pushing Sal in the chest.

'Don't push me,' says Sal.

'Make me stop pushing you,' says Eric, pushing him in the chest again. Eric is such a sap. It's like he reckons that Sharon is gonna get off with him, just 'cos he's started a fight with the biggest guy in our year. Luckily Sal ain't rising to it yet. He's a big guy. He takes time to get going.

'Leave him alone,' says Vern.

Suddenly everyone turns. We ain't even noticed Vern. Now, there he is, wearing his trilby hat like he's just begging to be smacked in the face. Eric grabs the hat off. You can see he's at boiling point. Any second, he's gonna fight someone. When Eric gets the rage, it don't go away, it just gets bigger. And usually it spreads to everyone else as well.

'Give back my hat,' says Vern.

'Yeah right,' says Eric. You can see him wondering where to chuck the hat. Obviously he can't give it back without losing face.

'Chuck it to me,' I say.

'Colin Bitchin!' says Eric. 'The tiny midget menace!'

He chucks the hat at me. I put it on my head. Trouble is, now the attention is on me, and Eric is definitely gonna fight someone. He walks up to me, and he takes the hat off, and drops it on the floor. Then he pushes his knuckles against my head, and he puts on his Hearfield voice and says:

'If we apply thwee unit of pwessure . . .'

Then he pushes some more. Everyone laughs a bit.

'If we apply thwee unit of pwessure against the head of the vewy special boy . . .'

No one's really laughing now.

'Eric,' I say, 'can you stop saying that?'

'Well, give me something else to say.'

And I know I shouldn't do this – I know it's gonna lead to big trouble – but I can't stop myself. I give him Verno's prayer out of my pocket.

Eric unfolds it, and he starts reading it in his Hearfield voice:

'O Almighty Father, we pway for the soul of Polly Fenula McBwien. Please send the Lamb of God . . .' Everyone is cacking themselves now.

'Don't do that,' says Vern. He is well tense. 'That is important. You must not disrespect it.'

'Do not diswespect the Lamb of God,' says Eric, in his Hearfield voice.

Vern can't take it no more. He rushes Eric. 'Cept Vern is no fighter. He totally spazzes out, and he's waving his arms and kicking. He's fighting just the way I used to. And it don't work. Eric steps out of trouble, and he punches Vern in the face three times, and Vern's glasses come off and he falls to the floor. I'm watching the whole thing in slow motion. I know I should step in. I started this, and I should have saved it, but at the same time, I'm on a mission. I can't take no passengers.

I can't help Vern. He was asking for trouble with his stupid hat, and now he's getting it.

In twenty seconds, Eric has got Vern in the headlock on the ground, and he's giving his signature: gobbing in Vern's mouth.

'Leave it now,' says Kriss.

Eric looks at Kriss. Then he gobs one more time to show that no one tells him what to do. Then he gets up.

I'm watching Vern. He can't stop it. He's definitely crying now. Definitely. He gets up slowly. But he don't walk off. He picks up his glasses. One of the lenses has got smashed, but still he puts them on. Then he straightens up his clothes. I pick up his hat, and I straighten it out, and I hold it out for him. But he don't take it. And he don't look at me. He just walks off. And I have never felt so ashamed in my life. I ain't the Ice Man no more. I am a maggot.

31

After school, I go straight back home.

Hoping maybe Jimmy's left a message.

There's nothing.

I call Sharleen. Polly ain't moved.

I go out. In the street I see Yussuf, who's out putting up one of his notices on lampposts. I'm about to cross the street to speak to him when I'm nearly crushed by a car the size of a tank. It's booming out the brainworm.

'*They started it/they started it/I hate 'em 'cos they started it . . .*'

This big guy winds down his window. I recognize who it is: Sharon Holding's dad.

'You better get back where you came from,' he shouts at Yussuf.

Yussuf don't seem too bothered. He smiles at Mr Holdings and he says:

'You are an infidel, my friend. And on the day of destruction, your armoured vehicle will not protect you from the holy fire. Turn to God.'

Mr Holdings ain't in the mood for talking God. 'You Paki twat,' he says. Then he holds up his phone and starts recording.

'You better watch out,' he goes, 'I can video with this thing.'

'Good,' says Yussuf, 'then I can broadcast a message for your infidel friends. Repent, and worship Allah. Or you will burn in the fires of destruction. Your armoured vehicle will not protect you from the furnace.'

Mr Holdings don't say nothing to this. He just switches off his phone, sticks his arm out the window, pulls down Yussuf's notice and puts it in the car. Then he drives off.

I go over to Yussuf.

'Why did he do that?'

'When a man is afraid, he is not accountable for his feelings. Or his actions.'

'Yussuf! Do people think you placed the bomb in Clissold Park?'

'Unfortunately that is the case.'

'And did you?'

'The Muslim bombers are a minority as small and as absurd as the Klu Klux Klan. I do not think all Christians wear white hoods and set fire to black people.'

'Sorry, Yussuf.'

'Don't worry. Listen, Colin, I have a message for you.

Each day at six o'clock, your uncle will wait for you in Butterfield Park.'

'Why didn't you tell me this before?'

'I did not see you. And you did not find me. Ask and it shall be given. Knock and the door shall be opened.'

'What's the time now?'

'Four-thirty.'

'Perfect. See you, Yussuf.'

I leg it to the bus stop, and I go over to the hospital to see Polly.

32

Polly's in a corner of a ward on the third floor. The place is bunged up with old people. A couple of them are sleeping. Most of them are sitting up and doing crosswords and eating grapes. As I walk over, Sharleen's just leaving.

'They're going to send her home so she can lie in her own bed,' she says.

'Does that mean she's getting better?'

'It means they don't know what's wrong. And they need the bed 'cos there's loads of kids coming in with the same thing. I'm trying to contact her dad.'

Then she goes.

So I've got Polly to myself. 'Cept I ain't. Her body's lying there looking green. And I don't think her lamia's inside. In fact I know it. Sharleen's put Polly's iPod on her, with the headphones in her ears. I check what she's listening to. It's a track by Ronan Keating. I know for a fact that Polly would rather die than listen to one of his songs. I don't even know how it got on there. So I scroll through the playlist, and find some stuff Poll likes, like Willie Mason, and Jewel, and Ed Harcourt, and I set it to Willie.

After that I don't know what to do.

I check round that no one's watching. They ain't.

So I bend down and I kiss her. It's the first time I've kissed Poll on the lips. In real life anyway, and it ain't the way I planned it. But Polly still smells of Polly, and so I stand there smelling her.

Then I say: 'Please come back to me.' And I go.

33

I reach Butterfield Park by 5:52 p.m. And right away I see Jimmy sitting by the trees on a rock. He's smoking. He smiles.

'You took your time,' he says.

'Jimmy, I know what's happened to Polly's lamia. The Master has got her. But what do you think he's doing to her?'

'*Where is he?* That's surely the first question.'

'We gotta project again, and find out.'

'Your mum isnae gonnae like that.'

'Jimmy, I ain't messing about. We gotta get her back. I need her.'

'Oh, come on. You don't need anyone. Look, your dad died and you carried on.'

'If Polly's gonna spend the rest of her life with a boiled head, just staring at the wall, then I'm gonna throw myself under a car.'

'Don't say that.'

'But, Jimmy, what can they do to her? Can lamias be killed?'

'It's very hard to kill a lamia. Have you ever tried to kill a jellyfish?'

'Yeah. When me and Dad were in Italy we went out in a boat, and we saw these jellyfish, and we chopped them up with our paddles. The bits just swum off.'

'Lamias are like that. If you chop the arms off a lamia, they grow back. They're basically immortal. Listen . . . I'll help you find Polly. But there's a condition. Afterwards, we're going to your mum and you've got to make her speak to me. Is that a deal?'

'I don't wanna see my mum. I'm mad at her.'

'Son, your mommy is a saint, and you give her nothing but abuse.'

'That's 'cos I'm upset. And I want her to help.'

'So ask for her help. Don't slag her off.'

'Jimmy, I know you just wanna see my mum 'cos you think she's fit.'

'There's nothing wrong with that. Your mother's been on her own for three years, and she's very attractive. You must see that yourself.'

'No, I don't.'

'You know what Freud said: All boys secretly want their mum to get sexy with them.'

'*I* don't, Jimmy. I want my mum to buy me trainers,

then keep away. Freud's mum musta been a right dirty cow.'

'I just wannae make your mommy happy. That's all I want.'

'Listen, pal. My mum is a Londoner. She don't wanna be happy. She wants to be rich. So she wants a bloke who can give her a job. Not some stinky hippy who can give her an STD.'

'Before you criticize a man,' says Jimmy, 'first walk a mile in his shoes. That way, when you do criticize him, you're a mile away and you've got his shoes.'

I stare at him.

'By the way, Jimmy,' I say, 'did you really spend time in a mental home?'

He looks at me.

'Your mum's been giving me a good write-up I see.'

'Did you?'

'Sure,' he goes. 'When you get lost, sometimes you need the security of four walls and three square meals. Just gotta watch the drugs. But don't think too much of it. I never get down. Not like your daddy. He got terrified. I don't want that to happen to you.'

Now I don't know what to say. I was expecting Jimmy to deny it.

'Right,' he says. 'Shall we try to project?'

'OK.'

'We gottae make sure we're not disturbed this time.

Luckily the government have told people to keep out of the parks. Which makes our timing perfect.'

We look about to try and find the quietest bit of the park. There's trees in one corner, but there's two blokes lifting an old TV over the fence. We find another quiet area, hidden behind the bushes, but you can tell a tramp has been using it for his tramp nest. The grass is all flat, and there's loads of Rizlas and tins lying about. I see some gash pictures but now ain't the moment to look. So then we go to the other side, and we push through a thick gorse bush, right next to the wall of a garage. There's a little space at the back. Jimmy says we should hide our bodies, so we get a few black rubbish bags, and we crawl in and hide behind them.

I'm lying on my side, resting my head on my jumper so I can hear the pulse in my ear. It's that swish-swish noise you hear when you're going to sleep and you're leaning on your side with your head on the pillow. Sounds like the sound of horsemen, coming to get you, swishing their swords in the air.

I lie there listening to the swish-swish, and then Uncle Jimmy talks. He does all that 'relax . . . think hazoom' stuff again, but much more. I'm fidgeting. At first I'm distracted by the smell of fag butts from the plastic bin bags, and also the petrol smell coming from the garage. And then I'm thinking of Sharleen saying 'I'm trying to contact her dad' and I'm picturing Polly seeing her dad again. And then I'm picturing seeing my own dad, and wishing I could see him again. But then I'm listening to Jimmy's voice talking, and waiting to get the light feeling.

But he keeps going for ten minutes, and I ain't getting nowhere.

I scratch myself. I open my eyes. Jimmy is saying:

'Leave your body. Enter your lamia.'

I look at him. Lying there with his Bob the Builder T-shirt on.

He says it again: 'Leave your body. Enter your lamia.'

I'm just watching him. Suddenly his eyes snap open: 'Right, let's talk.'

'What? We can't! We gotta get a move on!'

But Jimmy is already up. He pushes his way through the bush, and he goes into the grassy area. I follow him.

'Jimmy?' I say. 'What you doing?'

'This isnae working.'

'Why not?'

'Probably 'cos you're in too much of a hurry. And you've got too much on your mind. So have I.'

'But we gotta get after Polly quick. Anything could happen to her. QUICK!'

'Look, laddie. It isnae that easy to astral project. You're gifted. But maybe not that gifted.'

'I am! Do it to me again!'

'I can't!'

'We did it before!'

'We were lucky.'

'Jimmy, I still think they're gonna do something bad to her lamia. What will happen to Polly then? Will she die?'

'If she's lucky she'll spend her life in bed. If she's unlucky she'll get a contract presenting the *Holiday* programme. Listen, laddie, for this to work, your mind has got to be blank. And it's obviously not. What were you thinking about?'

'My dad. Do you know Mum said he wasn't in the SAS? She said he was weak. I know that ain't true.'

'Maybe your mum had a point. Maybe your dad wasn't everything you think. Maybe you need to hear what he was really like.'

I sit down on a log.

'Go on, Jimmy. Tell me about my dad.'

34

Jimmy sits next to me. He gets out his baccy and starts rolling.

'Your dad –' he says, 'my wee brother, Billy – was a good man. Both of us loved our mum, and were scared of our dad. We went to a school in Glasgow, where he had the reputation of being a live wire who would never back down in a fight. I had a reputation for being a nutter who would do ouija boards. I left to travel and write articles about the rave scene. Billy left Scotland and joined the army. Disaster. He was too much of a rebel. He only lasted a few months. He went to London. Drifted around, flirting with groups like the Socialist Worker crowd, but he always disliked extremists and people who know all the answers. He was writing newspaper articles on crime when he met your mum, who he loved very much. He was so proud when they had you. You were fascinated that he'd been in the army, and he would play up to that. I once heard him telling you he'd spent a winter on Ben Nevis, in an igloo. But he wanted to look after you and your mum, and it shamed him he never had money. So he was really happy when he got an advance to write his book on the history of British crime. He wanted to show crime in a global context. He thought all countries were like kids in a playground fighting for attention. He wanted his book to be a huge thing that you would read in years to come, and be proud. So he got overambitious, and bogged down, and skint. Meanwhile your mother wanted holidays and glamour and a fancy school for you. He realized your mum was disappointed in him, and he was stiff with a sense of failure. He became scared of the world. He used to hide away in the attic, reading loads of newspapers, and wasting money on spy equipment, the latest software, portable stoves for your camping trips. Madness. And he started to see ghosts and shakfiends and he thought he was going crazy because he didn't believe in all that. Gradually he got more and more isolated. Depressed people always do. Is isolation the symptom of depression, or is it the cause? I don't know. I know he was a good man, but he was also weak, scared, greedy and depressed. I reckon he'd decided to die by the time he was thirty-seven, and it took him a year to actually do it.'

'But how? And where?'

'You'll have to ask your mum that.'

We sit in silence for a bit. I feel chilled inside.

'Jimmy,' I say, 'I'm ready to find Polly.'

But at that moment another helicopter comes flying over. Whack Whack Whack.

'We need a bit of quiet,' says Jimmy. 'I hate those things.'

'That's an air ambulance, Jimmy. It's doing good.'

'It says Virgin on it. It may be doing good but it's also the noisiest advertising in the sky. I'd like to chuck rocks at those bastards till they crash.'

But the chopper don't move. It's practically overhead. And suddenly I see why . . .

I see Yussuf. He's at the other side of the little park, sticking up one of his paper signs. And right outside the park I see the biggest car in Stoke Newington, and I know who that is. Mr Holdings. He's standing outside the car talking into his mobie. And suddenly four police cars come hurtling up Palatine Road. They slam on the brakes, and eight coppers get out. They come into the park and sprint for Yussuf. They throw him to the ground.

Yussuf ain't helping himself. He's shouting:

'You infidels! You will all be exploded!'

The other coppers have kept guns trained on Yussuf all the time.

At first I don't even move I'm so shocked.

But then two cops have got Yussuf in a half-Nelson

and they're marching him back to the cars. And now I move. I'm running across the park.

'Leave him alone,' I'm shouting. 'Leave him! It weren't him! It weren't him!'

The policemen don't even turn. Yussuf does though. He sees me and he shouts:

'I love you, Colin! You are a Great One!'

But then one of the coppers punches him in the head and he shuts up.

They drive off.

I just stand there watching.

It takes me a while before I realize Jimmy ain't joined me. He's still sitting calmly on the rock. I go back.

'Come on, we gotta get over there and tell them they're making a mistake! I'll tell them I know Yussuf, he's my friend.' Then I think of something. 'Jimmy, do you reckon the bomb could be connected with the shakfiends?'

'Could be.'

'Then we should go and tell the police about them.'

'Good lad,' says Jimmy. 'Why don't you go over and tell them? 'Cos take it from me, the food in mental hospitals is of a very high quality.'

I look at him. He is right. The world is mad and there ain't nothing I can do to stop it. I'm empty. I just want to lie on the ground and die. But the good thing about that is: I ain't fidgeting no more. I know this time

I'm gonna go. I'm gonna leave my body behind. I'm gonna chuck it away like a piece of paper wrapped round a kebab.

'Come on then, Jimmy,' I say, 'let's find Polly.'

35

We get behind the rubbish bags. Same as before. Hide ourselves away next to the wall of the garage. We're just about to start. Jimmy says, 'Give us a smile.'

'Why?'

'Because, son, it's important to have a little fun.'

'But you said yourself: Polly could become a vegetable. This is life or death.'

'All the more reason to enjoy it.'

'Jimmy,' I say, 'why did you come here? Are you just trying to get jiggy with my mum?'

'Come on,' he says. 'Sure, I'd love it if your mommy liked me, but that doesnae matter. I came 'cos I wanted to see you were OK.'

'Well . . . thanks. But I didn't ask you to come.'

'And I was hoping, if possible, to have a laugh.'

'I don't feel that funny.'

Jimmy laughs. 'Oh, don't worry. You're always funny.

'Cos you're unusual. Come on. Let's try and find out what happened to your girlfriend.'

'She ain't my girlfriend.'

'OK, the girl that you have absolutely no interest in, but you can't live without. One thing before we go . . .'

'What?'

'Please say: *Ho-hum, what's all this then? Woof!*'

'*Ho-hum, what's all this then? Woof!*'

Jimmy laughs for about a whole minute. First he does one of them loud laughs. Then he does one of them silent ones when you ain't making any noise, you're just shaking, and crying. Then he gulps for air, and laughs some more. Then he actually wipes his eyes and looks at me.

'OK. I can now die happy. Let's go for it.'

And we mediate. Jimmy is speaking – *hazoom, relax the body, enter the ghost* – and this time it works.

I feel myself grow light, and I know I've left my body, and I'm drifting up.

I open the eyes of my lamia, and I see I'm three foot high. Hovering over the bushes, looking at our bodies tucked behind the plastic bags. Jimmy ain't managed yet. I can just see his head sticking out. He's looking calm though. Breathing regular. And then suddenly his lamia drifts out of his body. It's totally still at first.

Eyes shut. Just drifting out with the breeze. Arms by his sides.

'Jimmy,' I say.

His eyes open, and he looks at me.

'Colin,' he says, 'you made it. Good lad. Let's go then.'

And we drift up. Soon we've floated to the top of the eucalyptus trees that are in the middle of Butterfield. We drift up, over the grass, over the tramps' benches, and then we're drifting over Neville Road. I can't see any shakfiends about.

He turns to me in the air.

'Where first?'

'Let's try the warehouse.'

'You lead the way.'

We fly off down Allen Road.

Still no shakfiends in the sky.

As we go past the newsagent's, I see an old sofa sitting on the pavement. If you were walking by, that's what you'd see as well. But I'm a lamia, and I see more. There's the ghost of an old man sitting there, staring into space. We're over a hundred metres above his head, but even from up here I get a whiff of him. He smells the way a fridge smells when it's been unused for a year, but is still filled with old butter, and old plastic bags containing slimy stuff that used to be lettuce.

We keep going. Over Albion Road. Sharon Holdings and Trish Appleton are outside KFC talking to some boys that I don't recognize. We keep going.

Soon we're getting close to the warehouse, and I'm getting the fear something terrible.

'That's the place,' I tell Jimmy.

He keeps right on going. We go over the wall with the barbed-wire fence, and then we can see the big broken window where the shakfiends were bringing us in. I'm wetting myself when we get close. I don't wanna keep going. What will they do to us if they see us? I hover in the air, a metre or so from the broken window.

But Jimmy goes straight in and I can't see him.

I want him to poke his head round and tell me it's OK.

He don't.

36

So I fly in through the window. Jimmy is inside, just standing there.

I can see no one. Nothing.

Just then a pigeon flaps right past me. I scream.

But it goes out the window and off.

Now I look round the warehouse. There's nothing. No one. Not even a ghost.

We walk down the corridor. The doors are open to the goal cells. I poke my head in the one I was in before. Nothing there. Just a couple of plastic bottles on the floor.

'Jimmy,' I say, 'there's nothing here.'

'Good. Let's get out. I don't like it in here. Feels evil.'

'But where should we go?'

'Out. We'll stop on that main road, and look about.'

So we float out of the warehouse and we go back to

Albion Road and rest on the balcony of a big house. Across the street, some men are putting up a new billboard with glue. It says: **We salute the brave firemen who tackled the Clissold Park Blast (Sponsored by Amex Oil)***. I look down the street. There're three more new signs up.* **Fly away somewhere calm, somewhere safe. Fly Flyanair***. And . . .* **If you want a little bit of extra protection, call Captain's Insurance***. And . . .* **The new Mountain Rover is London's safest car – What Car? magazine***. There's a picture of the new Mountain Rover driving up the side of a mountain, whereas, if you ever see them cars, they're always double parked in Islington while posh mums drop off their kids.*

Jimmy checks what I'm looking at and he reads them himself.

'Why don't they just come right out and say it?' he says. **'Be scared. Be more scared. 'Cos we're making cash.'**

I check out the action in the road.

Down below us is a bus stop. A tired-looking woman is standing and reading the **Standard***. I can see the headline from here. It says: 'Fear Will Strike London Today'. Next to the tired woman is a bloke with greasy hair who wants to read her paper, so he's leaning in. When this happens, most people turn their papers away. They shield them, like Eric does with* *his exam papers, even though no one would be so stupid as to try and copy what he's written. But this woman don't mind. Her lamia is standing quiet next to her. So's the man's. I like the way they're strangers but they're getting along fine. Watching them reading the same paper, suddenly I feel like I love them. I ain't slept properly for too long now. I ain't thinking right.*

Outside the flower shop there's a young girl. Her lamia is dressed up in a fur coat dancing round the pavement. There's also a load of Hassidics – them ones with the black coats and furry hats and long sideburns. They're funny, them Hassidics. Like if you get on the swing next to their kids, they always take their kids away, like they're so different they don't wanna be contaminated. But their lamias are doing much the same as everyone else's. Women are testing different clothes, the blokes are trying to get off with them. 'Cept for the lamia of the oldest Jew, he's dancing round like he's a ballerina. Hilarious.

I realize Jimmy ain't there.

I look around, then I see he's slipped into the house just next to us.

I drift in. Makes me shudder as I come through the glass.

We're in a big room with ancient furniture from the olden days. Massive fireplace with marble all round.

Big mirrors with gold frames. One of them old clocks on the mantelpiece going tick tick tick.

Sitting in the corner, on a chair that ain't there, is a ghost of a woman in a long black dress like someone from Victorian times. She's staring right at us. She looks like a big old crow. Like she just knows we've come to nick her big mirror and ticking clock.

But the smell coming off her ain't what you'd expect. It's a bit like the smell in shoe shops. Like expensive glue. Kinda nice.

Then I notice it . . .

In the corner, there's another of them air-conditioner units, and it's whirring away, and underneath is a bottle filling with liquid. I go over, and I take it out, and I sniff it.

It trips me.

I feel like I did when my mum got me my Xbox the Christmas after Dad died . . . I'm lying in my bed, Christmas Eve, and I know it's wrapped up in the living-room, and already I can't wait to open it. I know it's going to be well perfect, all proper, tucked in its box with that polystyrene round it. Even thinking about it makes me feel important. I know I'm gonna get Kriss round and I'm gonna show it to him, dead casual, I'm gonna say, 'You wanna see my Xbox?' and he's gonna go, 'No, you ain't. Which one?' and I'm gonna say 'Yeah, it's the new one. I got it' and I'm gonna feel like

I got a boner. I really like the smell. I'm about to sniff it again, but then suddenly I get this terrible headache, like bang bang bang in my head, and then I get it.

'Jimmy,' I go, 'that's what they're doing. The shakfiends. Somehow they're collecting the smell off ghosts, and they're using it on the kids.'

'Why would they do that?'

'Think about it. You stay round a ghost and you feel what the ghost feels, and you start thinking about everything bad you ever done? This one makes you greedy. Some make you jealous. Some make you depressed. The question is, yeah: Why do some people become ghosts? And some get liberated?'

'The ghosts are just the ones who got stuck. And they stay stuck.'

'I don't think so. I think the shakfiends are keeping them.'

'They hardly need to. Ghosts are so obstinate. So stupid.'

'What you saying, Jimmy?' I go suddenly. He must know he's playing with fire. 'You saying that's what happened to Dad?'

'No . . . well . . .'

'Do you . . . think Dad is a ghost? Like, trapped somewhere? Tell me. Where did Dad kill himself?'

'In his office. Upstairs in the attic.'

I've got him.

'So he did kill himself?'

'Yes. Yes, I'm afraid he did. That's what he wanted.'

'And did he leave a ghost behind?'

'I don't know. It's your house, Colin. You go up there.'

'Mum won't let me. The hatch has stayed shut.'

We both go silent.

'Let's get out,' he says.

So we come out of the old crow's house, and right away I see it . . .

37

A supermarket lorry.

'Jimmy,' I go, 'one of them things was outside Poll's house when she got took. Let's follow it.'

'Right, pal.'

We keep fifty metres behind, but we follow the lorry up Clissold Road. It turns into the school. Goes through the gate, and round to the old gym. The gym has got big double doors leading to the outside. The lorry backs towards these.

We come down closer, but then we see 'em:

Must be about a hundred shakfiends all round the lorry. On the roof of the old gym. On top of the lorry. On the car park round about. They don't look like they've noticed us, and that's the way I wanna keep it.

Soon as we see 'em we dodge down to the ground. We're hiding behind the fence that surrounds the school astro-turf pitch. We're in a little alleyway *between the fence and the wall of the flats. It's filled with old leaves and plastic bags and chocolate wrappings. Also an old fridge and a broken VCR.*

'I know where she must be,' I go.

'Where?'

'In the old gym. When I was at school last week, I saw a snake guarding the door.

'Could be.'

'But there's a lot of them things out there. Reckon that's where the Master is as well?'

'Could be.'

I'm looking at a crow that's picking food out of a plastic bag.

'Is that where you are, Polly?' I say out loud. 'And is that where **you** *are as well, you evil son of a bitch?'*

Right away the crow turns, like it's heard me. Then its eyes go milky blue, and it opens its mouth, and I hear that Samuel L. Jackson voice:

'You got it, child. And don't forget. I been telling you for a while: I'm waiting for you to come and meet me. You're taking a long time. And I ain't gonna make it easy 'cos I'm only interested in seeing the pure in heart.'

'Why are you making your voice come from a crow? I know you're not in a crow.'

'God is everywhere*.'*

'Yeah, but you ain't God.'

'*God is whoever you pray to. God is whoever can help you. And I can help you loads. I'm more powerful than a nuclear bomb, and three times as pretty.*'

With that, the crow stops talking, and flies off.

'*Did you get all that, Jimmy?*'

'*Aye. She could be in there. He is in there. We're gonnae be scared. I'm feeling excited already.*'

'*You wanna be scared?*'

'*Abandon yourself,*' *says Jimmy, and his accent is more Scottish now – as it always is, when he's trying to be mystical.* '*Prepare yourself for strangeness. Smell the cheese, my friend. Smell the cheese, and weep.*'

'*Whatever you say, Jimmy. Let's go.*'

We pick our way round slowly to the front door of the school.

'*Jimmy,*' *I say,* '*you know that vision I had that there was a big snake guarding the way into the gym? What do you reckon?*'

'*Well there're two possibilities,*' *he says.*

'*What?*'

'*One: The Master is in that gym and he's got a huge snake guarding the door. A snake that exists in the spirit realm, like lamias and himself.*'

'*And what's the other possibility?*'

'*That you're a nutcase. And you were seeing things*

'cos you're scared of school. I'm hoping it's the second.'

'Yeah, but, Jimmy . . . what if there really is a massive snake there?'

'Well if it's massive, then it'll be a squeezer, not a poisoner. So we've got that going for us.'

'Why?'

' 'Cos it'd squeeze you first before it tries to swallow.'

'Is that good?'

'It gives us a moment to attack.'

'Right . . . What with?'

We're passing under a cherry tree that's ten metres from the front door of the school. Jimmy reaches up and he grabs down a branch of the tree. He tears off a good stick, about a metre long, and he tears it so the end is pointed. There're quite a few leaves on it.

'Great stick, Jimmy. But is there anything else you know about snakes that we can use?'

'Er . . . snakes have got no arms. That's why they can't wear vests. Maybe we could come at it with a string vest.'

'Be serious, Jimmy. What else we got?'

'Look at this . . .'

*Jimmy points at his long droopy moustache. It's a bit like the tash that the pimps in **Starsky and Hutch** have. 'Cept his is grey and filled with egg.*

'What's that?' *I say.*

215

'I've got the Moustache of Power,' says Jimmy. 'A magic moustache.'

'What does it do?'

'It does nothing. But it makes me feel cool.'

I can't help it. I do actually laugh at that one.

'Finally!' says Jimmy, and he tosses back his head and he laughs too. 'You're having a good time. Good! 'Cos I'm doing my best to entertain you.'

'Thanks, Jimmy.'

'That's all right, pal,' and he gives me a big, hairy, stinky hug, 'I love you, Colin. You're a great lad. And I wouldn't've missed this for the world. Right . . .' We're now outside the front door of the school. Still no shakfiends in sight. 'Ready to go in?'

'I am,' I go, 'but I still think this could be hard.'

'Well,' says Jimmy, 'life is hard, but what's the alternative?'

38

We go up the four steps. Through the locked door. And into the building.

School.

It's still got the school smell: all Pledge and trainers and bleach. I'm facing down the long shiny corridor with classrooms off to the left, and noticeboards pinned on the right. Of course it's empty, and it feels cold, but at least I know where I am.

We start walking.

It's too quiet.

It seems to take us ages to get to the far end. I know something bad's gonna happen.

We get to the locked door at the end of the corridor, where I saw the snake. I stop and take a deep breath.

'Wanna go back?' says Jimmy.

'No.'

But I'm scared about what I'm gonna see on the other side of that door.

I take a deep breath.

I step through.

I've come out in a corridor which ramps upwards towards the old gym. It's dark in here. The roof is made of white plastic which lets light through, but not much. It's all covered in dirt and dust.

I don't see a snake. I see something else.

Outside the door to the old gym is the lamia of a woman. On her own. No sign of her body nowhere. A woman with her back to us.

Even from behind, you can tell she's well fit. She's got on a tight white dress, and she's got one of them fleshy butts that is all round, just asking you to touch. And her hair is hanging down on her white shoulders, long and blonde.

The woman turns.

From the front, she's even more sexy. First off you look at her breasts, that are showing out the front of her dress. I'm looking at them. And looking at this nice crystal necklace she's got between them. And then looking into her eyes. She's staring back into my eyes with this dreamy look. I don't know how, but it takes me several seconds to see it . . .

It's my mum's lamia.

39

*F*irst time I seen it. She don't really look like Mum. It's my mum the way she was when I was small, when she had her hair long, and she didn't shout, and she hummed when she put me to bed.

'I knew I could find her,' says Jimmy. He smiles at Mum. 'I always said we had a psychic link.'

She walks halfway down the ramp, and he walks up towards her. She smiles. He kisses her right on the lips.

'Hello, darling,' says Mum, 'come and give your mum a kiss. We'll chat, and then I'm going to take you home. I think we've had enough of this nonsense.'

Jimmy's looking guilty.

Suddenly I see I was a fool to think I could get Polly back, a fool to think I'm gonna do anything. I'm got. I'm trapped. My mum is gonna take over and make me go home, and then make me go to school to get smacked about by Eric and Kriss and Trish. And I *ain't never gonna find Polly and she's gonna turn into a vegetable and everyone'll say that's the way she was always gonna be. Your mum always stops you in the end. That's what they're there for. All my fight has gone. I sit down on the floor. Mum turns away from me again, and kisses Jimmy.*

'Stop that,' I say.

But she don't. She turns back to Jimmy, and this time you can see she's really kissing him with tongues. Then he starts kissing her on the neck. I lose it.

'Stop that! Stop that! Stop! Stop! Stop!'

Mum pushes Jimmy aside. She turns slowly back to me.

'Colin, you have to accept it: I'm an attractive woman, I need a new man, and a new job, and new clothes, and a holiday, and I'm not going to hold myself back any more. And, my cross little flower, you could be an attractive boy. There's nothing wrong with that. Don't be shy if you want to kiss Polly. Or if you want to kiss Kriss.'

'What the hell you talking about? Shut up!'

'You're just scared of getting older.'

Nothing makes me more mad than someone saying I'm scared when I ain't. Except maybe my mum talking to me in her sugary voice, but saying stuff that's just wrong. She carries on.

'You're just getting older. It's normal.'

'You're the one spending all your money on hair dye and face creams. You're the one scared of getting older.'

'And, darling, accept your dad is dead. He's dead he's dead he's dead, and he was dead to us a long time before that. To be absolutely honest, I found him a drain, and, you know what, when he killed himself, a part of me was happy.'

I want to scream at her – '**Shut up, shut up, shut up, shut up!**' – but I don't. I just go quiet. So then Mum says:

'Colin, darling, it's not been easy for either of us. And I'm sorry if I've been difficult with you. But listen, I need you to go home, and to stop all this.'

'If I can't find Polly, life ain't worth living.'

'You'll move on. Just like you did with Dad.'

Now I lose it.

'I ain't moved on with Dad! And you know why? 'Cos you still ain't told me what happened to him! Tell me.'

Mum's lamia looks into my eyes.

'You tell him, Jimmy.'

And he starts up:

'Your dad came home,' he says, 'and he went up to his attic, and he took out a gun, and he shot himself in the head.'

'But, Mum,' I say, 'why? Was it 'cos I kept waking him? Was it 'cos I burned his book?'

Mum looks a long time into my eyes.

'Yes,' she says.

And I just fall down on the floor. I'm holding my head in my hands. My eyes are filling with tears. Only one thing worse than crying: that's having someone see you do it. Specially if it's your mum. But she loves it. Mums always love it when their kids cry, 'cos they can step in and take control just like they did when you were a baby. I can't take it.

My mum comes over and puts her arms round me. I kind of shrug her away. But she pulls me up to her chest, and she places her cheek against mine. No! She knows I'm crying. It can't get no worse than this. Her hair is on my face and it's sticking in my tears.

I turn my head to the side.

And that's when I see two shakfiends hobble through the gym door into the corridor. Soon as they see us, they come sprinting at Mum. They got their mouths open wide, so you can see their yellow teeth.

'MUM!' I shout, and she turns round, and just stands watching, fingering this chain round her neck. When they're a couple of paces away, she holds up the chain, and right away they stop. They close their mouths, and lie down like sleepy dogs.

'Go back in,' says Mum.

Right away the shakfiends turn and they head through the door.

This is weird. But now Mum turns back to me, like nothing's happened.

She pulls me into her. She touches me on the back of my head, and she kisses me on my cheek. As she takes her hand away, I look at it. The hand looks a little claw-shaped, and the nails are long and black. I'm thinking I ain't seeing things straight any more, maybe I been away from my body too long. Maybe it ain't right to go so long without proper sleep.

But my mum keeps holding me, and she looks me in the eye. She looks so different. Her eyes are beautiful and blue, and her hair is nice, and she even smells nice. She kisses me on the forehead. She kisses me on both cheeks. I'm starting to relax.

I see it. I been bad to my mum. I know that's what families are for: if you're feeling bad, you take it out on them. But she's trying her best. She lost dad as well. I gotta stop giving her a hard time. I look into her face, and I see how beautiful my mum is.

And that's when I see it . . .

Her tongue is long like a snake's, and it's orange and black.

It flicks twenty centimetres out of her mouth.

I scream.

And right away her face is changing.

Her nose flattens back on to her face.

Her eyes separate.

Her hair is falling out and underneath you see her scalp covered in scales.

She ain't looking like Mum no more. She's getting back her proper face.

Her snake face.

I'm trying to get away, but she's gripping me, and her eyes are bulging bigger and bigger. And now we're struggling, and I'm holding on to the necklace round her neck, and trying to push her off. And I'm kicking and spitting in her face, trying to get away, and suddenly I get an idea: I headbutt her.

I get her right in the nose, and she lets go.

Now she ain't fighting me.

Her neck gets fatter and fatter and her arms are disappearing and her body is changing back into its proper snake shape.

I gotta leg it quick.

I'm sprinting for the door back into the school, but the snake is getting longer and longer and its tail is now seven metres long and its head is starting to rise to attack and its mouth is opening.

That's when Jimmy attacks. He runs at the snake from behind, and he takes his branch, and he rams it into its eyes. Once, twice. Smack smack smack and the snake is squealing. The snake turns its huge mouth on Jimmy now, and he goes for it.

He smacks his stick into the snake's mouth, trying to wedge it.

But it just snaps like a matchstick.

Then the snake opens its mouth wide as it goes and it bites Jimmy on top of his head.

I'm sprinting to the door. I turn.

The snake has got Jimmy in its mouth so his legs are kicking out but his head is inside, and the snake lifts back its head and swallows him down. I once saw a cat swallowing a mouse and it's like that. He falls in some more and now I can only see the bottom of his legs. Then again, and I can only see his feet and I know I gotta do something quick to save him.

But then I see shakfiends coming from the gym in the background. Leaping through the gym door.

And I turn, and I leg it down the school corridor.

40

I'm through the front door of the school.

I lift up, and I fly off into the sky.

Where to go? Home? They know where I live. They'll head there. I'll go in the opposite direction.

I circle round, back over the school.

Down below the shakfiends are leaping out the door one by one. They land in the playground and they raise their heads to search the sky. I'm getting more time.

But then they see me.

They're looking up at me, their big mouths open, and they're hissing. They look less like old men now. They look more like bats. The first one spreads its wings, and it starts running along the ground, trying to get up into the air. But it's big. Three-metre wingspan. And it can't go straight upwards. Has to get going first. I'm getting a head start.

In five seconds, I've flown across the school grounds

and then I change direction again to throw them off. But I'm looking behind me, and I see the shakfiends come flapping back into sight.

It takes a second for them to see me, and it takes them a couple more to change direction. You can see I got an advantage. The shakfiends are big and strong, but they take time to turn.

But once they are going, they're moving fast. As I pass Clissold Leisure, I've got fifty metres on them. Their wings are taking big strokes through the air, flap flap flap, and they're gaining.

I'm flapping my wings as fast as I can, but it don't make any difference to my speed. I'm trying to get more streamlined, but they're gaining on me all the time. There's about twenty of them, and they're all staring at me with their big eyes – like they're huge dogs, dying to sink their teeth in my neck. Fifteen metres behind. You can hear them as well. Their wings are going sweep sweep, and they're whimpering like they can't wait to start biting and tearing.

And they're gaining.

I know they're gonna get me now, so I just close my eyes and wait for it to happen. Then suddenly it hits me where I should go.

Clissold Park! It's so obvious.

But I look up and I see five bats have actually flown right over my head. They're in front now.

Cutting me off. They're looking down at me, with their big bulgy eyes.

I'm panicking now. I'm praying:

'Help me help me I will do so many good things. Help me.'

They gather their wings in close, and they come shrieking down towards me. Not flapping, just falling out of the sky. Mouths open. Making a bat scream, all high-pitched like a metal nail dragged down a blackboard.

I know I gotta keep calm.

Two shakfiends come shrieking towards me with their yellow fangs gaping.

I wait. I wait.

*When they're a metre away, I **dart** sideways.*

But 'cos I'm watching the bats, I ain't noticed what's going on on the ground. We've flown into Clissold Park, and I've dodged into a tree.

A branch hits me in my stomach. Smack. I hold on to it.

I look up at the bats in the air. They seen me dropping down into the park.

Now they're hovering in the air, like they're wondering if they dare come in for me.

I gotta get further in.

I don't stop to watch. I leap out of that tree and I whizz off through the air, deeper into the park. Across the rose garden, over the field with the eight sick deer. Over to the river filled with terrapins and supermarket trolleys.

And I dive into the water. There's that panic you get when you dive in water, then, a moment later: I'm calm. The water ain't deep – half a metre at most – and I lie on the bottom, looking up, holding on to some pondweed. I wonder how long I can hide, and then I realize I can breathe underwater: I'm a lamia. I'm looking through the surface of the water, seeing if I can see black shapes arrive, but nothing does. A duck comes paddling overhead. I can see its chubby body and beating legs. I lie there some more. Totally still.

Then I see a black shape dart across the top of the water, and splash nearby. I push my head just above the surface and I see a shakfiend in the water nearby. It's thrashing about, and it's making a wheezy noise like it can't breathe. Its chest is going in spasms, and then it vomits. Its lungs burst from its mouth, and they hang from its lips – a bloody bag of mucous – and it dies.

41

I lie in the water for a while. The river has got a gentle
flow, and I can feel it pushing against my head. So I
imagine that the water is going right through me –
through my head and out my feet. I pretend I'm just a
part of the water, and it feels good.

Then I push my head out.

I stand up and look around.

Not a shakfiend in sight. Just the body of the one
that died nearby.

I hear something. I look up. It's just a plane flying
over, leaving a big trail of smoke. I watch that for a bit.
Then I look at the tree. It's a big conker tree. It ain't
got conkers yet but it's got big green leaves which are
in bunches which look like hands. And it's covered
with these triangular bunches of white flowers which
look a bit like candles. For a second I feel OK.

Then I look around.

The police musta opened the park again 'cos

people are everywhere. I start watching this group of kids. They look about five years old, and they're all huddling round the small stage. A little girl is in charge.

'I'm going to count to ten,' she says in a loud voice, 'then all the girls are gonna run and catch you. If we catch you, we're gonna kiss you. OK, one – two – three . . .'

Most of the boys run off a little bit, but they ain't going far. You can tell they're all hoping to get kissed. I watch one of the boys, who legs it as fast as he can. He's got blond hair and wears glasses and he looks younger than the rest. He comes over to where I am and he hides under the conker tree. After a bit I come a little closer.

He looks at me.

'Are you a ghost?' he says.

'Sort of,' I say. 'I'm like a ghost, but I ain't died.'

'Oh,' he says.

'You know something? You're the only person who's seen me.'

'I see lots of ghosts,' he says, 'but normally they don't speak to me. They talk to themselves.'

'What are you doing?'

'I'm trying to win at kiss chase. No girl is going to kiss me.'

'Is that winning?'

'I think so. But I don't care anyway. I'm pretending I'm hiding in an igloo.'

'Why are you hiding?'

' 'Cos of the bears.'

'What do the bears want to do to you?'

'Kiss me,' he says.

I like the boy. 'Where do you go to school?' I say.

'I'm about to go to Betty Leyward.'

'I went there.'

'Is it OK?'

'It's OK. But sometimes some of the people start on you.'

'Why? What do they want?'

'They want you to be like them.'

'So what do you have to do?'

I think about that one. But then I give him an answer: 'Refuse. Be yourself.'

'But I don't know how to be myself,' he says, 'because sometimes I'm a pirate and sometimes I'm a girl and sometimes I'm an eskimo in an igloo.'

'You stay like that.'

'Is it fun being a ghost?'

'Well, it's better being alive.'

'Yes,' he says, ' 'cos you can eat lollies.'

I laugh at that. I like it when people ask for my help, 'cos you can tell them stuff that's right, even *though you don't do it yourself. It makes you feel you know everything.*

'See you,' I say. 'Good luck with the bears.'

Then I walk off.

On the grass I look at two old ladies who're sitting on a blanket eating boiled eggs. They got their tights off and they're wriggling their toes.

Nearby there's a cricket game. It's got one batsman – a kid – one bowler – a grandad – and one fielder – a dog.

Everyone's having a good time and it makes me feel a bit better.

I go past where the café blew up. The place is roped off with police tape and there's police and dogs looking about, but you can tell they ain't expecting to find nothing.

It feels safe in the park. I wanna stay here, but then I'm getting the fear that someone's gonna find my body hiding next to Jimmy's in Butterfield. If some kids find them, then they're gonna think we're batty boys and they're gonna start kicking.

When I get to the fence at the edge of the park, I get scared that shakfiends are gonna find me, but I can't see any about.

I go through the fence and I head off for Butterfield.

Soon as I leave the park, I'm getting scared again. I'm trying not to think of Jimmy's legs sticking out the mouth of the snake, but now I keep seeing it in my head and I'm feeling sick inside. I'm walking slowly home and I'm trying not to get desperate. 'Cept I'm seeing ghosts everywhere. Every time I pass a ghost I see one of them air-conditioner things and I see a bottle of plastic liquid. So now I'm seeing how big this thing is. Dead people are everywhere. The whole of London is a city of ghosts, and it's in big trouble.

I'm fiddling with something in my hand, and then I look at it, and get a surprise.

A necklace. It's got a massive crystal which is blue and swirly, like it's got the ocean inside it. I can't remember where I go it. But then it hits me.

Mum was wearing it. 'Cept it wasn't Mum. It was the snake. I must have got it in the fight. I'm thinking I should chuck it away. But I don't.

Eventually I'm back at Butterfield, and I'm getting the fear as I go off to find our bodies. I go past the bandstand, past the tramp benches, and then I'm pushing through the thick bush where we left the bodies earlier.

They're just how we left them, lying behind the plastic bags at the wall of the park. So now I'm wondering how I'm supposed to get back inside my body. I lie down on top of it, hoping I'll just slip inside. I try that. But it still feels like I ain't back. I try to move my body's legs and I can't do it.

I'm doing everything we did before. But backwards. I imagine the golden light leaving. I imagine my head closing up. I try saying hazoom backwards: Moozah. Moozah Moozah Moozah. I'm trying to calm down. Trying not to think about the snake.

In a few minutes, I can smell the fag butts in the rubbish bins, and the petrol smell from the garage. And then I can hear the swish swish swish of the blood in my ear. The horsemen coming to get me, swishing their swords in the air.

I'm back. I wriggle my toes. Wriggle my fingers. I'm back in my body.

I get up. Ain't much room to stretch behind that bush, but I try. Then I look at Jimmy's body, and I feel sick inside.

42

His face is grey. His cheeks are sunk. He looks dead. Who knows what the snake is doing to his lamia? What can I do? Only one thing I can do: it's well dangerous, but it might be the only way of getting his ghost back in a hurry.

I gotta wake him up.

So I shake him.

Nothing.

I slap him.

Nothing.

I'm screaming: '*Jimmy!*'

His eyes open slow, and you can see there's a tiny bit of life left, but not much. He looks at me. He smiles.

'You shouldnae done that. I was just getting somewhere. I saw—'

'What?'

'Such things! . . . I gottae go back.'

'Jimmy! Jimmy! You can't leave me. I need you to help me.'

'You're too late, pal. I'm dying. But I tell you, Colin. I'm glad I came, 'cos I know something now.'

'What?'

'You've got a gift. And you're gonnae be OK.'

He shuts his eyes again.

He says something, but I don't catch it.

I crawl over, and I push my ear right next to his lips. Get a tiny trace of his breath. That hippy smell of rollies and wet jumper.

'Don't die,' I say again. And I hold open his eyelid with my thumb.

He looks at me again.

'I love you, Colin. Always will. Remember . . . You must give love, but not expect it. Generosity is its own reward. Specially if you're giving out pubic lice.' He smiles at that. Only a tiny smile. 'Please, one last time, "Ho-hum, what's all this then? Woof!"'

'Ho-hum, what's all this then, woof!'

He smiles again, and then shuts his eyes. And something happens. He shakes. It's like a leaf in the wind. And then I know he's gone.

And I'm feeling more alone than I ever done before.

And terrified about what's gonna happen now.

43

I walk back slowly to my flat. It's hit me but it ain't hit me too. Jimmy has gone. And Polly could be gone. And I need to rescue her but I ain't got Jimmy. And if I try to get to her, I gotta get past a snake.

And there's no one I can tell about all this.

I creep up the stairs to our flat, quiet as a ghost.

I push open the door slowly. Right away I get that smell of our home. Sausages and cherry lip balm. I hear something . . .

A voice. I listen. It's OB. I creep to the living-room door and push it open a crack. He's on the phone.

'I don't want to take Alison's job,' he's saying in his most friendly Aussie voice, 'I wouldn't dream of it. But perhaps there'll be an opening when she goes on holiday. Just for a trial period . . . OK . . . Anyway, you got the eight by tens, the pictures . . . yeah . . . I took 'em when I was back home last time . . . that's right . . .

I got some where I'm wearing even less – I did a sun-cream campaign . . .'

OB, you are so busted.

I swing open the door as noisily as I can. He turns. He looks at me. I look at him.

'OK . . .' he says. 'Listen, I better hustle along now. I got a meeting to get to. Call me if anything comes up. You've got my mobie number. Catch you later.'

He puts the phone down. He puts on his cheeriest I'm-a-kids-TV-presenter face. Makes him look like a killer.

'Colin, my old mucker! How's it going?'

'What was the phone call?' I say.

'Oh . . . A friend of mine runs a building site. I was just trying to get a little bit of casual labour. Could be fun – carrying bricks in the sunshine.'

'I don't think you should be sending him half naked pictures of yourself then. If you behave like that on a building site, they're gonna think you're such a gaylord they'll push you off the roof.'

He knows I've busted him. You can see it in his eyes. He's weighing it up in his head. How likely am I to tell my mum? What could he do to keep me on his side? How much does he want to keep Mum? I actually wanna see how he's gonna find a way out of this one. He don't.

'That's a good point,' he says. 'Anyway, tell Alison I dropped by. Catch you later.'

'Before you go,' I say, 'give me your key. I need another one 'cos my friend's coming.'

He thinks about it a second. Then he hands the key over.

'Give it back to me next time I'm round,' he says.

But both of us know he ain't never coming back.

So I'm standing in the middle of my home.

I keep thinking I might never see Polly again, and I'm definitely not gonna see Jimmy again. I open the fridge. There's a pot of old pesto, some of Mum's manky margarine, and three carrots that've gone bendy. Then I notice I got something in my pocket.

Polly's letter. I open it up.

Right away, I get her Irish voice in my head . . .

Dear Colin,

I've just come home because I'm depressed because I know you had a fight with Eric and you blame it on me. You think I shouldn't have asked you about being psychic. I just think you make everything worse because you won't explain what's going on in your head. You can be so funny, Colin. I hoped you'd just make them laugh a wee bit, and then everything would be fine. I'm sorry, Colin. I made a mistake. You keep shouting at me at the moment. I know it's hard because of your dad and everything, but it's also not fair. I hate it when you take it out on me when you feel bad. And I'm sorry I've been a bit intense with you recently. You know I've always wanted to go out with you, don't you? I've wanted it for a long time. But I know you don't, and of course I understand. I just wanted you to know that I know and it's fine. You'll always be my best friend, and I'll always love you to bits because I think you're an amazing person, Colin. So clever and so funny. (And so handsome.) Don't let anyone get you down, Colin. You're bigger than that. You have to fight back. But also don't fight back, when there's no fighting to be done.

I love you,

Your best friend,

Polly.'

I read it over several times.

Did I know she liked me? Why do I only figure everything out when it's too late?

The phone rings. I let it.

First of all I think it's Mum, saying when she'll be back.

But then I think: Now, relax, who is it actually gonna be?

It hits me right away. It's Polly's mum. She's calling to say Polly's home but still in a coma, do I want to come over? Sharleen's thinking that familiar voices could be a good thing.

The phone stops ringing.

Polly's mum has gone.

Just then I think if Polly's gonna be in bed for ever I'm gonna have to run away. I'll start in South America and find the bar where Jimmy worked. I could clean dishes there for a while and then I'll figure out my next move. I gotta get away 'cos this place is swag. I'm gonna fly me away.

The buzzer rings.

I think it's probably OB come back now he's thought up an excuse. I can't deal with that guy. I lean out the window. I'm gonna tell him to go and spin on a fence post.

But it ain't him.

There's two different people out there.

One of them is the old bag lady who wears the Chelsea strip. I see her everywhere, so she don't surprise me. But I definitely wasn't expecting to see the other person.

44

It's Polly. With a bike.

I go over to the door and buzz her in.

Her voice comes over the intercom:

'You coming, Bitchin?'

She never calls me Bitchin.

'Where?' I go.

'Sharon Holdings' birthday party. Meet Islington at six p.m. You forgotten?'

'No, I ain't forgotten.' I look at my watch. It's 5:42. 'I'll come down.'

I open the door. Polly's on the pavement, not looking at me. Looking like I never seen her before. Loads of make-up. And wearing clothes I ain't never seen.

'Where do you get the bike from, Poll?'

'Took it from my neighbour.'

'Oh.'

'Let's go.'

She sets off right away.

'Wait a second. I can't keep up with you.'

She stops and turns. She looks like she's pissed off with me, but she's too bored to say it.

'Why ain't you got a bike?'

She don't sound Irish suddenly. Her accent is like everyone else's, which is a kind of mixture of Cockney and Jamaican and Pakistani. It's easy to do. You just gotta sound like you got a cold, and you hate everyone.

'Where'm I supposed to keep a bike?' I say.

'Dunno, do I?'

And she sets off.

'What the hell are you doing?' I say out loud. 'And what the hell's going on?'

The bag lady turns.

Her eyes have gone milky grey.

'*I've sent her round,*' she says, sounding like Samuel L. Jackson.

'But what do you mean? Has she got her lamia back?'

'*No way, José. I'm holding on to that. You got her body though. And she'll be continuing on autopilot.*'

'What the hell does that mean?'

'*You'll find out. By the way, shame about your uncle. Still, that dude had a serious hygiene problem.*'

I leg it up the street.

Hundred metres on, Poll has stopped. I catch up, panting.

She's talking with Eric. He's showing her his bike.

He's put a flag on the back. He grins at her and he presses his Tarzan horn. She presses it as well. Eric sees me.

'You coming as well, Bitchin?'

'Yeah.'

'Did Shar invite you?'

'Sort of. Can you lend me a bike?'

'I can lend you my old bike.'

So now I'm cycling, trying to keep up. Eric is on his flash bike with the flag. Polly's on this gleaming mountain bike, I don't know who she's nicked it off. I got an old kids' bike that Eric musta stopped using when he was eight. It's the right size for me. But it's so rusted I reckon he ain't oiled it in five years. Also it says 'Action Bike' on the crossbar. I am so lacking in cred I might as well have stabilizers. What is Sharon gonna say when I show up? She didn't even invite me.

But I gotta keep an eye on Polly. The Voice said she's on autopilot. He shoulda said she's on Mogadon.

45

I'm squeak squeak squeaking up Essex Road, trying to keep up with them. A truck goes by. One of them ones that garages use for picking up cars. It's got a little crane on the back. It beeps at me – der dede der der *der derrrr:* the call of the cretin. I can't believe my eyes. Inside it's Kriss and Sal. Sal is driving. You ain't never seen someone look so proud. Ever seen a toddler get out of his own push chair and push it down the pavement? That's the look Sal's got on his face. He almost looks sweet.

I have to stop at the traffic lights at North End Road, just next to these two tourists. I can tell they're American even before they talk. They're carrying guide books. They're wearing them fanny packs that Yanks have round their waists 'cos they think everyone is a pickpocket. And they both weigh about twenty stone. They're sweating.

One of them says: 'Gee, I'm getting hot. I need to get

a lighter shirt.' He turns and sees me. 'Excuse me, sir. Where can we buy a shirt?' he asks.

'Mmmm . . . there, maybe.'

About ten metres away, there's one of them market stalls selling Chelsea tops, Man United tops, New York Yankie caps, and LA Raiders sweatshirts.

'Isn't that fantastic?' says one of them. 'Let's get ourselves Raiders strips!'

As I cycle off, they're trying to squeeze into their new clothes. They've travelled from America to England and now they're buying Raiders tops.

They say travel broadens the mind. It don't. Mainly it just broadens the arse.

By the time I catch Eric and Poll, they're all hanging outside the Nag's Head on the Essex Road. Sharon and Trish are already there. Sal's leaning on the back of his truck. Poll's sitting on the back next to Kriss. Kriss is eating a lolly, giving his I-don't-give-a-damn-about-no-one face. Poll's doing it too. He's wearing a New York Yankies cap, a bright purple T-shirt, and a powder blue tracksuit. I just don't get it. How come he always wears such clean clothes? His mum must spend all night washing. Eric is right in front of Sharon, showing her his Tarzan horn. 'Cos she's so tall she can see over his head. She's looking about. Maybe she's invited older people and she's checking out to see if they're gonna arrive and working out if she wants to be seen with us. Maybe

we're the B-Team. The ones you invite just in case the
A-Team don't show. 'Cept I wasn't even invited, so I'm
C-Team.

She sees me coming on my tiny Action Bike, and she
don't look as displeased as you'd expect.

'All right, Bitchin,' she says as I arrive. 'Didn't know
you was coming, innit?'

'Thought I'd swing by,' I say, casual-as-I-can, 'just to
wish you happy birthday.'

'Thanks!' she says sweetly. No one else has said hello
to me yet. It's a bad moment when you join a group. It's
the moment you find out if you're in or if you're out.

'Wassup, everyone?' I ask.

'All right, Bitchin,' says Eric, with a bit of a grin.
'Was the bike OK?'

'Yeah.' I leave it at that. Don't wanna draw too
much attention.

'Hey, Kriss,' I go.

'Ri, Bitchin,' he says, but he don't turn and look. He
keeps his eyes on the horizon like he's expecting a
stampede of bison coming up the Essex Road. I'm
watching him extra careful 'cos I'm trying to find out if
he fancies my girl. Polly herself ain't even turned. She's
eating a Flake. Just stuffing it in her mouth without
tasting. Flakes of chocolate are dropping on her chest.

She's got on a shiny white top which is showing off
her breasts like you would not believe. Her breasts might

as well have some of them searchlights scanning the sky like they have outside swag nightclubs. She's also got her hair in bunches which I ain't never seen before. Also eye shadow. Also lip gloss. I don't get lip gloss. It's like your lips are covered in jam. Also she's wearing some tight hipsters, it looks like she's borrowed them off Trish Appleton. Poll's shiny white top has got no shoulders and this is the bit that gives me the horn. I love Poll's arms.

Right now they're naked arms and touching Kriss's. This makes me bleed inside.

Suddenly Poll says: 'Stop checking me out, Tweek the Freak. Before you treat me like a shop window, let's see your cash.'

She says it without even looking. No expression in her voice. She's got the act right down.

Poll ain't never called me Tweek the Freak.

I can feel myself go red and I don't want no one to see. I pretend I'm sweaty, so I wipe my face with my T-shirt. I realize I'm wearing the same army camouflage top I been wearing for the last two days. I didn't even sleep last night. I smell bad. How'm I supposed to compete with Kriss?

'Right,' says Kriss. 'Shar, here's the dough. I think you better buy the drinks 'cos you look the oldest.'

He hands her a crisp twenty-quid note. How the hell has he got that? Everyone gets off the truck and goes inside. As Kriss goes in, Poll takes hold of his arm. Eric is the last to enter. Then me. I'm just stepping in the door, when Eric whispers:

'Bitchin, you better not come in, 'cos you look too young. Could get us all thrown out.'

I shoulda said, right away: 'Eric, you better not come in, 'cos you look too thick.' But I don't think of it right away. Besides, I'm so surprised that I've stopped. And now I don't know whether to come in or go out, but I don't wanna let Eric think he can give me orders.

I step into the pub and right away I think I could throw up.

46

They're having a Kimberley celebration in there. They got pictures of her. They got a cardboard cut-out of her. They got posters on the wall saying: 'Join Kimberley for her FIRST EVER SELL-OUT gig in THE BIG APPLE.'

I pretend to look at the pictures and it means I don't have to go over to the others and have Eric tell me I better drink lemonade. There's a telly on the wall and it shows Kimberley being interviewed. She's saying:

'. . . at the end of the day, I'm just a working-class girl from a single-parent family in North-East London. But I've got *righteous*. I've *learned*. And I say this to all the other girls out there: you don't want to be looking in a magazine and seeing stuff that you don't have, 'cos you'll feel bad. Go out there and *get* what you want. *Be* what you want. And don't get down. Get active. Get on a plane and see the world. Don't let anyone tell you you can't. Don't let anyone take from you the pleasures what're rightfully yours. It's about saying: I was here first, bruv, this is mine by right. It's about saying, you fight me, I'm gonna fight back more, 'cos you started it. It's about empowerment. It's about achieving your dreams. It's about faith . . .'

And then she fades into soft focus like she's an angel disappearing into a cloud. And then a drum beat starts. And the brainworm kicks in for the hundred millionth time . . .

'*I'm an individual*
I'm an individual
I got individual needs . . .'

I don't know why they bother with putting the song on phones and tellies. Why don't they just put it on a chip and insert it direct into our heads?

I can't take it no more. I step outside.

And I walk right into a camera crew standing in front of a limousine. There're four of them. One holding a light, one holding a camera, one bloke in geek glasses, and this leng girl. She's got a suntan and long brown bouncy hair that looks like it's come out of an advert. She's holding a microphone but she's still shouting:

'So here's our first ORDINARY PUNTER who's just come out of the LEGENDARY Nag's Head pub which was where Kimmy did her FIRST GIG.' She says all that looking into the camera, smiling like she's got something hidden in her pants. Now she turns, and she leans in right next to me so her gleaming white teeth are in my face.

'We've JUST HEARD,' she says. 'It's been OFFICIALLY announced that Kimberley HAS gone in at NUMBER ONE in the singles charts both in BRITAIN *AND* in the US of A.'

Now she stuffs the microphone in my mouth. It's one of them big ones with a big fluffy sock over it.

I'm thinking: Why did you have to SHOUT the ODD WORD as if SOME of the WORDS you say are IMPORTANT. Surely every word you say is IMPORTANT. If it ain't, why don't you SHUT UP?

I'm thinking: Why are you GRINNING at me?

I'm thinking: You ain't asked me a QUESTION. What am I supposed to SAY?

Now she asks a question: 'Just WHAT do you MAKE of the NEWS?'

So I go: 'It shows that ALL of the people can be ALL wrong ALL of the time. That song is so bad it could be played in a fairground. It ain't even a song, it's just a tune that tunnels into your head like a worm. Should just be called a BRAINWORM.'

She looks at the camera and laughs, like I'm the funniest thing in the world since that fat cat in *You've Been Framed* who fell backwards into the paddling pool. I don't think it's that funny. I'm only saying what I always think. I'm just saying it aloud 'cos I'm so mad 'cos I can tell Kriss is trying to get off with Polly. Ain't he supposed to be gay?

The girl is staring at me.

'Do I take it you're NOT a Kimberley fan?' she says.

So I say: 'She's a singer, but she can't sing. She's got a TV show but she ain't got nothing to say. She's in movies, but she can't act. How? I think she must be a witch who's playing with our minds. Someone must be. Why else is everyone listening to it? And why would anyone fly to America to hear it more? Why's *everyone* acting like window-lickers? Tell me. I'm serious. *What* is going on?'

I stop and I just look at the sket with the nice hair. She's laughing. The blokes with the cameras are laughing. The bloke with the geek glasses is laughing.

Then shouting girl says something that surprises me: 'BOY! Have we got a SURPRISE for you,' she says. (I'm thinking no one has said 'boy!' since 1958.) 'I'd like to INTRODUCE you to someone . . . it's KIMBERLEY GALLOWAY!!!!!!'

The limousine door opens.

And she comes out.

Kimberley. Followed by two enormous security guards.

I'm thinking: This is embarrassing.

Kimberley comes towards me.

I gotta say it . . . she's looking chung. Her hair is all tousled like she just got out of bed, but you know that it's been styled. She's got on a cotton top with embroidered flowers on it. And she's wearing hipsters but she's the right shape for them. You can see a little bit of hipbone and her hips are nice and brown. And she don't look as arrogant as you'd think, she looks quite nice and for a moment I feel sorry I been dissing her.

'*Hi*,' she says. And then she kisses me on the cheeks. 'Bet you didn't expect this!'

'Not really,' I go. 'Tell me . . . are you a witch?'

She laughs. 'I'm just a girl from a council estate, who had a dream.'

'You're lucky,' I say, ' 'cos when I dream I don't dream I'm famous. I dream I'm in a prison thinking about everything bad I ever done.'

She laughs again. 'You're a funny guy. You're an individual. I don't even care that you're boying me, 'cos at least you're keeping it real, so respect to you.'

'Thanks,' I go. I don't know what else to say.

'I have one space for one special person to come to New York with me to see my gig. Do you want to take a little holiday?'

At this point, Kimberley smiles. It's a real smile. She looks me in the eye like she cares about me, like we're friends. And I ain't meaning to tell her the truth. I ain't a fool. I always try not to do that.

But now I can't help it:

'Holidays are for people who are too uptight to have

fun the rest of the time. 'Sides, my friend ain't well and that's all I can think about right now. All I wanna do this weekend is go to Hackney Marsh with her.'

Then a weird thing happens.

'Good for you,' says Kimberley, 'I like you.'

Then she reaches forward and she kisses me.

When she's leaning in, I turn and I whisper in her ear.

'In there, you'll see this black guy, in a New York Yankies cap. Invite him. 'Cos he's like the best-looking guy in London, and you should get him to dance in a video.'

'Why?'

'It'll give you cred. And he needs to be round other dancers.'

I don't know why I said that. It just came out.

Right away the bloke with the geek glasses comes up to me. He puts his hand on my shoulder, and looks me right in the eye.

'You are *fabulous*,' he says. He sounds like Dale Winton. 'I need you to sign a release form.'

'What's that?' I go.

'We can't use the footage unless you agree.'

'Well pay me then,' I go.

'How much?'

'Two hundred and fifty quid,' I say.

'You drive a *hard* bargain, cheeky,' he says, giving me

a look. But then he takes a wallet out of his pocket, and he hands over the money right away. Five fifty-quid notes. I ain't even seen one before. They're red.

I put the money in my pocket.

I turn and I see Sharon Holdings looking at me. She's carrying a tray of drinks.

'That was unreal,' she says.

'Why?'

' 'Cos that was her, yeah? I wanted to talk to her as well, but she walked right by me like she didn't notice me.'

'Shar,' I say, 'you're way better looking than her. She noticed you, but she didn't wanna be on camera standing next to you. Woulda made her look bad.'

'Thanks, Col,' she says. 'I got you a half of lager. Is that OK?'

I could kiss her I'm so grateful.

Everyone else comes out.

'I can't believe it,' says Kriss. 'She gave me a card and said: "You should dance for me. Here's the number of my production company".'

'Did you see that?' says Eric, who's holding a pint of lager and a packet of crisps. 'She walked right by me. I flicked a crisp at her hair.'

'You shouldna done that,' says Kriss. 'I think those security guys saw you. What are you guys doing out here?'

I look at Sharon. 'Nothing,' I say. She smiles.

'We better not hang around,' says Kriss. 'I don't want her to change her mind.'

47

So we end up back at Sharon Holdings' house. Her mum is there so we don't drink more alcohol. Sharon Holdings' mum looks almost the same as Sharon 'cept with more hair dye and with lines round her eyes. They live in one of them new estates near Hackney Downs. Everything is brand new. White fitted carpets. New dining-room table made out of glass. Massive plasma widescreen TV. Kriss switches it on.

The words 'News Flash' come in. We all see a posh bloke standing with a microphone outside the Cop Shop on Stoke Newington High Street.

Eric pipes up: 'That's round the corner from my house!'

The posh blokes says:

'A man has been arrested on suspicion of the Clissold Park bombing. His name is Yussuf Mohammed Ali Khan and it appears the blast was intended as a protest against the decadence of Western culture.'

'Why would it be Yussuf?' I'm going. 'If Yussuf wanted to protest against Western culture, which he don't, then why don't he blow up *Heat* magazine? Or Harrods?'

'Don't say that, Tadpole,' says Trish. 'Ain't very nice.'

On TV, they got this really grainy picture of Yussuf which makes him look like he wants to eat children. They cut to him talking. I know exactly what we're watching. It's the stuff Mr Holdings recorded on his phone. Yussuf is going:

'I can broadcast a message for your infidel friends. Repent, and worship Allah. Or you will burn in the fires of destruction.'

'Oh my God,' says Sharon. 'I swear that's the stuff that was on Dad's phone.'

'He must've sold it,' I go. Giving her a dirty look.

'No!' says Trish. 'How much can you get for that?'

'What they don't say,' I go, 'is that your dad had just called him a "Paki twat".'

Sharon gives me a look back. I bet she knows her dad is racist and I bet it embarrasses her. Kids in Stoke Newington may be thick, may be violent, but they ain't never racist. Hackney is three-quarters immigrant so if you're racist then you're gonna end up in a very small gang. Racism is for farmers and Welsh people. Thing is, though . . . Sharon don't want me slagging off her dad, but she don't wanna get dragged into any conversation about whether her dad is racist 'cos we got Kriss, who's half-Jamaican, half-Nigerian, and we got Sal, who's Turkish. Plus Polly who's Irish. Sharon keeps quiet. So do I.

We all watch. The TV is saying how Yussuf is living off benefits. And then there's pictures of his flat, and I swear the whole place has been gutted, 'cos Yussuf's stuff is everywhere. The TV goes right on saying:

'A selection of threatening notices were discovered in the suspect's Stoke Newington home, and also a vast amount of aftershave which could have been used as bomb-making equipment.'

I can't help it. I lose it again.

'Yeah, he had tons of scent, 'cos when he was Lee he was always trying to get off with girls. This ain't right.'

Sharon wants to get away from the telly.

'Let's go outside,' she says.

So we go out and we walk to this car park round the corner from Sharon's house that's mainly filled with old fridges and bust-up cars. On the way round I see the same old bag lady that was outside my house. Again. It's like she's following me around. She's sitting on the pavement staring into space. She's wearing her Chelsea top and her grey hair is sticking up round the side of a baseball cap that says 'I've Been On The London Eye'. I think everyone's gonna stop and take the piss out of her, but luckily they keep moving. She smells of old meat and dirty bandages.

We get into a car that's got a smashed windscreen so there's a breeze coming through. I get into the back seat with Sharon. Kriss and Poll are in the front seat. I think he's putting his hand on her leg but I can't look without making it too obvious. He turns and looks at me. Gives me a long look. Why does he keep checking me?

'So,' says Kriss to Sharon, getting out a packet that's nicely wrapped, 'I got this for you.'

He hands over the packet.

'Thanks, Kriss,' says Sharon, and she opens it up. Inside is a blouse that's made out of turquoise cotton. It's got red flowers embroidered on it. Looks like the one that Kimberley was wearing earlier. I hate watching people open presents 'cos they gotta act like they love it, whatever it is. Even if they *do* like it, then they still gotta put on the right show. You can tell Sharon really does like it though. She knows she's gonna look good wearing this. She's gonna be hot like lava.

'My cousin makes clothes, yeah,' says Kriss. 'That's who I got it off.'

He's trying to say: I like you, but don't worry, I don't like you *that* much, I did get this for free. There's a fine line between being romantic and being a stalker.

'Got one for you as well, Poll,' and he gets out another.

Poll has been like a robot all evening, but this is the first time she smiles. She rips her present open right away. Hers is the same, 'cept it's green and the flowers are brown, which is a good choice 'cos of Poll's eyes.

'Thanks, Kriss,' says Poll. And she reaches forward and she kisses him right on the lips. Now I can't stop myself watching. She carries on kissing him. I don't think they've done tongues yet, they're just staying with full lip contact, oh my God this ain't right. I need to tell Kriss that Poll don't know what she's doing. I need to tell him all about the lamias.

Then he turns his head to the side. Oh my God. Don't be turning your head.

She turns her head. Poll, don't do that. Poll, you slag, don't do that.

And I see him open his mouth and I see his tongue come out. No no no no no no no no no no no no no no no no. They are definitely tonguing. Definitely.

Poll's leaning in towards him over the broken gear stick.

He reaches his hand right out and he puts it on her left breast. I wanna reach over and smack him on the side of his face right now. He's grabbing her like he's got to do everything as quick as he can. Like he's got something to prove. Now I'm figuring out what's going on, but it don't make it feel no better.

'You OK, Colin?' says Sharon. She holds my hand.

'Yeah, I'm good.'

'By the way,' says Sharon, and she takes my hand. I know I gotta stop looking at Poll. This is embarrassing.

I look right at Sharon Holdings. I check her out for the first time. She's wearing a white vest. Her hair is tied back in a ponytail, but she's got a few wispy bits that are winding down in front of her ears. She's got very small ears. 'By the way,' she says again, 'I'm sorry about what happened last week.'

'What?'

'You know ... when Trish hung you on the toilet door.'

'It weren't just Trish, Shar. It was you as well.'

'I know. Sorry. But it was Trish's idea. You know why she done it?'

'No.'

' 'Cos she's scared of you 'cos you're so brainy and she thought you were ripping the piss, talking about snakes. It was just a joke.'

I'm thinking: If you think of any other jokes like that, please keep 'em to yourself.

'You get me?' says Sharon.

'Yeah,' I say. I don't get her at all.

'Anyway,' she says, 'sorry, Bitchin.'

'Don't call me Bitchin,' I say.

'Why?'

'Ain't respectful.'

'It *is*,' she goes. 'Bitchin means good. Like if you've had a good evening, someone might say "Did you have a good evening?" "Yeah," you go, "it was *bitchin*." It's just saying you're bitchin. 'Cos you are. You're Colin Bitchin, and you're bitchin. Bitchin, and cute.'

And now she leans forward and Sharon Holdings pushes her lips against mine. I'm panicking. Don't get me wrong. I know that Sharon Holdings is officially the hottest girl in my whole school, and I can feel my cred going through the roof at this moment. But I'm still panicking.

Sharon Holdings pulls back.

'Wass the matter, Bitchin?' she says.

'I . . . I . . .'

'Don't you like kissing?'

'Not really.' I didn't mean to say that. But right now I'm so tired I can't keep control of what I'm saying. It's like pissing in the bath. It just comes out.

'Why don't you like kissing?'

' 'Cos . . . I dunno . . . I just got this stupid idea that . . .'

'What?'

I whisper. 'I can't kiss someone. 'Cos if I kiss 'em, I'm gonna kill 'em.'

'You're unreal, Bitchin,' she says, and she laughs. Sharon Holding's teeth are a bit crooked. It's the only thing that ain't perfect in her perfect face, which makes her look even more perfect. 'Let's try it out.'

And she presses her lips against mine. I keep my eyes open and I can see that hers are closed. So now I have a quick look to the side and I can get a good look at what's happening in the front. Polly is getting out of her seat. She's going over to Kriss's seat, and she's sitting on his lap. This ain't good.

But then Sharon Holdings opens her eyes, so I stop looking quick.

She pulls her head back just a few centimetres, and she rubs her nose against mine. You wouldn't think that would be nice, but it is. Sharon Holdings don't smell like Poll. I can smell some bubblegum she musta been chewing earlier. Her eyes are kind of grey blue.

Suddenly she puts her hands round the back of my head. She turns her nose sideways, and she thrusts her tongue in my mouth. I'm scared. I think I ain't gonna be able to breathe.

I'm thinking: Is this it? Is this what it's supposed to be like when you first lips?

But then I start getting turned on.

Sharon's tongue is like Sharon. It's long and quick like a fish. She flicks it fast over my tongue. She's snogging me. I ain't never done that to no one before, and this is it, my first time. It's Sharon Holdings.

Then she pulls back and smiles.

'See,' she says, 'I ain't dead.'

And it's at that moment the car is smacked from behind. BANG.

48

I turn round and I see Sal and Trish and Eric sitting in the front of their truck. They're laughing their heads off.

Right away me and Sharon jump out of the back doors of the car.

'What the hell were you doing?' I say.

'Your face!' says Eric. 'Shoulda seen your face. That was *hilarious*!'

'Were you getting off with Bitchin?' Trish is asking Sharon.

'Mighta been,' says Shar. 'He's a wicked kisser.'

Only now do I notice Kriss. He's looking well shaky.

'Something's wrong with Poll,' he says.

I run round to the front of the car.

Poll is now sitting in the front seat where Kriss was. He musta turned her round. She looks dead.

'Poll,' I say, 'POLL!' I slap her face.

She don't move. I try her pulse. Nothing.

'What the hell did you do that for?' Kriss is shouting at Sal and Eric. 'She musta whacked her head!'

'We hardly touched you,' says Sal. 'It was only a gentle push.'

'Right, Sal!' I say. 'Don't never try to be gentle. It ain't your special skill!'

'I hardly touched you!' he says again. 'I didn't do nothing.'

And I'm feeling round the back of Polly's head. I can't feel no bruise. No cut. Nothing.

I run across the car park to the bag lady.

'What the hell has happened to her?' I shout.

She turns to me and her eyes go grey-white.

'*You can't survive long without your lamia, child. I been saying for a while I need you to come and find me. If you don't come right away, I'm gonna do something to her. I'm gonna do something to all the bad kids that I been collecting.*'

'I'm coming right away,' I say, and I start walking off.

'*It's gonna be like going through a deep dark tunnel, coming to me. You're gonna be scared.*'

I go back to my friends at the edge of the car park. They're all staring at me.

'I know what's wrong with Polly,' I say. 'I'm gonna sort it out.'

'You're weird,' says Eric. 'You ain't like no one else round here.'

'Thank you,' I say. And I go.

49

I get on Eric's tiny bike and I speed back home. All the way back I'm running it by in my head. I gotta get to Polly. But I can't get to Polly 'cos she's with the Master and he's protected by a snake. So I gotta get something that's gonna kill that snake. Or if I can't kill it, I gotta get something that's gonna knock it out. Make it fall down and sleep. But what?

Then it hits me . . .

The liquid they're collecting off the ghosts. If smelling it is enough to make you wanna lie down and die, what's it gonna be like if you *drink* a whole bottle? Maybe if I can get a bottle of the strongest, most deadening stuff, then I stand a chance. But where am I gonna get some?

And I realize where.

I realize this whole journey has been leading up to this.

I gotta do it.

I'm gonna do it.

I gotta find my dad's ghost.

But is he actually there?

I'm gonna find out, but first I need a private place. I need to project. I'm about to go home, but then I think Mum might be there so I gotta try elsewhere. Where? Butterfield. That worked before. That's where I'm gonna go now.

So I go round to Butterfield, and head to the hiding place.

I get behind the plastic bags, and close them in after me. I close them in tight. The smell is rank. And I'm close to a vent from the garage and that's driving out petrol smells. Something about this don't feel right. Something tells me this could be dangerous. But I know I gotta do it. Like Jimmy said: Life is hard, but what's the alternative?

And so I'm lying there, and I'm breathing. Am I gonna be able to do this without Jimmy's help?

I gotta try.

I'm going innnnnn, ouuuuuuut. Breathing gold air in and cave air out. And I'm saying hazoom. And I'm saying: Help me, God, I need to leave my body, and enter my lamia. If it's the last time I do it, please grant me this wish.

And before I know it, I've drifted out.

50

I drift up straight away over Butterfield. I look down *and see the trees underneath me. A seagull is hovering in the air nearby. A few fluffy clouds in the sky, not moving. For a second I'm enjoying the flying. I see Vern cycling off to Coffee Corner. Then I fly over to Walford Road and I fly to our house. I fly up to the third floor. Our flat. Keep right on going. Upstairs to the attic, and I slip through the window at the front of the house.*

And I was right.

Down at the other end of the attic, Dad is sitting there at his desk.

Still working away at his book, like he ain't died, like I ain't burned it, like nothing's happened. He's sitting in front of an old dusty mirror. Surrounded by books and pages and hundreds and hundreds of newspapers.

'Cept Dad don't look the same. He's a ghost now. Black and white.

He keeps working. Just like he always did.
I keep watching.

Nearby, I see what I've come for. There's one of them air-conditioner things that's whirring away, and filling with liquid. I take the bottle out. It's full to the brim. Good, I'm gonna need all of that. I take a sniff of it. It's rank. It smells like my dad, if my dad had gone mouldy. It suddenly hits me: I come all this way to try and help Polly, but maybe Polly don't want me. Why would she? I'm still a tiny freak child. And I saw her with Kriss – I can't trust her. I couldn't trust Jimmy. Turned out he only wanted to get close to my mum. I definitely can't trust my mum. I can't trust nobody. And if I ain't careful, I'm gonna spend the whole of school getting battered by Sal and Kriss and Eric. And then I'm gonna grow up like my dad. A sad man sitting in an attic. I'm getting well depressed.

This stuff is definitely the stuff I need. I should get out of here.

But I should also talk to my dad.

I turn and watch him writing his book. He's scribbling something on a piece of paper which is covered in mad Biro marks and coffee stains.

Then suddenly he puts down his pen.

He reaches in his drawer for his gun.

And he puts it in his mouth.

And he blows his head off.

Then he carries on working.

Right away, there's something I wanna know. If there's a shakfiend who's keeping Dad's ghost from going, then who is the shakfiend pretending to be? I work it out right away . . . It'll be my grandad. My dad's dad. Dad was so scared of him, and thinking that makes me feel sorry for my dad. So then I'm just looking at him some more. Looking at his skinny body, and the hair on the back of his neck that he ain't shaved. Then I smile 'cos I know he's a ghost but I'm still about to see my dad's face again.

I put the bottle down, and I walk slowly towards him, picking my way past all his piles of boxes. When I get to his side, first I just look at the gun. I pick it up and hold it. The gun that killed my dad. Its lamia anyway. Then I just look at Dad. I look at the lines on his face. I look at the little tuft of hair at the front of his ear. I look at the hair growing in his nose.

'Dad?' I say. 'Dad?'

He looks up and he sees me. I grin at him.

'It's me, Col. I figured out a way to come and see you again.'

He nods.

' 'Cos I been missing you, Dad. And I thought you might need to see me, and you might wanna hear what me and Mum are doing. And we wanna know what you're doing, and how you been.'

If Dad's surprised to see me, he don't show it. He acts like he saw me yesterday, but he's a ghost – maybe that's how it feels to him.

'I must work,' says Dad. 'There's a lot to get through.'

That's definitely what Dad'd normally say. But I ain't letting him get away with it. I give it to him.

*'Dad, there **is** a lot to get through. But you ain't never gonna finish it. 'Cos you're a ghost.'*

'I know that. But I've still got my papers, and my coffee, and the newspapers. It's hard, but when something's hard, you've got to just keep going. Something you should learn, Colin . . .'

I'm getting that I'm-with-Dad feeling. Any second now he's gonna start drowning me in advice.

'You're wrong, Dad,' I say. 'When things are hard, you ain't gotta keep going. You gotta do something different. You're a ghost, Dad, you can go.'

He ain't listening.

'This is important,' he says. 'This is vital. Do you know the justice system has released over a hundred dangerous criminals who should've been deported back to their own countries?'

*'Dad, I don't wanna hear about this. All I wanna know is how I can get Mum to cheer up, start telling the truth and actually **listen** to me, and how I*

can start having some fun, and how I can get Polly back.'

'Never mind that. Terrible things are happening in the world. You should be scared. I'm doing this for your sake, you know? So you're prepared for what's out there. And so you can feel proud of what your daddy's achieved.'

'I don't care, Dad. This stuff is cold.'

'Shut up! If you can't appreciate—'

He's about to lay into me now like he used to. But I'm older now. I come right back at him.

'**You** shut up. Maybe I ain't never gonna see you again. So this is your one chance. Shut up and listen. Dad, I'm angry. I ain't had a dad for three years. All my friends've got dads, even Polly – her dad ain't there, but at least he's **alive**. So for three years I've been thinking if I could only see my dad it'd be OK. I'm mad 'cos you left me with Mum going mental. I'm mad 'cos you ain't there. And I'm mad 'cos you might as well have left me long before, 'cos you never listen to me!'

'I know,' says my dad. 'I was a terrible dad anyway . . .'

'Shut up.'

'That's probably why I've stayed upstairs. I know you found me boring—'

'Shut up.'

'You all hate me, I know that.'

'No we don't. You think we want to hate you? We want to like you.'

'And it's so hard, isn't it, liking your own father?'

'Shut up a second! This ain't what I want to say . . . I'm trying to . . . LISTEN . . . Just . . . Tell me why you shoot yourself? Why? Did you do it 'cos of me? 'Cos of Mum? Why?'

'Yes, yes, yes, yes! I know what you're saying. I failed. I'm a failure of a father.'

'No! **No!** SHUT UP!'

'Well, anyway. I'm not coming back. It's too late. There's nothing I can do about it now.'

'No. I know you're not coming back . . .'

God, I wish I ain't said that. 'Cos suddenly my stomach has fallen away and my throat is really hurting, I can't stop it, I know I'm going to cry.

'. . . I know you're not coming back. But I wish you ain't done it. And I wanted to say . . . I wish I ain't always been so mad and . . . 'Cos . . . Dad, I . . . I . . . miss you . . . and . . . I want you back . . .'

And now I can't say nothing else, 'cos I'm really crying. The tears are running down my cheeks, and I'm shaking so much I have to sit down.

'I can't come back,' says Dad. 'And I've got to get on with my work now.'

'Look, Dad. You took on too much, and

*that's why you can't finish. And the whole situation is
so negative, you're getting bogged down. Just stop it
now. 'Cos it's stupid, and I don't wanna read a word
of it 'cos I know it's gonna depress me.'*

*'Well, that's you hiding from the truth! That's you
being weak.'*

*'I ain't weak just 'cos I ain't depressing myself like
you! I am strong. Least I know how to have fun.
Unlike you, you prat! Look at you. Sitting up here.
Not helping no one. Doing nothing but writing and
eating and buying stuff no one needs. You are a selfish,
stupid, waste of space!'*

*And I take out the brass lighter, and I do it all over
again.*

I set fire to his papers.

*'Don't do that,' he shouts, and he tries to put it out.
'Don't!'*

*I skip away from him, and I'm setting fire to all the
books in the attic. They go up quick.*

*'Now go!' I'm shouting. 'Get out of here! Do
something with yourself! Go! Get out! I don't never
wanna see you again!'*

And the flames get bigger and bigger.

*And then I'm thinking: Are these real flames? Are
they lamia flames? Am I really setting fire to my own
flat?*

And then I pick up this old rug from the floor, and

I throw it over Dad's desk. It damps down some of the flames. I do it more. I damp down the burning pages that have fallen on the floor. I put the flames out.

Then I look around.

I can't see no sign of Dad.

He must've gone.

I just stand there for a moment.

Then I approach the desk and pick it up: his gun. I think, Right, this is mine.

And just then a shakfiend comes flying on to the windowsill outside. I don't believe it. He's wearing a baseball cap that I used to wear when I did the army gang with Kriss. And maybe there's reflections and the shakfiend can't see through the window, 'cos as soon as he arrives he starts talking in a weird child's voice:

'Come on, Dad, you gotta get this work done. 'Cos I need it, Dad. If you can't do it, everyone's gonna cuss me raw.'

I don't believe it! That's how they've been keeping my dad's ghost here: they been pretending to be me. Doing the most lame impression as well.

I don't even stop to talk to that shakfiend.

I shoot him in the face.

He drops out of sight.

And then I look in Dad's old dusty mirror.

And I jump.

51

'os there's someone behind me.

It's the lamia of the old bag lady. Sitting there with her mad cap and her grey hair and her legs covered with bandages and pus.

Right away her eyes go milky-blue, and she talks. I can smell her breath, which is all rank like old garlic and ashtray mixed together. And she starts to talk to me, in the Samuel L. Jackson voice.

'**You're starting to annoy me now. You're messing with my good deeds. Besides, I been telling you to come and find me, you been delaying. I don't believe you got what it takes. So now, I'm gonna make it harder for you. I'm gonna make other kids come and find me as well. I'm gonna create a little competition.**'

The bag lady stops talking. Her milky-white eyes go back to normal. Then she smiles and I see her yellow teeth. Right away she drifts up, through the *window, and disappears.*

It takes me a moment till I've stopped shaking. I look round Dad's office, which is filled with Dad's books and ashes of his paper. Then I pick up the bottle of liquid. I scrunch up same paper to use as a cork.

Then I notice a clock. It's saying 11:50 p.m. Ten minutes to midnight. How did it get so late?

I step through the window.

And I jump into the hot black night. And I fly across Stoke Newington towards my school. I'm going over houses and some of them have got lights on, so I'm thinking of all the people who are in them, tossing and turning on their sweaty sheets.

On the way over I stop off at the house of the old crow on Albion Road. I pick up the liquid that makes you feel greedy. And I put that in one pocket of my combat trousers. In the other, I've got the bottle from my dad's attic.

Soon I'm flying down towards the playground.

Right away I see something I never expected to see.

52

'Cos in the playground, there're lamias. Without bodies. I recognize them . . . Kriss, Sal, Eric, Sharon Holdings and Trish Appleton. They're sitting on the ground, about ten metres from the school front door. They turn and look up at me as I come flying down. I look down at them. Also I notice something else. Shakfiends are hanging round the edge of the playground. Not getting involved, just watching. I land amongst my friends.

Sharon's lamia has got dark purple wings. She looks worried.

'All right, Shar,' I say, 'what's going on?'

'Well, I fell asleep, and then one of them things came and got me. What are they?'

'Shakfiends.'

'A shakfiend took me here and I saw Kriss and Trish and everyone else. And then he told us all that we had a chance: we have to walk through *the school and get to the Master – whoever he is – who's waiting inside there. Only one person can go to him, and whoever gets to him is gonna get a lot of power. Whatever we want, he can help us get it.'*

'So why ain't no one gone in and tried to reach him yet?'

Sal looks at me: 'We are about to go.'

'We? I thought he said only one person can go?'

'I'm going in there with Kriss and Eric. We're gonna share the power.'

'But he says he's gonna help one individual. It's everyone out for himself. If all three of you try and get to him, then you're gonna have to knock the other two out.'

'No we ain't,' says Eric.

I ignore him. I carry right on . . .

'Who's it gonna be? Who's gonna cheat on the others first?'

Sal and Kriss and Eric are all kinda smirking. They're doing that look guys do when a teacher's told 'em off – grinning behind their hands like to say: 'You can tell me off, but you're still basically a loser. I'm cool; you teach Maths.' That the way they're grinning. They're trying to show me they don't care. I know I got 'em, though. You can tell I'm saying what's on their minds.

'What's it to you, Bitchin?' says Kriss. 'What you gonna do to stop us?'

'Listen. I think the Master's got Polly's lamia, and I need to go in and get her out.'

'No you ain't.'

'I am.'

'Try it. We're gonna fight you.'

'I don't care.'

'Nang,' Kriss says.

And he walks over to the bottle bank at the edge of the playground. He reaches in and gets some out. He passes one to Sal, and one to Eric. And then he smashes the bottle on the floor, so he's holding jagged glass. Then he smiles at me.

Soon as he does this, I see I've made a big mistake. I don't know what happened. I got carried away. What was I thinking? I gotta fight. But how? How can I fight them all? Specially since I never win fights 'cos I close my eyes and turn into Tweek the Freak. And I've fought these guys before, and they've always wasted me.

53

*K*eeping my eyes on Kriss, I back away. I sit on the floor, and I hazoom. Hazoom, hazoom, hazoom. That surprises them for a start. I'm asking a question in my head: **What do I do?**

Right away, a voice comes into my mind.

It's Jimmy.

'You're doing great,' he says. 'Keep calm. And speak to Kriss.'

And he tells me a plan.

When he's finished, 'Kriss,' I say, 'I wanna tell you one thing. Let me whisper to you.'

'I don't wanna speak to you, Bitchin.'

'You want me to speak to Eric instead? 'Cos I know more about what's gonna happen in there than you. I could help you.'

I walk towards him. He don't know whether to fight me. But I approach him nice and easy. It's very hard to fight someone when they're calm. I pull him towards me, and I whisper in his ear:

'Kriss, I know you're gay, and you were just getting off with Polly to prove something. I ain't telling no one. I don't mind. But if you don't fight Sal, I'll tell him.'

Then I back off.

'What's going on?' says Sal.

I reach for the little plastic bottle that I took from the old crow ghost. I look at them. Sal is waving his smashed bottle like a nutter, trying to psych me out. Eric is smirking at me. Kriss is just staring.

Hazoom, stay calm. Hazoom. I walk backwards a little way.

I hold up the plastic bottle from the old crow, and I get the quickest whiff of that new magazine smell, and I lob it over to the three guys. My throw is perfect, 'cos the bottle lands at their feet – clonk – and then it spins, and a whole lot of liquid spills out.

The boys are interested in the smell. Kriss picks the bottle up, and sniffs it.

'That is nice, man,' he says. 'Smells like your mum.'

And Sal grabs it off him.

And then Eric grabs it off him.

Sal says, 'Give it back.'

But Eric just gives him a look and he pours the rest of the liquid from the bottle on the ground. Then he chucks it away.

I know they must be surrounded by that smell. So now I make my move:

'Guys,' I say, 'I wanna give you something.'

'Shut up,' says Kriss. 'I don't want none of your stuff.'

'Look at this,' I say, taking off the crystal necklace I got from the snake. 'This is a gold chain with green crystal beads, of a stone no one has seen before. I got this necklace from in there. It gives you control over them things. Here, I'll show you . . .'

I hold the necklace up in the air, and I shout: 'I need two shakfiends NOW!'

Right away, two shakfiends are standing in front of me. I command them:

'Fly inside and speak to the Master. Tell him I'm coming.'

They do exactly as I describe. They go over the top of the school towards the old gym at the back.

So it's official. That is where he is.

I grin. I can't help it. I'm getting off on the power myself. But now I really surprise the guys.

I lob the necklace at them.

'There you go,' I say. 'Whoever has this, controls the shakfiends.'

Sal grabs it. Kriss pushes him in the chest.

'That is mine, man!'

'I want it!' says Sal.

'No way!' says Kriss.

And it kicks off. Sal swings his bottle at Kriss's head. He gets a good swipe in. Buries it in Kriss's shoulder. Blood coming out. Kriss goes mental. He's pushing his broken bottle towards Sal's face, and trying to get his bottle. In seconds, the two of them are rolling on the ground towards me, wrestling, holding each other close, stabbing each other in the back, with blood going everywhere. Stab stab stab stab. Doing a lot of damage. Sal is stronger, but Kriss is quick, and vicious. He's stabbing and stabbing, and he manages to cut Sal's left arm so it's bleeding bad. It looks like Kriss is winning, except then Sal stabs the bottle at Kriss's throat. Now Kriss falls to the ground, and his body is twitching like a fish on the river bank. Meanwhile Sal's wobbling like a drunk, he's got so many wounds on his back. He falls, and then both of them lie still like they're dead. I know they are lamias, they can't truly be hurt unless they're ripped to shreds and eaten, but this is still damage. This is wrong. I feel disgusted just seeing it.

'Great,' says Jimmy's voice, in my head, 'now turn and look at Eric.'

I face Eric. I'm thinking: Right, I'm gonna pay you back for everything you've done to me. I'm gonna pay you back for gobbing in my mouth. For gobbing in Verno's mouth. His face is twitching. He's starting to look nervous. I'm still as a rock, waiting for him to come. I can see it already. I know what he's going to do.

'Just let him come to you,' says Jimmy. 'Keep calm. Don't get scared or you tense up.'

He's holding his bottle in his right hand.

He lifts it.

Then he charges, screaming. He's like a bull the way he comes at me.

I wait.

I wait.

I wait till he's just a step away from me.

Then I jump to the side, as quick as I can. He stabs down with the bottle and he misses. He turns. But he's off balance.

I jump in, and kick him really hard in the shin.

Then I jump back out the way again.

He swipes at me again. Again I dodge.

Now he's unsteady, I jump in and kick him in the shin, same one as before, right leg. You can tell that's really hurt him. Right away he has trouble putting weight on that leg. Now I punch him in the face. Put my leg behind his. Knock him off balance. Get him on the floor in a headlock. I've won.

I look into his face.

'If I were you,' I say, 'I'd be gobbing in your face. And I tell you: I am tempted. For everything you've done to me. You waste man.'

*And he starts to cry. And then I know something.
. . . I don't need to fight him. I just gotta take control.
I look at Sal and Kriss, who are groaning on the
ground.*

'I don't want you guys messing me about no more.
Now you back off. You go and wait at the side of the
playground. If you try anything, I'm gonna stab Eric in
the face, and I don't wanna do that.'

Kriss and Sal get up unsteadily and limp off.

'Eric,' I say, 'get up and walk.'

'My leg really hurts,' he says, 'it hurts . . .'

'Get up and walk. Go and join your friends.'

He gets up.

I look at Sharon Holdings. She is grinning at me.
You can tell she's impressed. Three guys came at me
together, and I finished them off. I am the champion.

54

I say *hazoom hazoom hazoom until my head gets clear. But then I realize I've been staring at Sharon Holdings all this time. And she is looking at me. Just staring, deep into my eyes. She looks beautiful. Not just beautiful. Good. Kind. And she's staring at me, and her eyes are blue, and her lips are red, and her hair is blonde and it's all tied back in a ponytail. And she looks so athletic, and so* **perfect***, wearing her white vest, and her Adidas tracksuit. She walks forward, and she holds both my hands. She looks me in the eye:*

'Colin, are you OK?'

'Yes.'

'You fought well.'

I'm shaking bad. She hugs me. I like the way she feels taller than me. I like the way her back feels under my hands. You can feel how fit she is. She whispers in my ear:

'You fought well. But you gotta look after yourself. OK?'

'I don't like fighting,' I say.

'No. But you gotta do it. 'Cos you fight well.'

'Yeah.'

'It's the truth, bruv. **Believe**.'

She holds my face in her hands. And she smiles at me.

'Listen, Col, you're gonna go in there and see him and you're gonna get the power. Then you and me are gonna team up. I'm gonna be your girl, and I'm gonna help you. And you're gonna help me, and we're gonna make a gang and we're gonna rule.'

And she holds my face in her hands, and she looks at me, looking so caring, and so beautiful, and like an angel.

And then she reaches forward and she kisses me on my lips.

I kiss her back.

But then she opens her lips, and she is snogging me. I've got my hands round her back. And I'm pulling her towards me. And she's sticking her body against me. Like she **wants** me. And I want her. I'm glad her legs are so long, 'cos she can't feel me against her.

But then I see stuff in my head.

I see Polly. The way she'll be if she don't ever get her

*lamia back. She is sitting up in bed like an old person.
Fat and grey looking. Dribbling and staring at the TV.
Music comes on – the theme from **Emmerdale** – and
she smiles a little. Then she goes back to dribbling.*

*Then I see Jimmy. He's saying: 'It might not be safe
to leave your body for so long.'*

*So then I'm thinking: Maybe I can't do this much
longer, so I gotta choice. I could go in there quick and
get Polly's lamia. But I don't know where she is, or
whether I can rescue her, or even if she'll want to come
away with me. Or I could get back to my body, quick,
because it ain't safe.*

*And then I open my eyes, and I see there's another
option.*

I could just stand here, snogging Sharon Holdings.

But then she pulls away.

*'OK, Col,' she says, 'you gotta do it. I'll stay here
and wait for you.'*

*I stand at the door of the school. Then I think about
the bottle I got from my dad. I don't wanna be
fumbling with it when that snake comes, so I gotta
open the bottle now. I get a whiff. Just quickly. For a
second I see this ain't gonna work. I think I should go
home and then come back and burn down the school.
I think I should go over to Sharon Holdings and snog
her again, but hurt her this time. I know this is the*

stuff I need. This is pure poison. I don't wanna spill a drop. I'll need all of it, and besides, I don't trust myself with this stuff sloshing about.

'OK,' I say, 'I'm going in.'

'What you gonna do?' says Sharon.

'There's a snake down there. I'm gonna chuck this bottle in its mouth.'

'How are you gonna get its mouth open?'

'I'm gonna let it attack.'

I stop a moment. I know that as soon as I go in there, whatever I'm scared of I'm gonna see. I'm ready.

I push open the door.

55

I'm saying hazoom under my breath. But then
I hear a noise in front. Coming down the corridor,
there's a swan. It's flying straight towards me, its
wings flapping, and its head pointed at me like a
spear.

I whisper under my breath: 'You ain't real you
ain't real you ain't real you can't hurt me.' But the
swan is going faster with its wings swooping down,
and the neck pointing at me like a gun. At the last
moment it's about to smash into my head, and I can't
help it, I close my eyes, and I hunch my shoulders, and
I wait for it to smash into my head.

But it don't.

I open my eyes, and there's nothing there.

I'm still holding the bottle. Nothing spilled.

I set off. Feet tap tapping on the shiny floor.

To the left is the Year Eight classroom. I turn to it.

And I see Polly sitting there, on a chair, with her

back to me. So it hits me . . . I don't need to go further. There's Polly. I can just get her out, and we can leave.

I go to the door. I tap on the glass, but Polly don't turn. I go in.

'Polly,' I whisper.

She turns.

She has no face. Where there should be a face, there's just a hole, and it's filled with worms.

I'm scrambling to get out of there. But at that moment, a huge dog leaps up from behind the door. Rottweiler. It springs at me, but it's on a chain, which yanks it back and upwards, so its face is at the same height as mine. Its yellow eyes are rolling, and its teeth are gnashing and full of slobber.

I freeze.

I've completely tensed up. Hazoom hazoom hazoom, gotta stay calm.

I come out of the classroom.

On the right is the noticeboard. A notice says: **Colin Hitchin. Your body is being suffocated. Go back now if you want to have any chance of surviving**.

This is just a trick. Must be.

But then I move on to another noticeboard. This one usually shows photos of sporting stuff. Now it shows pictures of my body. It's where I hid it in the park behind the bins. The mouth of my body is pushed against the black plastic, and not enough breath is getting in. And it's worse than that. Behind me is the vent from the garage, and it's blasting out car exhaust. 'Cept it ain't going into the air. It's going against the black plastic bags, so the air I'm breathing is full of fumes. So I see now that the game is up. If I keep going, I'm probably gonna die. I gotta go back.

But I keep going.

Taking tiny steps.

I keep walking. Tap tapping.

Then I realize something's going on above me.

I know I shouldn't look up.

I look up.

There's my dad hanging by his neck. Suddenly he opens his eyes and mouth, and he has long teeth like a wolf. He says: 'Colin, you wee sod. You're going to spill that liquid. You're so self-indulgent.'

I keep walking.

I look down at the floor.

I'm stepping over a void. It's like a huge ravine, and at the bottom there's water smashing its way over rocks. But I'm in midair above it. It can't be real.

I keep walking. Feet tap tapping. Not spilling the liquid.

But then I notice something about the bottle. It's filled with wasps. They're crawling out and walking up my arms. One is on my neck as well. And when I look at them, they ain't normal wasps, they're hornets. Just as I work that out, I feel one crawling up my nose. Oh God, oh God, oh God. I'm losing it now.

But I keep going. And I'm reaching the end of the corridor. I look at my feet. The void has gone. I look at my hands. The hornets have disappeared.

And it's at that moment that it happens.

Suddenly I see the snake that killed Jimmy. It comes slithering through the locked door. I freeze.

I pull out dad's gun, and I shoot it.

Makes no difference.

The snake gets closer and closer and closer, and then it rears up, and it attacks. Its huge mouth gapes and it lunges.

56

*A*nd I fling the bottle straight down that mouth.
I can't believe how well I've flung it, 'cos it goes
right in. Immediately the snake freezes. Then its mouth
slowly closes. And this calm look comes over its face.
And it sinks to the floor, and its eyes close, and it's like
it goes to sleep.

I've done it.

And at that moment, another snake appears – just
as big as the first one – and I scream. I freeze, and
close my eyes. I'm waiting to die.

But when I open them, it's gone. I'm sure of it now.
I really have done it.

And I go to the locked door at the end of the
corridor. I jump through it. Suddenly I feel so tired. I
feel the way I feel when I've got a fever: like someone's
sucked all the power out of my bones with a syringe.

I'm walking up the corridor which connects
the school to the old gym. At the end the door is

locked, so I can't see through it, but I can hear noise. Sound of engines.

I get to it.

I take a deep breath. I step through the door.

The sun is coming in, and it looks sweaty and hot in there.

It's a big gym, with the walls all charred from the fire.

And there he is – at the other end of the room. The Master. He must be forty foot high. His head is right up to the ceiling, and he's sitting on the floor of the gym. He's huge and fat. He looks like a Buddha or maybe like a big evil baby. He's got huge earlobes and big jowls and big, fleshy, greasy lips. Giant bulging eyes.

Just seeing him makes me weak. My heart's beating hard. Mouth is dry. He's surrounded by smashed glass and motorbikes with their engines running. Also cans of petrol. He's holding one of them now, and he's sucking from it with a huge straw made out of a scaffolding pole. Then I look at his hands. He's got three fingers which are fat like big German sausages. And he's got one finger that's thin and long and it's sort of waving in the air and rubbing against his nose. He looks like a baby drinking his milk.

There's something else just next to him . . . It's a huge glass box like a massive fish tank. It is full of lamias. They're crammed in there like commuters on a tube train. Must be a couple of hundred at least.

I look into it. And I see her, pushed against the glass . . .

Polly's lamia. Looking terrified.

The Master don't seem to have seen me. He's naked 'cept for a big dirty towel round his waist, and I'm seeing his massive spotty body. His skin looks thick like an elephant's 'cept it's smooth and wet from his sweat.

And his whole body is covered with big red boils. They're ten centimetres wide and they're leaking pus. Just then he lets go of the scaffolding pole, and he pokes his long thin finger into one of the boils on his chest. It goes in a long way – nearly half a metre – and then he squelches it in and out like he's scratching. Then he takes it out and licks his finger. Then he carries on sucking through the scaffolding. There's stuff moving in them boils. Like big maggots. As I watch, one of them comes wriggling out of the hole he's been scratching. Its head is transparent and wet.

I'm feeling sick.

Then he throws down the can of petrol. And he turns to me.

It's like it takes him a moment to notice me. 'Cos his face changes slowly. He's got these huge hairy eyebrows and they go slowly up up up his *forehead so he looks more and more surprised.*

Then he smiles this huge beautiful smile:

*'Colin **Bitchin!**' he says '**Alleluia!**'*

He sounds like Samuel L. Jackson and now I see his eyes are milky-white. I see what I always knew: somehow he was entering the pigeon and the baby and the bag lady, and he was talking to me. He's beaming. Like I'm his best friend, and he's never loved anyone so much. I can't help but smile back at him.

'Come here,' he says.

I walk across the gym, stepping over old petrol cans and shattered glass.

'Lordy-lord, child, you took your time! Where you been? I been waiting for you, child.'

'Why?'

'I been watching you.'

Just then I see his legs. He don't have feet. His legs stop at the knee in big stumps.

'How do you know me?' I say. 'How do you get around?'

'I get around with my mind. I can enter anyone I want.'

Just then he closes his eyes. He keeps them shut and he talks.

'Right now I'm inside your mother. Mmmm. I'm stepping into a red hot bath. Mmm. People are like baths. The ones you get stuck with: they're lukewarm.

The ones you want: they're red hot. The ones that scald. The ones that burn.'

He opens his eyes and smiles at me again.

'And you burn, child. You got talent. Your every contradiction makes sense to me. Your intelligence. Your anger . . . I got plans for you. I gotta fix you up with some powerful friends. People who run the banks, people who sell the arms, people who make the money.'

'That ain't power, if I gotta hang with them.'

'Child, that's what power is. You fix yourself up with the greedy people, and you do everything they say. Look at Mr Doubleyou. An ex-alcoholic retard who's flunked out of every school he went to – how does he come to be the most powerful man on the planet? Answer: he had faith. And he came to me. I'm gonna make you more powerful still. You got way more faith. Damn! Mr Bitchin! I been hiding here two years, and you the first person to get past the snake. First one. Of course, you have a special motive. And I know what that is . . .'

He takes the lid off the glass tank and reaches inside.

'You want her,' he says. He pulls out Polly's lamia, holding her between his chubby fingers. She's frozen. Just looking at me. Not daring to turn. He smiles at me. He holds her in front of his mouth, like any second he's gonna open up and start chewing.

302

'Mmmm,' he says.

Then he lifts her over to me with his big arm and lets her go.

'There's your prize. You run along now. And you come back and see me soon.'

Polly runs to me, and she puts her arms round me. She's shivering. She whispers in my ear.

'Colin, let's get out of here.'

'No.'

'What do you want, child?'

'You need to let the others out too.'

'I was looking forward to them,' says the Master. Then he smiles. 'But 'cos you is my main man, and 'cos you and me are gonna work together, I'm gonna do you a favour.'

He turns the giant tank on its side. The kids come out, very scared, and they run one by one towards the door and out of it. When the last one is gone, Polly nudges me.

'Let's go.'

I whisper back: 'OK.'

And we turn, we go back to the door. We step out of the gym.

When we get into the school, we see the other kids sprinting off down the corridor.

The snake is still lying nearby.

Polly sees it, and screams.

'Stay calm,' I say.

'Is it dead?'

'Not dead. Just sleeping.'

'Let's run.'

She grabs my hand, and she heads off down the corridor. I pull away from her.

'What?' she says, turning.

'I can't go yet,' I say.

'**Why?** Why the hell not?'

'There's still something I gotta do.'

'What?'

'I gotta go back in.'

I make to turn. Just then the snake twitches its head.

Polly screams:

'Colin, don't go back! It looks like the snake is waking up. Then you'll be stuck in there!'

'Polly, I gotta do this.'

And I turn, and I go back through the door.

57

*H*e smiles when I come back in.
'Colin Bitchin,' he smiles. 'You left, but now you come back.'

'Yes.'

'There's something else you want to do.'

'Yes.'

'You wanna kill me.'

He says it like that, like he don't care. And it's strange, 'cos I know he understands everything, and I can be honest with him.

'That's right,' I say. I even smile at him.

'What you gonna do? Bite my stumpy leg? Here . . . come over here, my friend.'

And I really see it clearly: people are only violent when they're scared. This guy don't give a damn: he ain't gonna hurt me. He smiles again.

'Colin Hitchin! I been waiting for you a long time. You the man! We goan help each other! I can change *your life. I can redesign your world. What do you need?'*

'I wanted Polly back.'

'And she's outside. You need anything else?'

'Definitely. My mum goes out with this bloke called OB, and he's a chief.'

'He's gone.'

'I didn't . . . I don't want you to kill him . . .'

'I ain't killed him. I just arranged for him to walk out of your mom's life. But to be honest, it looks like you managed that already. Anything else?'

'I feel bad about Vern. I like him, but he looks like such a chief I can't hang with him.'

'You wanna make him cool?'

'Yeah.'

'Be careful, child. Our greatest fear is that we have ultimate power. Careful what you ask for.'

*'Make him cool. And give him a nice bike. He'd like that. One with thirty-six gears, and one gear that's really **really** stiff, so even if he's going full speed down the hill on Hampstead Heath, he can still pedal faster.'*

'That bike is sitting in his shed.'

'Thanks.'

'Stop thanking me, child. This is your first lesson: you could do this yourself. Everybody could. You just gotta ask yourself what you need, and you get it.

Everything starts in the brain. You can design the world you need.'

'What you saying? It's all like . . . perception?'

*'I ain't saying that, I'm saying **you are an angel. You are God**. Anything you wish to manifest, you just gotta **believe** you need it.'*

'Yeah? OK, I want a squirrel with red eyes that can fire bullets with its arse.'

'Don't fool with me, child.'

'You said I could have whatever I wanted.'

*'I didn't say you could have what you **wanted**! I said you could have what you **need**! What else you **need?**'*

'My mum's doing my head. She keeps saying she needs money.'

'She just got herself a new job.'

'Thanks.'

*'I keep telling you, child, don't thank me. You told her to make the call. Come on . . . What about you? What do **you** need?'*

'Well . . . I want everyone to like me.'

'There's a good reason why people don't like you, and you know what that is?'

'No.'

'One: You're different. You about ten times more intelligent than most people. And second: They don't like you 'cos you don't like them. That's fine! I don't

want to see you **popular**. I want to see you **feared!**
And when you are truly feared, living in your palace,
sending out guards to behead your enemies, then
everyone will say how kind and noble you are. Why?
'Cos people are dogs. They follow the leader. **Come
on!** Popularity is a booby prize given to the man who
lost the race. We gotta get you to **win** the race. So tell
me again: what else you need?'

'Nothing.'

'Come on. There's bombs going off. There's gonna be
a war out there soon. You should get yourself a tank. You
should at least get yourself a Jeep.'

'No no no no! How's it gonna be if everyone
thought like that? Whole town would be filled with
massive Jeeps too big to get past each other. We should
all just stick to our bikes.'

'**Other People Just Think Of Themselves**. You
gotta think of **yourself**! Everybody's doing it, so why
can't you?'

Suddenly I figured it out. How come I've been so
slow to get it?

'I got it. That's what you want: to get everyone
to think like that. People are greedy. But they ain't
stupid. They know if everyone has Jeeps, no one
will be able to breathe. It's obvious. But you're
making them so scared, they think they need
that stuff.'

'Come on, brother, get righteous. I'm trying to help you here.'

'You're the one who's helping himself. And I know why. You got creatures under your skin, and they're gonna **hatch**. And then there's gonna be a load more of you, ain't there? And this city is perfect for you, 'cept for one thing: a tiny bit too much oxygen. All the time I been trying to find you, I thought you was making a bomb. But you don't need a bomb. You just need people driving Jeeps and travelling to Malta for the weekend. I worked it out, and so have you. If people are happy, they don't travel. They don't buy stuff. 'Cos they just walking up and down the street, talking to their neighbours and chilling. So you're keeping them afraid and unhappy.'

'Mmm! Stop preaching at me.'

'Just tell me one thing. Who planted the bomb in Clissold?'

'Listen, child. It don't matter who did it. Long as people are scared, someone's gonna do it.'

'But it wasn't Yussuf, was it?'

'That dude is beyond temptation. Pisses me off.'

'So get him out of prison. I like him. In fact, can you go back and get rid of all the bombs?'

'Mmm, don't push me, child. A lot of work went into those things. But since we're gonna do business together, I grant your wish.'

'That's good. So everything's OK again.'

'Ain't you listening to me? Everything is not OK. Wake up and smell the petrol. The world is finished. It's too hard to save.'

'It's **easy** to save. Stop flying, stop driving, stop buying stuff you don't need. Bosh. The world is saved.'

'Bullshit! Oxygen is going. Ice caps are melting. There's islands going underwater. Ain't nobody can stop that. People smoke, people drive, people throw their trash in the park. How're people supposed to stop the world getting dirty, when they can't even keep their own park clean? Their own bodies clean? Meanwhile there's six billion people, and they're all pecking away like chickens and they're scared 'cos there ain't much grain. Fact: you can be the one to get the grain. Fact: everyone else's gonna die. That's why everyone's scared.'

'I ain't scared.'

'You're all scared, and I'll tell you why. 'Cos you're alone. 'Cos when you close your eyes, you don't see nobody else.'

'You're wrong. When I close my eyes, I see **everybody**.'

'You're alone.'

'I ain't alone. And I tell you why. I ain't here now. I'm in Butterfield, hiding behind some bags. I'm only here 'cos I have **imagined** my way here. All this is like a dream I wanted to keep dreaming. I've imagined **everything** I've seen. Imagined every**one** I've seen. And I've imagined you.'

'Like I say, you are God. Everyone is in your head, and you are in theirs. Ain't that a beautiful thing. You are God! Alleluia to that, brother! Your greatest fear is that you become powerful beyond measure.'

'You keep saying that. Don't make it no more true.'

'Listen to me, child. Your greatest fear is that you have ultimate power.'

'Don't say that again.'

'You have ultimate power.'

'I know that. But that don't make me scared! That makes me happy!'

And with that, I pull out my dad's gun. And I point it at his head, and I fire.

58

The noise is so loud it makes my ears ring. It takes a few seconds for it to clear.

I don't move. He don't move.

But then he smiles.

*'Colin Bitchin! You **fother-mucker**!'*

I just stare at him. He looks exactly the same, apart from a tiny pin-prick you can see between his eyeballs: the place where I shot him. It's leaking a black liquid.

Now I'm scared.

'Colin Bitchin! You scared now. You feel alone now. I knew you was going to do that. I knew you had a gun. You think I woulda let you stay conversing, if you coulda killed me? You can't kill me. I ain't filled with blood. Look at that . . .'

He wipes the pin-prick, smearing the black blood on to his finger. He holds it out to me.

'Look at that. Pure oil. I'm filled with the good stuff. You couldn't kill me. 'Cos I'm big. And you

*small. And you alone. The only way you could ever kill **me**, is if you got **every**body, all at once, to march on me. And that ain't never gonna happen. In two years, you the only guy who's ever come here. The only guy who ever had enough faith. So deal with that. I finished with you now. Finished with all of you. The whole human race is a plague of maggots under a stone. And I'm gonna lift the stone, and I'll pour boiling water on your squirmy little heads!'*

And with that, he reaches out with his big chubby hand.

And he swipes me so he's squeezing me in his hand.

He places me next to the door of the gym.

He opens it. And he flicks me like a bogey down the corridor of the school.

59

*I skid ten metres down the shiny floor. I look round.
Everyone's gone.*

I am alone.

I get up, and I start walking straight back.

Then I hear someone speak.

It's my dad's voice. I look up.

*He's still there, hanging from the ceiling by his neck.
Eyes bulging. I keep going.*

'What the hell are you doing, Colin?'

'Going back to kill him.'

*'If you go back now, you're going to die. The snake
will wake up in moments, and, next time, the same
trick won't work.'*

'So I've got to hurry. It ain't woken yet.'

*'But, Colin, you are about to die. Your body is
being suffocated. You have to return! It may be too late
already.'*

'So what's to lose?'

'Wait! Wait!'

I stop.

I turn round, and look up at my dad, hanging from the ceiling.

'Listen to me,' he says, 'there's no point you going back in. In two years you're the only one who's made it. The only way you could even tackle him would be if loads of people came at once. It'd be like a revolution of human consciousness.'

'Well . . . then that's what I need. I'm seeing that, right now, in my head.'

I turn and walk.

*'Wait! Wait wait wait!' My dad is screaming. 'That's it? You imagine everyone will come at once 'cos you called for them **in your mind**?'*

'No. I imagined Polly out there, telling them to come back.'

'What? That's it? That's it? Is that your plan?'

I notice the snake twitching again.

'That's my plan.'

I turn and walk calmly back inside.

60

*A*nd suddenly I think something: Is this it? Have I now definitely gone mad? 'Cos I know the truth. No one is coming to help me. Course they ain't. Why did I ever think they would? Is this it? Is this the moment I'm gonna die?

And I look up, and I see the snake. It opens its eyes.

And at that moment, the door bangs open behind me. I turn, and I see Polly, and behind her I can see a crowd of lamias. Looks like all of the ones that came out of the tank. I also see Kriss and Sharon. They're running through the door, and everyone is holding a broken bottle.

'Come on!' I shout. 'Run! The snake is about to wake up! Run!'

And they sprint down the corridor.

As they reach me, I yell: 'Quick! Get on the snake, and start stabbing. As many as possible.'

Now there's about twenty of us along the back of the snake. It looks like one of them big bananas that get towed behind motorboats. 'Cept the passengers have all got broken bottles, and they're stabbing.

The snake opens its big mouth, and it tries to lash about. But the weight of the guys is holding it down. And they're stabbing everywhere. The first stabs go right into its eyes. And the next are going in its nostrils. And soon they're stabbing all along its back, and the scaly skin is coming right off, and they're cutting away big hunks of flesh.

I stand on top of the back of the snake, and I shout again:

'We're all going to rush the Master, and we're all gonna stab him!'

And I run down the corridor into the gym.

The Master turns right away. You can see all the different thoughts go through his mind. First he smiles, then he looks confused . . . then he looks scared.

He chucks a big glass bottle at us. We dodge, and it smashes on the ground. That don't stop us for long. A few of the kids have got glass in their legs, but they're still running.

And then he flings a can of petrol.

It lands near me, and the petrol spills out and I get a mouthful of it. I'm choking. And the kids behind bang into me, and I'm knocked to the floor. I'm on my hands and knees, and kids are kicking me in the head as they jump over me. And still I can't breathe. I'm choking. I can't breathe.

I see a piece of glass on the floor.

I pick it up, and manage to get to my feet.

The first kids have reached the Master. A few of them are climbing on his big chubby legs, and they're stabbing into him. He's trying to get up. But they're hanging on to his legs and climbing up and gouging his flesh. Then he slips on the oil.

I run. I want to be part of the action. The Master is trying to brush kids off, flicking them away. But there's too many of us and the kids are all going mental and climbing on and tearing and slicing. He tries to get up, but again he slips, and his head knocks on the floor.

I leap on it, and I'm clinging on to his hair. It's thick like cable. I climb right up on to his face. I'm slipping and sliding, but I'm digging in my glass and scrambling up. I get over to his big nose, and I stick my glass dagger upwards into his nostril, and that helps me to cling on. I think he's going to throw me off any second. But he don't. He is covered in kids. They are all over him, and they're all stabbing away, and blood is gushing out everywhere, and it's all black and it smells of petrol. It's only taken seconds, but already his big body is being ripped to pieces. Chunks of his legs are already being cut off. Then kids are taking them chunks and slicing them up. I take my bottle out of the nostril, and I stab down on to his top lip. It slices right in, and black blood bursts out of there. I stay on top of his face, and I'm cutting into his mouth, and cutting away lumps of his lips. A wheezing sound is coming out of him.

I can't tell you how long it goes on. Soon the whole place is a mess. I can see a group who are trying to cut one of his hands clean off. But the Master is still moving.

He's still moving!

And it ain't just that. The maggots under his skin, they're all coming out. We're helping them hatch.

Just then I see it. I know it.

This ain't a big baby we're dealing with. This is the most powerful being the world has known. Any second he's gonna come back at us.

61

I *stop a second.*
I'm standing in the middle of his gored face, his flesh all black and slimy under my feet. I see it. It ain't enough just to stab him. Even though there's so many of us.

I'm feeling in my pocket, and suddenly it hits me.

I know what I have to do. I know what this whole journey has been about.

I remember what Dawnelle told me in the park.

I reach into my pocket, and I find my dad's lighter.

'GET OFF, EVERYBODY!' I shout. 'GET OFF! GET OFF! GO BACK THROUGH THE DOOR! GO BACK!'

But no one's paying much mind to me.

'GET OUT!' I say. 'HE'S GONNA COME BACK AT US!'

This gets the attention of a few kids who are on his belly, cutting right into it, hacking pieces away.

'HE'S GONNA COME BACK AT US! GET BACK BEHIND THE DOOR!'

People are listening to me now. You can see them getting scared. Then panicking. They're scrambling to slide off his body. It don't take long. Soon the kids have all left the Master, and they've all pushed back through the big door.

And that leaves just me. I'm standing on his face. I look down at him. The smell coming out of him is rank, like the mankiest smell you ever smelled from the bottom of a dustbin.

I know what I have to do.

62

I take the lighter out of my pocket. I hold it down towards the mess of his ripped-up cheek. Using both hands, I light it.

WHOOSH!

There's actually a noise as his flesh lights up. The flames jump up out of his ripped face, and they spread in a moment all the way down his body, down the remains of his legs, and over his hacked flesh.

Result.

But there's only one problem with this.

I've set myself on fire too.

63

I look down. My legs and feet, covered in his oily blood, are on fire. I'm burning so quick, I can hardly even feel the pain, 'cept for my eyes, which are scalding. And the noise of the flames is roaring in my ears. The whole place is filled with black smoke and flame, and I can hardly see nothing.

I fall over, and my hands fall down into his flesh, which is burning fast and it's slimy like rubber. I try to stumble to my feet, but I can't get up. I'm still on my hands and knees.

And then something moves in front of me. It's like the flesh opens.

It takes me a moment to see what it is.

It's his eye. He's opened his eyelid. I'm on all fours looking into his eye, which is as big as a table. It's staring up at me, all frightened. Round the edge are eyelashes, and they are all on fire, so the eye is surrounded by flame.

*What Dawnelle said is going round and round my head: '**Fight hard, then jump into the eye**.'*

And now I can feel my whole body is about to burn up, and I see that there's only one way out of these flames.

And the Master seems to see it the moment I do. 'Cos his eye goes wider still. Full of fear.

And I reach up my piece of glass and – down – I stab right into the middle of his eyeball.

I cut a slice through it, as wide as me. Then I step out on to it.

I get a last glimpse of the fire blazing all around me.

And then I slip, out of the flames, into his eye.

I fall.

The slit eyeball closes above my head. And for a tiny moment, I'm in darkness.

But then I feel something else.

I feel light. I felt lighter when I left my body to enter my lamia, but now I feel even lighter still. I'm like a locust who's lost his skin.

Then my eyes are adjusting to darkness.

There's a little bit of light coming through the eye.

I turn. And I see there's a tunnel behind me.

A big black squelchy tunnel.

It don't look good.

But it's the only way out.

And when you've only got one way out, you gotta take it.

I jump.

64

Suddenly the tunnel is lit up with bright light. I shut my eyes it's so bright.

I feel like I'm floating. Like I'm on a lilo and I'm on water, in an underground pipe, and I'm moving fast towards the sea.

I open my eyes a moment, and I see I'm going through something. It's the door to the shed in Clissold Park.

It gets brighter still and I shut my eyes again.

It's like my lilo has stopped.

I open my eyes.

I feel as if the drugs have worn off again, and I'm staring at a new reality I ain't never seen. I like it.

I see grass. I see big trees with the sun shining through the leaves. Everything looks yellow and soft and beautiful. It looks like the way you remember a summer's evening when you were five.

It looks calm.

It looks safe.

It looks shady.

I'm standing up to my knees in water. It's beautiful. It's like I'm seeing water for the first time. And I can hear it as well. It tinkles.

A dandelion seed drifts by, swaying in the breeze, and I can hear the air rustling through the fine hairs of the parachute.

I don't know how long I'm standing in the water, looking around, but I suddenly realize something: I can hear people talking, but their voices are faint. It's like their volume has been turned down. And the volume of everything else has been turned up. And the colours have been changed as well, 'cos they're so much brighter. And the smells are stronger too. I can smell the sweet scent of the water. A bee flies by, and I can smell the honey on its wings. And it lands in a bright pink flower and I can smell the perfumed petals.

Then I look for the people I heard, and I can see them, but they're faint. They got no colour. They look like ghosts. I see a boy with a skateboard. He jumps, the skateboard turns in the air, and he lands. And I look around, and suddenly I see something that's so obvious, I don't know how I didn't see it straight away.

I'm in Clissold Park.

I feel there's someone behind me.

I turn.

65

It's Dawnelle. She's smiling.

'Colin,' she says, 'welcome.'

'Hey, Dawnelle,' I say.

And we both smile. Then she hugs me and I smell coconut oil and palm butter.

'I said I'd be waiting . . .' she says.

'What do you mean?'

'. . . when you reached heaven.'

At first I can't take that in. I just look at her.

'**What**?' I say. Then . . . 'Is this it?'

'What?'

'Is this . . . **heaven**?'

'Yes!'

'No! It can't be. Heaven is **Stoke Newington**?'

She laughs.

'Part of it is.'

'It can't be!'

'Why not? How do you want heaven to be?'

328

I think about that. 'Mountains . . . Maybe heaven should look like a Greek island.'

'What do you know about Greek islands?'

'I went on holiday to one with Mum and Dad.'

'You can go there again now. But I thought you said holidays are for people who are too uptight to have fun where they are . . . Here. Come with me.'

Dawnelle floats into the air. Then she glides across the park towards the big pond. I jump up and float after her. That feels good. I catch her up and I'm gliding next to her in the air and she turns to me and smiles. I still don't quite get it though. I've got to ask her again.

'So . . . **This is it**?' I say.

'You still ain't got it. How do you want it to be?'

'People should be happy.'

'I'm happy. You happy?'

'Yeah. I am.'

I realize I am as well.

'Good. 'Cos that's all you gotta do, to be in heaven. Be happy. Come. I'm gonna show you some angels.'

We're drifting towards a tall figure, who's standing under an apple tree. He's got big wings like a swan. 'Cept some of them are muddy. And the angel has got some dirt on his face.

And he's got a moustache.

'Colin Hitchin!' says the angel. 'You brave beauty!'

'Hello, Jimmy,' I say. 'Hang on . . . . this is doing my head. **You** . . . are an angel?'

'I always was. A dirty angel. A heavy angel. A shady angel. And so are we all. Here . . . Look at this.' He holds something out. It's a green-white apple. 'Bite it,' he says.

I bite out a big chunk. It's got green-white flesh. Crunchy and slightly bitter. Jimmy shows me the middle.

'Look,' he says.

In the apple, where the seeds should be, there's something wiggling. Looks like a pink tadpole.

'What is it?' I say.

He smiles. 'It's the lamia of a baby waiting to be born.'

He strokes it with his finger.

'Hello, child,' he says, 'your name is Pablo Escusias, and you are going to be born, in nine months' time, in Homerton Hospital. Go with love! Relax, listen, laugh!'

And he blows on the apple, and the lamia flips off into the air.

'Right,' he says. 'You're just in time.'

'For what?'

'Go up into that tree and find out.'

He points his head at a huge apple tree which is right next to the pond. Its branches are reaching right over the water.

'Aint you coming?'
'I'm staying here.'
'But . . .'
'You scared?'

66

I float up into the apple tree. There's someone standing on a big branch, holding the trunk with one hand.

It's Dad.

'Colin,' he says, 'you've arrived. Give me a hug.'

He smells of rollies and coffee and shirts worn for the third day running.

'Let's sit.'

So we sit side by side on the branch with our legs swinging down.

'Dad,' I say, 'you ain't mad at me?'

'Course not.'

'You know that I . . . I burned your book?'

'**Did you**?'

'Yes. Sorry.'

He laughs. 'I thought **I'd** done it. I thought I must've been drunk,' he says, 'and knocked cigarette ash on it. I was so angry with myself.'

'It was me. Sorry, Dad.'

'Don't worry. Listen . . . I didn't think how it would affect you when I killed myself. I'm sorry.'

'But, Dad, I was doing my best. I wanted you to be happy. I—'

'No no no no, Colin, it wasnae your fault.'

'Yeah, but if maybe I'd tried to—'

'No, it wasn't your fault. And I'm sorry.'

'But—'

'Colin, really . . .' I look him in the eye. He smiles. 'It wasnae your fault.'

And I get it. 'OK,' I say.

Then he goes: 'So how has Mum been?'

'Mmm, not good. Why didn't she stop you dying?'

'Oh . . . she couldn't.'

'Why?'

'You know . . .'

'No?'

'Over the writing of the joint Christmas cards, during the eating of the shared dinners, something happened. Our love died. I needed to be a great writer. She needed me to earn some cash. It wasnae her fault. She's a wonderful woman actually. She put up with a lot. I was so gloomy. That's why I've come straight here.'

'What do you mean?'

'In a minute, I'm going to jump down into the pond. And you know what'll happen then?'

'No.'

'I'll turn into a tree. And all the memories of my stupid selfish life will get drained down.'

Suddenly, I'm panicking. '**What?** Dad! Wait. You . . . you can't just go . . . Every time I see you, you disappear. I need you.'

Dad looks at me, and he holds my face in his hands.

'Colin,' he says, 'you don't need me. And I don't need me any more. My life is done. Finished. Hazoom.'

'But . . .'

'I just waited for you, 'cos I wanted to say that I'm very proud of you, Colin. I love you – so much. And thank you for rescuing me back there. Thanks for everything.'

'Thanks yourself, Dad.'

'For what? What did I ever do?'

'Well . . . you were selfish sometimes. But I loved it when we went camping, and when you took the piss out of Mum. You were, sometimes, a wicked dad.'

'I was horrible. But next time I'm gonnae be fantastic. Hazoom. Goodbye.'

And he kisses me on my forehead. And for a moment I get that little trace of Dad smell. Then he walks to the end of the branch.

'Dawnelle!' he shouts. 'Goodbye!'

'Bye, Billy!'

'Jimmy!' he shouts. 'You're not as clever as you think you are, you smell like pish, and it was me who stole your pornographic collection.'

Jimmy tips back his head and laughs.

'You were welcome to it! See you around! Go with love!'

'Go with love!' says Dad.

And he jumps.

For a second, I think nothing's gonna happen. 'Cos he just falls ten metres into the pond, and he stands there with the water going up to his knees. And he raises his arms.

But then, I watch, amazed.

Leaves sprout on my dad's hands. First they're buds, then they get bigger, then they're proper leaves.

And I look at Dad's face. He looks relaxed.

He turns browny-green. His face slowly melts.

And he changes into a tree. A man-tree. Six foot tall. Standing in the pond.

For a second, I wanna fly down and drag him out.

But I don't.

I just watch. The tree sways, and the leaves shake, and a shape appears amongst the foliage. It ain't real, *this shape, it's like a ghost thing. It's pages of words, going up and disappearing in the air.*

It's my dad's work. All the hundreds of pages of **The History of British Crime**. *Everything that's in my dad's head. It starts to go.*

First just a few pages. Then page after page.

Blowing off into the air and disappearing like ash from the top of a bonfire.

And then finally the pages stop, and other stuff comes out. It's like there's a film being projected above the tree.

I see our flat. The way it was when we first moved in. With the little tree growing outside that the council cut down.

And I see my mum. Standing next to him in church, about to get married.

I see her the way she was when they first met. Really young. And she's got a nose ring and she looks great and she's laughing.

And then I see Uncle Jimmy, and he's with my dad, but they look about eighteen and they're drinking beer and laughing.

And then suddenly everything I see is to do with me.

I see me as a baby. I'm grinning, 'cos I've got a rattle.

And I see me going to my first day of school in my new uniform.

And then I see stuff about me I never thought my dad would've noticed.

*I see one of my exercise books from school, and the teacher has written **V good work. Well done. A.***

And there's me, learning to swim.

And then suddenly it's me now: the way I was earlier today. When I turned up at my dad's room.

And then that goes.

And then nothing.

And then the tree starts to grow.

It's slow at first, but then it gets taller. Two metres, four metres, seven metres.

It shoots up. Twenty seconds later, Dad has turned into a twenty-metre tree, standing with its roots at the edge of the pond.

And then Jimmy flies up from the ground. He goes into the branches of the dad-tree and then he floats down and lands on the branch beside me.

'Here,' he says, handing me another apple, 'he's in there. You wanna be the one to let him go.'

'I'll hold on to it for a bit,' I say.

And I reach into the pocket of my combat trousers and I find a crisp packet from some crisps I got a lifetime ago. I put the apple in the packet. And then I put the packet back in my pocket.

Jimmy puts his hand on my shoulder.

'Right . . .' he says. 'Dawnelle reckons you think

Greece could be heaven. So I'm thinking we could fly there like three geese and have a few days splashing about in the clear sea.'

I look at Jimmy. And I look at Dawnelle, who's standing on the ground smiling at me. And I think of all the fun we're gonna have.

And then I run to the end of the branch.

'Colin!' they both shout at once. 'Don't do it! NOOOOOOOO!'

67

I jump into the pond.

Squelch.

I can feel I've landed in the mud. My feet are cool in the water.

And then I feel myself stiffening.

So, quickly, I raise my arms up above my head, and leaves sprout from my fingers.

And suddenly my whole life is rushing through my head . . .

Snogging Sharon Holdings in the burned-out car.

Flying from the shakfiends into Clissold Park.

Me and Vern listening to Johnny Hodges.

Eric gobbing into my mouth.

Me and Polly sitting on the bus talking about who we'd take to a desert island.

Then I'm going further back.

Me and Mum sitting next to Epping Forest pond talking about Dad.

Me and Mum and Polly and Vern, and we're all younger and we're going to Alton Towers for my birthday.

Me and Dad and we're making a camp site on a hill.

And then me and Polly and it's when I first met Polly at Walford Road playschool. She's in the little house playing with an orange teapot, and I give her a red plastic plate.

And then it's me, and I must be a baby, 'cos I'm being carried by my mum and her hair is on my face and I'm patting her face with my pudgy hand and she's smiling and I love her so much.

And then nothing.

And then I feel myself grow.

Up up up I go.

I'm reaching up, I want to stretch as high as I can into the sky.

Pretty soon I'm rising above the top of the apple tree. I rise up up higher, and I'm higher than all the houses round Clissold Park. I can see all the way to Finsbury Park, where I can see more plane trees and it's like they're all waving at me. And then I can see all the way to Parliament Hill and I can see beech trees and I feel like we're all in the same team. And I feel golden light coming down from the air, I can feel cold air coming through my roots, and I say hazoom.

And then it hits me. This is it. This is heaven. And all we gotta do to save the world is just keep breathing. And then something else hits me: I am dead.

68

I should not be dead.

And as soon as I think that, I get this evil pounding in my head.

I feel like I been grabbed.

And I'm being whooshed through the air.

And then I feel sick. And weak. And I smell fire and oil and burned flesh.

And that's when I hear a loud scream.

'COLIN! **COLIN!***'*

And I open my eyes.

I'm in a black ball.

I look up. A girl is looking down at me, and she's screaming. I stare at her. I feel sicker than ever. I'm looking at this girl, trying to work out who she is, and why I'm here, and why I'm not back in Clissold Park, breathing out love. Then I see it.

It's Polly.

'Colin!' she says. 'You got to get out of there! Hold me!'

She drops her hand down.

'Hold on to me!'

I look at her hand. I know what she wants me to do, but I can't get my body to move.

But then I hold her hand.

She pulls me, and soon I'm squelching up, and I tumble out into a stinking, black place.

'Polly,' I say, 'what's happening?'

'I saw you do it. I saw you set him on fire. And then I saw you slip inside his eye. You're a genius, Colin. How did you know that was gonna keep you safe?'

I look around. I see what we're standing on. It's the charred remains of the Master. His flesh is slimy and still warm.

'Come on,' says Polly. 'All the other lamias have gone. We should get out of here. Do you think you can move?'

'I dunno.'

'Hold my hand.'

I hold Polly's hand. And she looks into my eyes, and she smiles.

She's all covered in black slimy stuff, but somehow I like it. It's Polly.

'Colin,' she says, 'I thought you were dead. I couldn't believe it when I cut into his eye, and found you moving.'

I just stare at her eyes, with their thick lashes.

'Polly,' I say, 'I love you. I love you so much.'

Polly grins.

Then I realize where I am, and what I've just said.

And then I realize you shouldn't go round saying stuff like that.

I gotta get out of here.

'Come on,' she says, 'let's go home.'

69

*W*e walk out of the gym. Into the school. Down the long shiny corridor. Out into the playground. Outside the streetlamps are on, but there's still light in the sky. Summer night. Polly turns to me, and she says: 'Shall we fly?'

I smile and we lift up above the playground, over the streetlamps outside. We fly down Clissold Road. Over Albion Road. Then we're flying along Walford Road. And then we stop on the roof of her estate.

I'm looking at Stoke Newington. I see all the pylons and the adverts and the cranes. I see a helicopter that needs shooting out the sky. And then I look at all the houses and the trees and the people walking along the street, not noticing their lamias flying around them. It looks good.

'OK, Coll,' says Polly, 'this is nice. But I'm gonna go back to my flat and get back in my body.'

'OK.'

'You better go back to yours.'

'I will.'

'Then go and sleep. I'll see you tomorrow at school.'

'Yeah.'

She kisses me on the cheek. Then she turns and she flies to her house and through the window, into her bedroom.

And I turn and I fly off towards Butterfield. It's dark and quiet. I come down through the trees, and I see my body lying there, against the wall behind the bags. I touch my body. I can't believe it. It feels cold. It feels dead.

I crawl over the bin bags, and I lie myself down on my body, and close my eyes.

I say it: 'Moozah moozah moozah.'

And instead of seeing gold coming into my head, I'm thinking it's all leaving.

Till I'm just normal. Just me.

70

I smell the fag butts in the rubbish bin. And I smell petrol coming from the garage. And I hear the *dvd dvd* pulse of blood in my ear, and it sounds like horsemen coming to get me, waving their swords in the air.

I open my eyes.

I'm lying on the ground in Butterfield Park. I move my fingers and toes. It feels odd moving my body again. I feel all heavy. I sit up.

I stand.

The park is empty, and dirty. Everything looks grey.

I feel alone.

I don't know who I am. Or what I should do. Then I remember a dream I had, where I was Colin Hitchin, and I lived in a flat nearby.

I might as well go back there.

I pick up my rucksack and walk across the park. It's quiet and dark.

I leave the park. There's no one in the street outside.

And I walk home.

I go trudge trudge up the stairs to our flat and suddenly I'm so tried I feel I won't even make it to the top.

But eventually I'm opening the door and smelling the smell of home. I don't go to the living-room to see if Mum's there. I go straight to my room. I look around at the SAS pictures, and the clothes on the floor, and the mirror. It looks like the room of someone I used to know, and a thought comes into my head: My whole life is a dream that I chose to keep dreaming.

I get on my bed and I sleep.

71

Next day at school, I'm tired but I'm mellow. Everyone else is as well. Before Assembly. Kriss comes up to me in the playground.

'Colin!' he says, grinning. 'Hey, bruv, did you see yourself on telly?'

'No.'

'You were on *London Tonight* last night, right at the end.'

'What was I doing?'

'They showed you with Kimberley outside the Nag's Head. You gave her this evil look, and then you said: 'Are you a witch?' It was *hilarious*.'

And Sal and Eric come up.

'Bitchin,' says Eric, 'I'm sorry about . . . you know . . . the fight last week.'

I look at him.

'Forget it,' I say.

'But . . . don't be mad at me. 'Cos if you're mad at me I'm gonna fight you again.'

'Eric, I ain't got time for this. I need to speak to Verno. You need to sort him out with some software.'

'What's that?'

'He'll tell you in a second.'

And I leave Eric, 'cos Vern's walking past. I go up to him, and give him a hug. This surprises him, but he don't mind.

I get something out of the pocket of my combat trousers. It's an envelope.

'This is for you,' I say.

'What is it?'

'It's cash, Vern. I want you to get the chess software. Eric'll sort you out.'

Vern grins. You can tell he really wants it. But then he says, 'I can't take that.'

'Yes you can, Vern'. 'You're my best friend. Apart from Polly. I want you to have it.'

'No.'

'OK then. It'll still be mine, but install it on your computer.'

'Thanks,' he says, 'you can come and use it whenever you want.'

'I will Vern, thanks.'

'By the way,' he says, 'is it true what everyone's saying?'

'What?'

'That you got off with Sharon Holdings?'

'No. We just . . . Nothing happened. You know I wouldn't do that. It's Polly I like.'

'Did you hear what happened to her?'

'What?'

'Apparently Sal hit her with a car.'

'Oh.'

'And she didn't move for an hour. They took her home and called a doctor, then suddenly she recovered like she was fine.'

'Right.'

Polly arrives late into school and so I don't even manage to talk to her. But she smiles at me when she sits down. After that I just drift.

The only interesting bit happens before break. Barker says he ain't teaching his normal class. He says he's here in the capacity of Head of Year. Basically he wants people to come up and talk about what they want to do with their lives. Right away, Trish Appleton gets well vexed. She's saying: 'You ain't asked us to prepare this. It ain't fair.'

Barker tells her to relax. Then he gets everyone up one by one.

Vern goes first. He says he wants to be a chess Grand Master. If he can't do that, he wants to be a teacher, he says, and he'll run a chess club in his spare time. No one disses him for this. No one even laughs. Something unreal has gone on. It's like being a chess Grand Master is now as safe as being an MC.

After that Barker asks for Polly. Teachers always get Polly up. It's 'cos they know she will always give an answer, but she's got cred as well, so after her other people will join in. She says: 'I want to write loads and loads of songs and I'd like to make my money touring round, and singing. I'd like to be in the Shepherd's Bush Empire, but if I could be onstage in the Vortex Jazz Bar in Dalston, I'd be laughing. And I also wouldn't mind working at Lea Valley Stables. If I could do that, I'd be laughing as well.'

After that Eric comes up. He says he wants his own bike shop. I'm thinking that ain't a bad idea. You can see him in twenty years' time, with a bit of a belly, fixing bikes and listening to bad music. Taking the piss out of all the kids that come in.

When Sal gets up, it's hilarious.

Barker says: 'What do you like, Sal?'

'Food,' he says, and everyone laughs and he smiles. 'That is why,' he says proudly, 'I am going to work in the Best Turkish Kebab Shop in Stoke Newington.'

'Which one would that be?' says Barker.

'It's called the Best Turkish Kebab Shop, 'cos it is the best Turkish Kebab shop.'

'Why do you think you'd like that?'

' 'Cos my cousins work there, so we'd be together.

We'd work together. We'd go drinking together. Then at the weekends we could watch Arsenal. Plus,' says Sal, 'you guys could all come in and visit, and I would feed you. I wouldn't give you shish kebab for free, but I'd give you extra.'

'Fair enough,' says Barker. With anyone else, he'd probably say: 'Why don't you aim a bit higher?' But Barker aint no fool. He knows what he's dealing with. Besides, Sal is looking so proud. In his mind, he's feeding the whole of Stoke Newington like he's a fat Jesus working with shish and garlic sauce.

Kriss says he wants to be a model. You can tell Barker is about to say yes, well, that's a career that lots of people want to have, but very few make it, etc etc etc. But then he looks at Kriss, who is so good-looking it's unreal. Kriss is saying: 'I like clothes, you know what I mean? I got a cousin who's a hairdresser and he's always got loads of tight threads made out of satin, or made out of velvet. I like stuff with a bit of colour, you know what I'm saying?' This almost makes me laugh. I'm thinking: Kriss, you are *so gay*. You're as gay as Elton John.

Sharon says something about herself that I never knew. She wants to be an athlete. A high jumper. She gets out this picture of herself.

'This one was in the paper,' she says. 'That's me, at Crystal Palace, UK Youth Championships. Last summer holidays.'

Everyone passes the picture round. I gotta admit it, it's a good picture. In the background you can see a massive bank of people who are watching. And Sharon is way way up in the air, like she's on her back, but she's flying. She's wearing some of them tight athletes' shorts which show her long long legs right the way up to the top. I pass the picture to Vern.

'How many people were watching?' asks Barker.

'About ten thousand,' says Shar.

'Weren't you nervous?'

'Not about them watching. I was nervous about getting my run right. If I can get the run right, then I know I can really take off.'

'How did you get on?' says Barker.

Sharon smiles. Her whole face shines. She's so beautiful, the world shines with her.

'I won,' she says.

How come we didn't know that? We all start clapping. So now I'm looking round my classroom and I think that I like them. I wouldn't say I feel connected to them, like trees in the park. But it's hard not to like people when you know what they want.

Near the end, Barker gets up Trish Appleton. She's still grouchy.

'What would you like to do?' says Barker.

'Dunno.'

'Well . . . what do you like?'

'I don't like them mums you see walking down the street pushing buggies and smoking fags and looking pissed.'

'OK,' says Barker. 'But what *does* matter to you? What do you think is important, about life?'

'It's love, innit?' says Trish.

Then she goes back to her seat. So we don't never find out what Trish wants to do. I look at her belly poking over her jeans, and I think she's a fool. But then I think . . . Everyone was asked 'What matters most?' and she was the only one to give the right answer – 'It's love, innit.'

When I come up, I don't know what to say neither.

'What do you think you might do?' says Barker.

'I would like to be a basketball player,' I say. Everyone cracks up at that. 'To tell you the truth,' I go, 'I don't know what I'd like to do.'

'Well,' says Barker, 'what do you think is different about you? What's special?'

'Loads of things,' I say. 'I'm clever. I'm very small. I'm good at football 'cos I've got a low centre of gravity. I'm good-looking but not as good-looking as Kriss. But the thing that is probably most special about me, is that I'm psychic.'

The whole class goes silent. They just look at me. A long pause.

'Well,' says Barker, 'that's . . . that's marvellous. But

probably not something you can make money out of.'

'First off, you're wrong 'cos I don't need much money. But second, you can make money from being psychic, because people visit and you advise them. I'd like that.'

'OK,' says Barker, 'if you're psychic, then surely you can see the future. What future do you imagine for yourself?'

'Don't rush me,' I say. 'It's a good question. I ain't never tried this before.'

And I close my eyes, and I take a deep breath. Right away pictures cram in my mind . . .

I am sitting on a chair, looking out at water. I know right away where I am: one of them little houses next to Lea Valley Canal. It feels good in the house. Full of peace and power. But there's something wrong.

I open my eyes.

Everyone's looking at me.

'Well?' says Barker.

'Thing is,' I go, 'I started to see it, but then right away I saw it don't matter what I do, or how much money I got. I realized that . . . the only thing that matters to me, about my future, is that I spend it with Polly. 'Cos I wouldn't, ever, want to be away from her again.'

I really didn't mean to say that. And I sort of wish I hadn't. 'Cos just saying it has done something to me. I'm standing in front of the class, and I'm crying my eyes

out. I don't care. I ain't gonna rush this. I close my eyes.
I take a tissue out my pocket, and I wipe my face. I look
at my friends. Polly is crying. Sharon Holdings is crying.
Kriss – looking so gay you wouldn't believe it – even he
is looking like his eyes are a bit red.

He sticks his hand up.

'Yes,' says Barker, 'what is it?'

'I'm thinking . . . Bitchin is seeing ghosts. Ghosts are
sometimes called shades. And I'm thinking Bitchin is
shady 'cos what he just said was real. So I'm thinking
that, from now on, we ain't calling him Bitchin no
more. We're calling him . . . the Shade.'

Everybody laughs at that.

'Thank you, Kriss,' says Barker. 'That was excellent
. . . Why don't you return to your seat, er, Shade?'

72

When school finishes, I take my time walking home.

When I'm going down Albion Road, I pass KFC. Trish and Sharon are hanging outside. Trish is smoking a fag.

'Hey . . . *Shade*!' says Trish. 'You wanna puff?'

'That's OK,' I say, 'it stunts the growth.'

They both laugh. Sharon looks even prettier than she did earlier.

'Col,' she says, 'can I talk to you a second?'

'Yeah.'

She nods her head like she wants us to be on our own. So we walk a couple of metres away till we're outside the health shop.

'I was . . . I was wondering, if you wanted to go out with me?'

I smile at her.

'Sharon,' I say, 'you're an amazing person. But I like

Polly. And I think you should pick on someone your own size.'

'OK,' she says, and she laughs. 'Anyway, see you around, Shade!'

'See you.'

I walk off to the health shop feeling like a giant. A horny giant.

When I turn into Walford Road, I see someone near a lamppost.

It's Yussuf.

'Hey, brother,' I say. 'So they let you out?'

'Yeah,' he says, 'they didn't have any evidence. Just asked a few questions.'

'That's good.'

I walk off. This day is going so perfect, I can't wait to see what's gonna happen next.

As I'm walking up Walford Road, I see Kriss and Sal and Eric playing on the football pitch. So I go round. Kriss takes a penalty, and Eric, in goal, jumps forward, and saves the ball with his legs. So then Kriss says:

'You can't jump forward on penalties. Ain't allowed.'

And Eric says: 'Everybody does it, so why can't I?'

And I think: People are still saying that. Some things never change. But then the guys see me, and Eric shouts:

'Hey! The Shade! Wanna come and play?'

'That's OK,' I say. 'Maybe later.'

So Sal lines up to take a penalty against Eric. And Kriss comes to speak to me. He leans in and talks quietly in my ear.

'Shade,' he says, 'I just called that number, and I spoke to that producer who was working with Kimberley. He said it was you who told her to pick me. I wanna say thanks, Shade. And thanks also for, you know, keeping my secret.'

'Kriss,' I say, 'I wanna say two things: one – your secret is safe with me. And two – I wish I could come and see you play football for England, but I'd also like to see you on the catwalk.'

'Thanks, bruv. You will.'

As I walk into the house, I see something's happened. It's all been tidied, so it looks great. Flowers on the table. I'm wondering where all the stuff is. Then Mum comes down the ladder from Dad's attic. She looks wicked. She's got this denim outfit on, and her hair is all different. She smiles.

'Malcolm called this morning,' she says. 'He's launching a new design magazine, and he's given me a job, starting next week, as Editor. I get a twenty-K raise right away. So I thought I'd make some changes round here. Fresh new start.'

'That's excellent, Mum. Well done.'

Then she comes over and kisses my cheek.

'Colin,' she says, 'we've really been arguing recently, haven't we?'

'Yip.'

'Let's stop that now.'

'OK.'

'I mean, I know it's not been easy for you. But sometimes I feel you take it out on me, whenever you're annoyed about something. And I can't be your punchbag all the time.'

'*Some* of the time – would that be OK?'

She laughs.

'But, Mum, what got me was this. One: you didn't tell Dad I was having dreams he was gonna die. Two: you made Juvanji give me medication. And three: you didn't never tell me what actually happened to Dad.'

She looks at me a long time.

'OK, fair enough. But one: I did tell Dad. It freaked him out. Two: OK, Juvanji gave you pills, but he didn't get you put down like a sick dog. Which frankly I could've done with at the time, because you were waking up every night and shouting. And three: you were eleven. Your dad had shot himself in the head. What was I supposed to say? You do know that was what happened?'

'I know.'

'OK . . . And, Col, I know you don't like it when I've had boyfriends. Especially straight after Dad went, but . . .'

361

'I know, Mum.'

'I was lonely too, you know. And they weren't too bad.'

' 'Cept OB. He's a fool. He's so thick it's amazing he can fit through doors.'

'Good-looking though,' she says with her eyes smiling. 'But . . . not as good-looking as Polly.'

I'm blushing.

'Col?' she says. 'It's not been easy for either of us. We both missed Dad.'

'Yip.'

'Even though he was so lazy when he was alive.'

'And selfish. And depressing. And he smelled.'

Mum laughs at that. 'Actually, I liked his smell,' she says. 'Anyway, we both loved him. He's gone. I'm sorry if I've been a bit of a cow.'

I look at my hands.

'Mum,' I say, 'you know I don't say sorry. So . . . forget it. By the way,' I get something out of my pocket, 'I got this for you, Mum.'

'What?'

'Soya milk.'

She smiles at me and hugs me. She smells of clean hair and freshly-washed denim and expensive perfume. I let her hug me for a second, then I push her off. I don't want to give her too much of a good thing.

Then I go down to my bedroom. I got pictures on

362

the wall that are three years out of date. I've even got a Dennis Bergkamp picture on the wall. 'Respect to you, Den,' I say, ' 'cos you don't fly.' Then I rip it down. Then I rip down all my SAS pictures.

Then I quickly shower and I put on my combat trousers and a clean shirt.

Then the door rings, and I look out the window.

It's Polly.

I run down the stairs.

73

She's got her hair tied up in a blue scarf and she's got on nice flared jeans and also the top Kriss gave her.

'Hey, Colin,' she says, 'do you fancy going to the Marsh?'

'Sure.'

So we walk down the street to the bus stop.

She reaches out and takes my hand. I take hers.

Then I say: 'What do you think of what's happened?'

And she says: 'What?'

Then I talk. I go through the whole story, starting with hearing the Samuel L. Jackson voice coming from the pigeon, and then I talk about the ghost at school, and then the bomb in the park. And I tell about the dreams, and the shakfiends, and how I saw her lamia taken away. I go right through to the bit about the Master and about how I killed him and then went to heaven and turned into a tree and then she rescued me. I don't tell the bit about where I snogged Sharon

Holdings – which shouldn't've happened – but otherwise I don't leave nothing out. I want Polly to see the truth: I've saved London, and everyone in it.

While I'm talking, we get on the bus, we travel all the way to Clapton, and then get off the bus. Then we walk along the canal. Past the houseboats and the swans. Then we go over the bridge, and into the Marsh.

I finish the story just as we reach our normal spot under the trees.

Then, at last, I go silent. Polly don't say nothing.

So then I say: 'So what did you think?'

'I think it was a good story,' she says, 'I like the way it was all about you trying to rescue me. But I don't like the way I spent most of it in a glass tank.'

'Anything else?'

'Well . . . that bit where you turned into a tree . . . I liked that bit. But I didn't like that Kriss fought Sal and they nearly killed each other. By the way, has Kriss told you yet that he's gay?'

'How do you know about that?'

'He told me, in the park on Wednesday. He was asking me if I thought you were gay too.'

'*What?*'

'Yeah. I said you were.'

'You *what*? I'm not gay!'

'Prove it then.'

'Is that all you're going to say?'

'What do you mean?'

'Don't . . . Didn't you hear everything I just said?'

'I heard it. And I thought it was a good story.'

'It wasn't a story. It was true. What do you think you've been up to? Why did you fall into the coma?'

'I wasn't in a coma. I was just well depressed 'cos you were out of order with me. And then I just couldn't wake up. I don't know why my mum panicked.'

'But do you remember going into Islington and snogging Kriss in a car?'

'I didn't do that!'

'So how did you get in the car?'

'I gotta be honest. I don't know. But I don't think my "lamia" had been captured by a massive baby.'

'But . . .'

Just then I see someone speeding along the towpath beside the canal. It's Vernon Watkins. He's on a new bike, and he looks tight. He's got on a purple shirt that's flapping in the wind and he's got on his thick geeky glasses and another trilby hat. He looks like a freak, but a cool freak, who'd be singing in a band.

'But look . . .' I say, 'there's Vernon. He's totally changed.'

And Polly looks at him.

'He always looks like that. He's a Style Master all right.'

And then it suddenly hits me. I've got evidence. I can prove everything.

'The apple I got from my dad!' I say. 'Maybe ... maybe you could eat it with me and we could watch him go. It'd be the perfect way to end this.'

I sit down in the grass. Polly sits down next to me. I search in the pocket of my combat trousers, and I find the crisp packet.

I open it.

But inside there's no apple. There's just some old chewing gum that's gone hard.

I show it to Polly. She laughs.

'Colin,' she says, 'you feeling OK?'

I look at her.

'Yeah, Poll, I feel bitchin.'

And I reach forward and I kiss her. She's pressing her lips against mine, and I feel orange inside. I smell her lemon cheeks, and then I open my eyes and see her bushy eyebrows. And then I close my eyes and I kiss her again. I feel amazing. It's like when you eat a doughnut and you get this warm feeling inside. 'Cept the feeling ain't just inside, it's everywhere.

Acknowledgements

I got a phone call one day from my friend Lou Gish, who I met eight years ago when we were both young actors. I used to make her laugh by walking into her dressing room in the nude. In this way we struck up a deep friendship. On the phone, Lou told me she'd got cancer to her bones and was taking to her bed to sleep off the chemotherapy. So I started writing this book and sending her chunks, because I wanted to keep her hooked, and I wanted to give her something to look forward to. After a while it became Lou who was being benevolent, not me, because she kept reading and enthusing. The book was a lot wilder then, and not easy to follow. The shakfiends chased Colin to an abandoned oil rig and then he went under the North Sea where the Master was hiding out in an empty oil well. But because Lou kept enjoying it, I worked and worked until it turned into the altogether slicker book that you've just read. Just after it was sold, Lou died, and I still wish I could thank her. Or just see her. I know she's now one of my own dirty angels, but sometimes I miss the real thing.

I'd also like to thank all the friends who've read the book, and have given me help: Adam Baron, Katie Bond, Wendy Cooling, Michael McManus, Laura and Trish Lankaster, Tif Loehnis, Ruth Fielding and Tom Guard. My editor, Emily Thomas, has been excellent. She's patient, she's good fun, and she doesn't need to look up how to spell Freddie Ljundberg. It's my first novel, and it's come out quick, but I've been writing almost every day since I was 16. During that time I've sometimes been tempted, like Colin's dad, to push away the keyboard and blow my face off with a gun. So I'm immensely grateful to the golden people who've kept me going by praising my writing: Stephen Adams, my first history teacher, Copstick, Malcom and Tony Hayes, Dom Collier, James Dreyfus, Jewel Kilcher, Lizzie Roper, Eleanor Mills, Catherine Story, Wilf, John Pollock, and, espeicaly Gary Reich. Also Glasgow Jimmy, homeless poet, freelance angel, the original Uncle Jimmy. Paul Sansome, who inspired the figure of Vernon Watkins, in that Paul was one of the funniest and most loyal friends of my childhood, and I sometimes responded by treating him shamefully. I want this book to help me find Paul Sansome; I'll do him whatever service he asks. I particularly want to thank Livy, who gives me love.